# Heart OF THE West
## ANN JACOBS

Ellora's Cave
Romantica Publishing

## What the critics are saying...

❧

**5 Lips** "*Roped* is an extremely emotion filled and sexually charged book. Ann Jacobs has done a remarkable job creating two characters able to heal each other's souls. […] Ms. Jacobs writes with passion and is able to create BDSM scenes that left me wishing I was the heroine. I am anxiously waiting for the next installment in the ***Heart of the West*** series." ~ *Two Lips Reviews*

**5 Angels** "Ann Jacobs has brought us another tantalizing BDSM story in *Hitched*. […] The story was well written and delivered. I'm looking forward to reading the next story in this erotic series." ~ *Fallen Angels Reviews*

**5 Blue Ribbons** "The HEART OF THE WEST series has come to an end and I'm very glad I had the opportunity to read it. The world of BDSM is at the heart of this series. […] The end came all too soon. I highly recommend LASSOED and have placed it in my e-book keeper file next to ROPED and HITCHED." ~ *Romance Junkies Reviews*

An Ellora's Cave Romantica Publication

www.ellorascave.com

Heart of the West

ISBN 9781419958021
ALL RIGHTS RESERVED.
Roped Copyright © 2007 Ann Jacobs
Hitched Copyright © 2008 Ann Jacobs
Lassoed Copyright © 2008 Ann Jacobs
Edited by Sue-Ellen Gower.
Cover art by Syneca.

This book printed in the U.S.A. by Jasmine-Jade Enterprises, LLC.

Trade paperback Publication October 2008

With the exception of quotes used in reviews, this book may not be reproduced or used in whole or in part by any means existing without written permission from the publisher, Ellora's Cave Publishing, Inc.® 1056 Home Avenue, Akron OH 44310-3502.

Warning: The unauthorized reproduction or distribution of this copyrighted work is illegal. Criminal copyright infringement, including infringement without monetary gain, is investigated by the FBI and is punishable by up to 5 years in federal prison and a fine of $250,000.
(http://www.fbi.gov/ipr/)

This book is a work of fiction and any resemblance to persons, living or dead, or places, events or locales is purely coincidental. The characters are productions of the author's imagination and used fictitiously.

# HEART OF THE WEST
∾

### ROPED
*~11~*

### HITCHED
*~91~*

### LASSOED
*~167~*

# ROPED

# Trademarks Acknowledgement

∽

The author acknowledges the trademarked status and trademark owners of the following wordmarks mentioned in this work of fiction:

Honda Ridgeline: Honda Motor Co., Ltd

Humvee: Ren Acquisition Corp./C/O The Renco Group, Inc.

# Chapter One

*Water. Got to find water.* Sand swirled around Jared McTavish, each individual grain pelting his hands and nose, the only parts of him not covered by the all-encompassing robe and headdress he'd stolen from the man he'd killed.

The man—an insurgent, one of the bastards he and his men had been searching for—had shot up Jared's Humvee and murdered his driver moments before this sandstorm had blown up on the western Iraqi desert. Jared shuddered when he recalled the explosion that had rocked the desert road ahead of them, and the resultant blood and broken body parts of the soldiers who'd taken the forward position on this hellish assignment.

Trying to ignore blinding pain in his legs, he stumbled forward—toward his platoon headquarters, or so he thought. He hunched his shoulders, his head dropped to his chin to keep the wind-whipped sand from blinding him for real. It seemed like he'd been heading toward nowhere for hours, praying for shelter…an oasis…anything but the desolate grave that had already claimed so many of his comrades.

*Can't. Can't go on much longer.* His throat parched, every cell in his body screaming from pain as well as thirst, Jared lifted his canteen, let the last precious drops of water dribble through his cracked lips. His whole body ached from the effort of moving against the forces of nature.

There. In the distance, barely visible over shifting dunes nearly as tall as he was, he spied some stately date palms bent nearly double in the wind. He redoubled his efforts, moved faster, his eye on his goal. *Shade. Water. Gotta make it, can't be far now.*

Jared clawed his way over a dune, the last impediment between him and life. On his knees now, for he was becoming too weak to walk, he crawled the last fifty yards, only to look up and see the palm trees disappear, the verdant vegetation turn to arid wasteland. A mirage, he thought as he sank face down on the sand and took one last labored breath.

Blackness. A sensation of hot sand scorched the palms of his hands, his cheek. Then a halo of light. And a blessed breath of cool, soothing air swirled all around him.

Thank God. It hadn't been a mirage after all. Jared inhaled deeply, aerating his parched body, his dry throat. "Water," he croaked, sensing another presence yet too exhausted to open his eyes.

Soft hands cradled his head, tucked what felt like fat fluffy pillows beneath it. The sound of fluid hitting a container was music to his ears—ears that had last heard the cry of the wind as it tossed desert sand around him like a shroud. This was better, he thought, lying on a silken couch while a lusty *houri* tended to his bath. He'd turn the tides on her, ravage her in payback for the way she'd been caressing him. Jared rolled her beneath him, restrained her for his pleasure while she whimpered eagerly in an Arabic dialect he couldn't understand.

"Wake up, Captain, and open your mouth." The voice was female, the tone firm but still somehow seductive, the language English. "I've got some water for you."

A slow stream of cool water bathed his parched lips, wet his swollen tongue. "More."

If this was a dream he didn't want to wake up. Not now, when he had his lover tied hand and foot to the four posters on his bed. Not when he'd stroked her silky skin until she begged for more, and drunk his fill of her sweet-salty essence. Not as he'd listened to her whimpering his name and begging him to take her. And particularly not now, when he was on his knees between her thighs, set to sink his cock into her sweet pussy and fuck her until they both were wrung out and hung up to dry.

No, this was definitely not the time for anybody to tell Jared this was only a dream, that like the oasis he'd seen in the desert that had damn near killed him, the erotic interlude he'd been experiencing the past few minutes was only a mirage.

"Sorry to bother you, Captain, but it's time to change your dressing."

Opening his eyes reluctantly, he looked into the face he'd begun placing on the *houris* in his recurring dream. Nurse Ninia Barker. For the past few days she'd been his waking nightmare, bullying him into taking care of himself when he didn't really give a damn. But yet, in the dreams he'd been having lately, it was always her face on the woman who was tied, begging him to take her. Jared let out a string of curses that would have sent most women running for cover, but it didn't seem to faze Ninia. As if he'd smiled and said "Thanks," as though she didn't notice his hard-on tenting the blanket, she went about her business, folding back the sheets and baring the wound that had brought him here, to a small VA hospital in Cheyenne, not far from the home he'd left ten years ago when he'd opted for a military career.

He hadn't gone back to his squadron in Iraq or to his home base because the roadside bomb that had riddled his lower body with shrapnel and ended up taking part of his right leg had ended what he'd planned as a lifelong career in the Marines. They hadn't wanted him taking up space at Walter Reed once they'd done all they could and determined he'd never be fit enough to go back to his Special Force Reconnaissance Team. Part of him couldn't help wishing his second-in-command hadn't risked his own skin to come back and drag his miserable ass out of the desert, especially at times like this when he was lying more or less helpless, either pretty much in constant pain, or with the pain masked by drugs that also dulled his wits.

"Okay. Looks like another piece of shrapnel has worked its way out." The pretty blonde tyrant stood and motioned for an orderly to come help take him to the procedure room so they could fish out the tiny shard of metal. "What will this make?"

Jared shrugged. "How the hell would I know?"

"Don't get upset with me. I was just making conversation. Lots of you guys like to keep count of how many pieces of your Humvees have made their way out of your bodies."

"Well, I couldn't care less." He realized a lot of his irritability came from his situation, but part of it came from watching her, wanting her so much but knowing there was nothing more pathetically cliché than a wounded soldier falling for his nurse. She tended him, saw all his weaknesses, while his cock hungered to show her it wasn't exactly helpless.

"You couldn't care less about a lot of things, right, tough guy?" Ninia reminded Jared of a particularly hot Domme he'd once observed in his brother's Laramie dungeon. Only thing was, that Domme had taken it easier verbally on the sub he'd watched her playing with than this nurse did on him and the other patients in the small post-trauma rehab unit at the Cheyenne VA Medical Center. "You got banged up a little, so the world's come to an end."

"What the fuck would you know about what's going on in my head?" Jared usually tried to be civil to the people charged with helping him, but Ninia was getting on his nerves. Not only because she'd just fucked up the best dream he'd had since coming back stateside, but because she'd been the main focus of it. "Or about what I've been through for that matter?"

Her lips went white underneath the pink lipstick she had on, and all of a sudden she got so quiet Jared felt like squirming, especially when he noticed dampness gathering in the corners of her big blue eyes, a barely perceptible tremor in her usually steady hands. Still he wasn't ready to cut her any slack. "Well?"

When she lowered her gaze, he saw the pain in her expression. "I lost my husband," she said. "In the fighting in Afghanistan. I'd have given everything I own if he'd come home no more battered than you."

He reached out, ashamed he'd taken out his frustration on her and chagrined that she'd had to remind him the whole world was filled with people who'd lost their dreams. Mostly he felt bad for hurting her just because he wanted her so damn much. Jared noticed how her expression softened when he grasped her hand, so he tightened his grip, taking a chance she'd think he was coming on to her like any other pathetic bastard in the place. "I was being an ass. I didn't mean to take my annoyance out on you," he told her, moving his thumb over her palm.

She didn't move for a moment. Then her hand tightened somewhat on his, and he thought he saw the pulse in her throat speed up. For a moment, he forgot he was in a hospital bed again. He wanted to tug her closer and see if he could taste her there, make her…

"It's all right." She pulled her hand away, her cheeks slightly flushed. Damn, he'd flustered her. But he was also a fucking cripple, helpless to get off that bed and pursue her under his own steam. The jarring reminder made him turn away when she spoke, her irritating composure restored. "Come on, let's get you into this wheelchair and down to the procedure room. The sooner this piece of shrapnel's gone, the sooner you'll be able to get up on your feet."

"Don't you mean foot?" He swung himself into the wheelchair the orderly had brought. It had become second nature for Jared to correct his caregivers when they referred to his prosthesis as though it were part of him instead of a bunch of plastic and titanium. Not that it didn't work surprisingly well, but nothing could hold a candle to the real thing. Ninia looked stricken, though, so he made himself grin. "I'll start thinking of feet in the plural when I can actually put the other one back on," he said, gesturing toward the lower portion of the stump where shrapnel had been coming to the surface lately, requiring removal and keeping him from using his new state-of-the-art prosthesis while each tiny fresh wound healed.

"Fair enough. Come on, let's make that happen ASAP. We need to get you out of here and free up your bed for a guy who really needs it." She managed a smile, and it seemed to have as much effect on his libido as that erotic dream. Man, did he have it bad.

\* \* \* \* \*

Nurse Ninia stuck in his mind, even now, a week after he'd been released from her inpatient ward to get his physical therapy three days a week at the outpatient clinic. Jared closed his eyes and envisioned the bossy blonde as he half-listened to a sports announcer on TV going on about the Broncos' chances in the upcoming NFL season.

If it hadn't been for his leg hurting him like hell, he'd probably have fallen asleep in the living room, but it did, so he grabbed his crutches and made his way into bed where he could elevate the stump. The noise from the TV gave the illusion that he wasn't alone, lulled him off to sleep.

*Sand dunes white as the snow back home on his Wyoming ranch stretched as far as he could see, past date palms swaying in the hot, dry desert air. A soothing breeze bathed his cheeks when he pulled the flap back and looked outside the luxurious tent where he'd awakened moments earlier.*

*He must have died and gone to heaven. Jared could think of no other explanation. The last thing he remembered was crawling, clawing his way across the Iraqi desert in a blinding storm, struggling to reach an oasis. An oasis that had only been a mirage.*

*He remembered that. Remembered gasping for air, taking in sand instead. But apparently he'd been wrong. Apparently just past his line of vision the oasis had been here after all, and God had helped him find the way.*

*This was no mirage, but a miracle. He closed his eyes, said a silent prayer this wouldn't all be gone when he looked again. Relief* washed over him when he saw the same welcome scene, when he turned back and found the tent still there.

And the woman. Ninia? Blonde hair like spun silk swaying loose against her tanned shoulders, sky-blue eyes made more compelling because they were set off by the veil that showed just a hint of her full, red lips, a chin with a dimple that softened its stubborn set. Voluptuous, smiling, graceful, she'd danced for him. Bathed his sunburned body with cool, fresh water. Dipped her fingers ever so slowly into the cool, clear liquid then held them just over his lips so it slid drop by drop between his parched lips and down his throat. Now she beckoned to him with outstretched arms, temptation beyond anything he could resist.

Tired. He was so tired. Back inside the tent now, he found the silk-draped sleeping couch, paused only for a moment before letting his unfamiliar Arab garb drop to the floor. He stretched out, naked, against cushions soft as goose down. Foreign sounding music, dissonant to his American ears, soothed him – yet it aroused him too, for it conjured pictures in his mind of dancers undulating to its haunting rhythm.

Dancing – for him. The woman who'd been tending him sat on the floor beside his feet, gently massaging the bruised, blistered soles, his toes...his ankles. Her fingers moved in time with the music, making him aware of her female heat – her desires.

His desire too. Rolling over, he started to lift her in his arms, only to wake up hard and sweating...and once again, alone.

He blinked, disoriented for a moment until he recognized the bedroom of the Spartan apartment he'd rented when he first arrived in Cheyenne for outpatient therapy. "Closer to home," the brass had told him when they'd tossed him out of Walter Reed three weeks ago and sent him here. Well, he'd seen precious little of Cheyenne so far, since he'd freaked out during his first visit to the VA hospital three blocks down from this apartment complex.

Yeah. He'd made a real ass out of himself, letting the sight of a badly burned soldier set off a full-scale panic attack.

Besides the fact his action had embarrassed the shit out of him, it also resulted in him spending more than a week back in a hospital ward. And meeting a nurse whose face now showed up in damn near all his dreams.

Jared glanced around his darkened bedroom, looked out the window at the clear surface of a small lake illuminated by a fat new moon. The throbbing in the stump of his right leg made him want to scream, but he refused to give in and take more of the pain medications that dulled his mind.

Sooner or later he'd have to figure something to occupy himself with or he'd go fucking nuts. Not now, though. Now he was struggling, trying to accept that his plan to spend thirty years in the Marines was history. He hadn't even begun to wrestle with the concept that he was no longer well-equipped physically to enjoy the BDSM lifestyle that had been the cornerstone of his personal life.

Would the take-charge, sometimes bossy Ninia surrender to a Dominant male? Jared couldn't help imagining her melting in his arms, giving over control to him the way she never had when he was her patient. He'd stroke her soft skin, pillow his head on her full breasts, nibble at her nipples until she squirmed and begged him for more. *Stop it, idiot, or you'll be taking another cold shower. Sex with your nurse is the last thing you should be thinking about, because it ain't gonna happen.*

Jared didn't have the foggiest idea of what he might do, professionally or personally. Not that he needed money—his grandfather had left him and his sister and brother a prime piece of southern Wyoming ranch land near Tie Siding, along with enough money to live on comfortably for the rest of their lives. As long as the stock market didn't crash, the principal would keep on growing even if the oil wells should dry up. What he needed was to find something to do with the rest of his life.

And a real live woman to put this recurring dream to rest. Be damned if he wanted to keep fucking a mirage, and only in his dreams. As if there was a chance in hell he'd find a sub to love the scarred-up has-been Master he was now.

No chance he'd sleep any more tonight.

He sat on the edge of the bed and transferred himself into the wheelchair they'd lent him at the hospital when he refused to take a prescription for one of his own. Rolling it to the patio doors that led to a balcony overlooking the courtyard, he let the cool mountain breeze bring a small measure of relief to his heated flesh.

* * * * *

There he was. Jared McTavish. Captain, United States Marines until his medical discharge had come through last week. Her patient. Ninia had no business on earth staring out her bedroom window at the man whose battered body she'd tended…would likely tend again when more shrapnel was ready to be removed. She had no right whatever to be imagining him wanting to pleasure a woman under his will as a Master.

Across the courtyard with its small man-made lake, she watched him stare out at the night. The light of a silvery moon reflected off the water, accentuating the rugged planes of his face and making her want to caress him there with her fingertips, bring him peace from whatever demons kept sleep at bay for him tonight. *Ninia, he's your patient. You must be insane, fantasizing how he'd master you…how his rough, rugged hands would feel when he touched you. How it would make your body sing when he claimed you the way a Master would.*

But she couldn't help it. Jared McTavish fascinated her as no one had done in the four years since Earl had died. There was something about him…the way he looked and talked, the way he mumbled arousing, erotic orders in his dreams…

Once, when she'd leaned over him to soothe him as he cried out in one of those dreams, he'd reached his hand out, closed it over her throat. He'd caressed her, made her want to drop to her knees when he mumbled the order for her to do so, his voice hoarse, intense. She'd imagined then that if she'd complied he'd have clasped her head between his two big hands, guided her to his cock, ordered her to take him in her mouth and suck. God how she'd wanted to do just that, to encroach on his sleep and taste the massive male flesh she hadn't been able to ignore.

Captain McTavish was a wounded male. From the moment he'd surfaced to consciousness in her ward, even before that from the things he'd muttered in his sleep, she could tell he was used to controlling all aspects of his life, commanding those around him. Not only did that part of him make her weak with desire in spite of her fiercest admonitions to herself to remain professional, it made her want to be the one to help him reclaim that self-confidence…and perhaps claim her. God, she'd lost her mind. Maybe it had been pure accident that she'd glanced at his address on the hospital record and noticed he lived in her apartment complex, in the unit directly across the courtyard from hers. Or had it been fate? Ninia had never been one to discount destiny. She couldn't lie to herself. She wanted more than to make Jared well. She wanted him. Perhaps it was impulse. The beauty of the night sky. Maybe it was the ache of her lonely body. She didn't care and wasn't going to take the time to analyze her actions.

Lifting off her sleep shirt, she stood naked in front of the open patio door, using a vibrating dildo to massage her breasts the way she longed for him to do. She skimmed her hands down her body, spread her legs apart, pretended the gentle breeze was his breath on her pussy, his fingers on her aching clit.

She kept her gaze on him, so she knew the moment he saw her. His gaze drifted past the open door then snapped back. Her face was mostly in shadows, but he could clearly see her body as she loosened her hair, let the breeze lift it as she stepped out on her balcony. His eyes were on her, scorching her flesh. She wished he were sitting here, within reach of her eager arms as she displayed herself for his pleasure, showing him in every way that she was his for the taking. Even with the distance of the courtyard between them, she offered herself as if that were the case. Tendrils of hair curled around her breasts, her waist, caressing her bare skin as she bent and braced one hand on her side balcony rail and the other against the frame of the patio door, giving him a birds-eye view of her damp, swollen pussy.

*See what you could do to me?* She braced herself with one hand on the rail, used the other to reach between her legs with the dildo. A cool night breeze caressed her swollen flesh when she rubbed the toy along her slit. The heat from his gaze made her hotter, so hot she plunged it into her pussy, balls deep. The vibrations sent shivers through her, but no more so than the knowledge that *he* was watching. Watching and wanting.

He'd be hard as stone, hot and throbbing as he sat across the balcony watching her do herself. He'd be doing himself too, jerking his long, thick cock in his left hand—she'd noticed when she tended his wounds that he was left-handed—and cupping his balls in his right. His face would be flushed, and his tongue would go out to moisten the thin but sensual lips she longed to kiss. He'd be imagining eating her pussy, ramming his cock hard into her cunt, her ass…

Or maybe he'd order her to suck him off. Her mouth watered at the thought of going on her knees, taking him in her mouth, serving him that way and any other way that would bring him pleasure.

Ninia turned up the vibrator, let sensation wash through her, bringing release of the sexual tension but not the desire. Maybe it was time to go back, find a Master to fill the empty spot in her heart that losing Earl had carved out.

Maybe…

\* \* \* \* \*

What the fuck?

He lived across the courtyard from a female exhibitionist? Jared should have rolled his chair back inside and crawled back into bed. Instead he stayed and watched. It might have been his imagination, but he could have sworn he smelled her coming. No question about it, he'd seen the waves of ecstasy undulating through her naked body. Damn, he'd come all over himself before he realized he'd curled his fingers around his cock and mimicked the rhythm she'd set with her dildo.

He wished to hell he could have seen her face. Her body was dynamite, all slender curves with just enough meat on them for a man to get a hand-hold. When the new moon darted out from behind the clouds, he saw she was pale, with long light hair that cascaded around her, caught the moonlight. She'd gotten herself off with a dildo at the same time he was getting himself off with his hand. Before that, she'd been a surreal shadow, like the oasis in the desert that looked so deceptively real in his dreams.

She looked so much like Ninia, Jared imagined… Fuck, he was a fool, imagining anything happening between him and the woman who'd nursed him through panic and pain, seen him at his worst. He had to forget her. Once no more shrapnel could be removed he'd be gone and she'd be nothing but a memory. And that was all the better, because he was going to end up embarrassing himself, asking her out or imagining for a moment that he might pursue a relationship with her, like a hundred other guys who she'd helped through the pain of rehabilitation. She'd probably have patted his hand, given him a sympathetic smile if he approached her. But then he remembered that flush on her cheeks. *No. Don't be an idiot.*

Dawn was breaking in the eastern sky. Soon it would start getting light. He'd be able to see her then…except that now she'd gone back inside her apartment, closing the drapes against his prying eyes. Damn, he'd better get his ass inside as well, or the cops would be paying him a visit. Wouldn't do if he got caught on the balcony staring at a window across the courtyard and salivating over a neighbor whose pussy he could describe in more detail than her face.

\* \* \* \* \*

Showered and shaved now, he checked his legs, proud of himself because he hardly winced anymore when he looked closely at the below-knee stump. Good, the latest wounds where they'd taken out more shrapnel seemed finally to be healing. Satisfied that infection wasn't setting in, Jared pulled on boxers and jeans, pulling the right jeans leg up over the knee of his stump.

He didn't kid himself that his body had shed the last of the hardware. Seemed he had half a fucking Humvee inside his lower body in minute bits and pieces, mostly concentrated in what was left of his right leg. It had pissed the hell out of him when he was flying commercial for the first time after his injury, realizing he made airport metal detectors go bonkers when he passed through. Recognizing the pity in strangers' eyes when they noticed his wheelchair, or the crutches he'd still needed even when he was wearing his prosthesis. He hated it. Hated them for their sympathy that reminded him he was a fucking cripple.

He eyed the stump, wondered why he hadn't let them re-amputate the leg at mid-thigh, the way the orthopods at Walter Reed had suggested. They'd have gotten most of the metal fragments, and by now he'd have been up and running—or at least walking fairly well if he'd applied himself as hard as he had when he'd been trying to pass the fitness tests so they'd let him stay on active duty. But returning to his unit had been a possibility with the below-knee amputation. He'd known fellow officers who'd done it, had been certain he'd be able to overcome this disability as well. If not for the shrapnel his body kept rejecting piece-by-piece, he'd have succeeded. He'd have been a man, doing a man's work, not the object of anybody's pity.

In any case, he wouldn't put up with stares today. After re-bandaging the two wounds that would come in contact with his prosthesis, he rolled on two stump socks and snapped the stump into its custom-made socket. Getting carefully to his feet, he put weight on the prosthesis, found the pain bearable. More bearable than having people try so transparently not to stare at the empty space where his lower leg should have been.

He winced as he took the last of six steps from the bathroom to his closet where a selection of his shirts hung neatly in a row. The damn wounds weren't as healed as they looked. Choosing a burgundy print shirt he'd bought two years ago while on R&R in Hawaii, he shrugged it on, then gave in and picked up the forearm crutches he'd sworn he'd never use again. Better to use them than to end up passed out on Cheyenne's famed Greenway Path and somebody have to carry him back here.

Shoving his wallet and keys into his pockets, Jared made his way to the elevator, ticking off his plans as the outside-mounted cab made its way down the twelve floors of apartments to the ground. He'd take it easy, walk a little way along the pathway lined with fragrant evergreens and an occasional massive cottonwood tree, enjoy the wildflowers and the animals that always reminded him he was home. Maybe this time he'd make it to that spot where his neighbor kept saying he could enjoy a spectacular view of distant mountains that still had small caps of snow, even now, in midsummer. If not today, he'd make it there someday soon.

## Chapter Two
### ಐ

She shouldn't have done it. But what the hell? Almost four years now, and she'd never stopped mourning for Earl. Until last night. Until she'd obsessed about the tall, rugged cowboy-soldier with all the pain in his eyes, to the point she'd consciously exposed herself to him. For him.

Ninia was about to do something equally stupid, if not more so. She stood in the office of Boundless Pleasure, the dungeon where she and Earl had played, waiting for the dungeon master to prepare an invitation.

"You sure he's a Dom?" Marshall Wallace asked, his gnarled fingers hesitating as he handed her the form. "If he's not and if he doesn't care much for our lifestyle, this could get us in a world of trouble."

She met the dungeon master's gaze, saw grief there for his friend who'd been almost like a son. Marshall's compassion for her had kept her stable in the months after they'd learned about Earl's death. "A submissive knows," she said, remembering the snippets of dreams Jared had verbalized in his sleep, his bitterness that seemed to go deeper than the death of his dreams for a career in the Marine Special Forces. "Besides, he mentioned he'd gone to a club in Vegas—a dungeon I visited once with Earl."

Never mind he'd talked about it in his sleep, and not, as far as she could tell, in the context of a D/s encounter he'd had in the place. Ninia just knew.

"Okay. It's on you if you're wrong." Marshall's frown morphed into a smile when he handed her the envelope inviting Jared McTavish to visit the exclusive dungeon where Ninia hadn't played since before Earl had left with his squadron to fight the War on Terror. "It's about time you stopped mourning and started living again. I assume I'll be seeing you here again, as well."

"Maybe so." While her intention—at least her conscious one—had been to shove Jared kicking and screaming back into the world she sensed he thought he'd forever lost rather than joining him in his rediscovery, that was before something had compelled her to strip naked and masturbate for his viewing pleasure. "I'm still afraid the memories will hurt too much, but I believe it's finally time for me to move on."

Marshall took her hand, massaged her palm with his callused thumb. "Good girl. Earl wouldn't have wanted you to bury yourself along with him, and that's what you've been doing."

No, Earl had been as generous as any man she'd ever known, never satisfied until he'd brought her pleasure. No way could she imagine him looking down from Heaven and faulting her for celebrating life. "I know, Marshall. But it's taken me a long time to tell him goodbye."

"Sure. I understand. Bring yourself on over here tonight. Play with your wounded Marine. Master Chad has booked the room with the observation dome for some suspension bondage play. Should be interesting—nobody else around here is better at rope bondage than Chad."

Earl had been better, at least at *Karada*, or net bondage. Many a day she had worn the confining ropes beneath her clothes, felt the arousal he'd intended when he put them there. But Earl was gone. The reminder didn't hurt Ninia the way it usually did. "That should be interesting, watching Chad do his magic. I don't imagine that demo would appeal to McTavish, though. Unless I miss my guess, his tastes in rope play will be pretty much limited to tossing lassos and restraining his partner."

"A basic sort of Dom, then." Marshall smiled then glanced out at the public room, where a member was working his flogger with less skill than Ninia was accustomed to seeing here in the club. "Go on. That guy just joined last week. Looks like I need to teach him how to flog his sub without doing her serious bodily harm. Don't be a stranger any more. We've missed you."

Ninia had missed this too. The arousal that came from being controlled, being forced to shed her inhibitions and experience the ultimate in sexual pleasure. Lured by a black leather corset with pink side lacings on a kneeling dummy in a display window, she stopped in the dungeon's toy shop. If she was going to get back in the dungeon scene, she'd need some new trappings.

What would turn Jared McTavish on? Earl had always wanted her to wear pastel colors, lots of lace and satin. Girly-girl stuff, he'd always said, and he'd brought her home something new every time he came back from a trip. Something made her believe Jared would prefer seeing his subs in leather and denim. A cowgirl outfit, complete with curled brim hat and knee-high boots to go with the denim short shorts and plaid shirt that tied below the breasts, caught her eye, so she laid it on the counter along with a slender riding crop she hoped he'd use on her.

Hmmm. She trembled slightly when she eyed a cat o'nine and imagined Jared wielding it with exquisite skill. It cost a bit much, considering her nurse's salary, so she decided that if he wanted one, he could buy it for himself. After perusing the selection of sex toys, she came back to the counter and bought the outfit she'd picked out, along with a length of silken rope whose royal blue color made it impossible to resist. Her pussy creamed at the thought of wearing it tonight. Wearing the rope bondage to honor Earl's memory, and later on the cowboy fantasy outfit for Jared's pleasure.

\* \* \* \* \*

A few hours later Jared returned from his walk on Greenway Path, sore but feeling good that he'd managed pretty well with his prosthesis on the uneven terrain. The burger and fries he'd eaten at the restaurant across from his apartment complex had hit the spot, along with a longneck bottle of Blonde Ale. One good thing about being close to home, he thought—his favorite locally brewed libation was readily available.

When he stepped inside the door, he saw it. A large, cream-colored envelope with nothing but his name scrawled on it in bold, masculine print. Setting aside his crutches and bending carefully—a motion that was damn tricky to make on one gimpy leg and a prosthesis—he picked up the thing and made his way to the nearest chair, a leather recliner.

Fuck. It was an invitation to a dungeon. Who the hell around here had guessed he'd been into the BDSM lifestyle? *Had been* being the operative word.

He searched his memory, trying to figure out who might have contacted this guy Marshall Wallace at a Cheyenne club called Boundless Pleasure. It had to have been his older brother Brad, who owned the club in Laramie where Jared had been a frequent visitor before enlisting and when he came home on leave. Nobody else Jared could think of was likely to have known his sexual tastes as well as his present location. Pulling his cell phone off the waistband of his jeans, he put in a call.

Nope. It wasn't Brad, although he'd been glad to hear Jared had gotten hooked up with what he'd heard was the best run dungeon in Cheyenne. Jared looked at the invitation again. It didn't matter who'd sent it, he wouldn't be going. Brad had apparently forgotten he wasn't the same guy he'd been a year ago. The Dom in him was gone, left somewhere on a windblown desert in western Iraq with his career…his future.

If he ever went out looking for a woman now, he'd be in the market for a nurturer, not a sub who needed nurturing. A strong woman, not one who'd look to him for strength and pleasure. When he'd first been discharged from Walter Reed and come home to Wyoming for further rehabilitation at the hospital where Ninia worked, he hadn't imagined he'd ever reach the point of wondering if a woman existed who'd take him as he was, love him for whatever he might have inside and not for the battered outside wrappings. But being close to home, getting a little more mobile every day, he was beginning to think about his future. To imagine someday there might be a woman who'd want him as he was.

Jared's gaze drifted to the expanse of glass that led to the patio. Wrong vantage point, but still he remembered as clearly as though her image were etched on his brain. Moonlight and a mystery woman as lonely as he, pleasuring herself on her patio for his entertainment. His arousal. A woman who might be able to drive the recurring dreams with Nurse Ninia out of his head, even though he'd put Ninia's face on her when she aroused him.

Could his captivating neighbor have been the one who arranged this invitation? The more he thought of it, the more he figured maybe she had… Maybe he'd figure out which apartment his mystery woman lived in, find out who she was. Maybe he'd even go to her, offer her his cock instead of her dildo…

Would she like him to restrain her, pleasure her beyond anything she'd ever known? Damn it, he had no business fantasizing about an encounter that never would take place. Setting aside the invitation that had started his mind to wandering in a world of make-believe, he heaved himself out of the chair and limped off to bed. He'd rest a while, then maybe if he felt up to it, he'd check out the place called Boundless Pleasure.

So what if he found himself standing on the sidelines, observing other Doms pleasuring their subs? He figured there was nothing like a rude awakening to keep him focused on how his life had changed and reminded that since his injuries, some people inevitably would look at him not with desire, but with thinly veiled pity for what he'd lost. Figuratively as well as literally.

## Chapter Three

Would Jared come tonight? Ninia hung out in the dressing room at Boundless Pleasure as long as she dared, counting goose bumps on her nearly naked body and toying with the full-face mask she was trying to work up enough courage to leave in the locker with her street clothes.

Four years. That's how long it had been since she'd come here with Earl the night before he shipped out. He'd shown off a new pattern of rope bondage he'd learned just for her, or so he'd whispered when she'd reached that delicious level of pleasure-pain that had her on the edge. As if it had been just yesterday, she felt the roughness of his hands, his callused fingertips. He'd caressed her throat, her back, everywhere but the spots he'd known would send her tumbling into a haze of Nirvana. A state he'd granted her—finally—by giving her his cock and fucking her before a dozen pairs of eyes, glowing like predators in the forest, attracted by the sexual energy he'd roused in her and himself. By giving her permission to come in his gruff, beloved voice when she'd thought she couldn't hold out a minute more. Then he'd untied her, tenderly, tugged on the slim gold chain he'd put around her neck the day they'd married. And ordered her to wait for him until he came home.

But a Taliban insurgent's bullet had come between them, kept him from keeping his promise. Ninia shed the mask, wiped a tear off her cheek. Her usually steady hands uncharacteristically clumsy, she fumbled with the elaborate clasp that undid the slender chain, letting the gold links slide through her fingers like tears of farewell.

She'd endured four years of loneliness and grief, but the memories weren't so painful now that she couldn't consider living…satisfying another Master's needs, taking pleasure from giving pleasure to him. It was almost as if Earl were there, guiding her, lifting her hand and placing it in Jared's. His deep voice rang in her ears, almost as if he were beside her. *This was mine, but now I'm gone. Now she's yours to care for.*

Would Jared find the *Karada* bondage she'd decided to wear in Earl's memory arousing? She closed her eyes, imagined Jared tightening the confinement she'd always loved. He'd caress her with calloused hands the way he'd touched her last night with hungry eyes. Her mouth watered when she pictured him, still hard-muscled despite the ordeal of surgeries and recovery.

No, she shouldn't have surreptitiously managed to be the one accompanying him to the physical therapy rooms. But she had, and she'd nearly crumbled emotionally when she'd watched him working out his upper body so fiercely, as though he were still fighting insurgents. How he'd struggled, how he'd pushed those muscles he obviously had deemed too weak. She'd felt his determination in every grunt, each droplet of sweat that dotted his brow…in the tight set of his mouth as though he'd force the still-working parts of his body to be more powerful than ever or be damned trying.

He hadn't seen her watching. Hadn't known how much she'd wanted to tell him then that he wasn't weak. To whisper how he made her wet just looking at him, imagining him claiming her, taking her. To show him he was perfect in her eyes.

She visualized his long, thick cock, imagined as she had so many times when tending him in the hospital how satiny it would feel in her hands. Her skin tingled when she thought about the way he'd explore her body with his callused fingers before ordering her to take him in her mouth, her cunt, her ass.

Her pulse raced. Her heart pounded in her chest. She wanted a Master tonight—not just any Dom who might hit on her, but Jared. The wounded soldier who'd come to dominate her dreams. When she stepped into the main dungeon, she saw him.

Gorgeous. Bare-chested, with a light dusting of dark hair over well-developed pecs and impressively muscular arms, he wore low-riding black chaps over snug black jeans...and cowboy boots. Her gaze settled on the coiled black leather whip he clutched in his left fist. She'd guessed right—the cat was his specialty. Made sense, with him having come from the rugged Wyoming ranch country near the Colorado border, as he'd mentioned the first day while she filled in the blanks in his patient history after he came onto her inpatient unit at the hospital.

Jared stood in the entryway to the main dungeon, not yet certain if he'd stay. Then he spied a familiar face. Ninia.

Not that he hadn't pictured her in a dungeon like this. But he'd imagined her decked out in black leather and stiletto-heeled boots, whip in hand. Not like the submissive angel who stood, eyes downcast, decked out in loosely tied *Karada* bondage that drew his gaze to her naked breasts and pussy.

There was something more seductive than plain bare skin about the intricate pattern of royal blue rope against her pale, creamy body. He watched her eyelids flutter, her full lips curve upward in a shy smile. Her eyes remained downcast, as a good sub's should, yet he sensed she recognized him, that she'd singled him out somehow even before he'd noticed her. Like the woman across the courtyard last night, she wore her blonde hair loose, trailing down her back, soft curls caressing each womanly curve. Who had wrapped the intricate pattern of blue nylon rope? Apparently not her Master, for she waited with the other unattached subs for an invitation to play.

Jared figured he might fit the role of submissive better now that he wasn't all he'd been, but that thought didn't set well. He'd planned to say he was just here to observe tonight and not commit to either preference, but when the dungeon master had asked him his chosen role and orientation he'd answered automatically, "Dominant. Heterosexual," as he'd done countless times in dungeons around the world.

Old habits died hard. Real hard.

Making a conscious effort not to limp, he made his way across the room, not realizing until he stopped in front of Ninia that he'd been headed for her all along. It shocked the hell out of him because she already knew his physical limitations when the other subs wouldn't have seen them right away. He'd assumed his nurse, who'd seen him helpless and battered, would be the last one he'd want, for fear it would be a pity fuck. But it was as if his recurring dream had become reality. She had his cock rock-hard, his balls aching. There was no other woman in the room he could see past her.

"Without your uniform you are one hell of a beautiful woman," he told her, reaching out his hand in invitation. "Come with me."

When he noticed her eyes glistening with tears, he remembered she'd lost a serviceman-husband. Undoubtedly a Master, since she was obviously a practiced sub. He met her gaze and knew. This was her first venture into the world of BDSM in a long, long time—most likely since before her husband had shipped out for the last time. Would Jared, limited as he was by his injuries, be able to wipe out the pain he'd glimpsed so briefly in her eyes? He didn't know, but there was no way he could turn away, deny her whatever pleasure he could give her.

As though she sensed his doubts, she smiled, her tongue darting out to dampen her lips in shy invitation. "Yes, Master Jared." He could barely hear her, but he saw the longing in her eyes. "What can I do to please you?"

If he'd told her all the things he'd fantasized her doing to him, she probably would have run, so he stroked her satiny arm the way he might gentle a skittish mare. "Many things, but first I'd like to know I'm not stepping onto another Dom's property. Who tied your *Karada*?"

"I did, Master. My husband taught me how, and I thought of doing it because Master Chad is presenting a demonstration of the art tonight for everyone to view. The binding is loose, so if it pleases you, you may tighten it."

If it pleased him? He couldn't remember feeling as alive—as whole—as when he felt the softness of her skin beneath his fingers, the rhythmic pulsing of a delicate vein. Jared reached out, traced the intricate pattern of rope around her slender neck, down between her breasts, around and down past her hipbones over her downy mound. She'd done this to seduce him, and knowing that made him feel a Master's responsibility to bring her pleasure. "I'm not an expert in the art of Japanese rope bondage, so I will think of this as merely an arousing wrapping for an incredibly erotic package. I want to shave you here. I like eating a smooth pussy."

"Whatever gives you pleasure. Master." A tiny tremor went through her body, made him wonder…

She was being too damn compliant, even for a sub. Suspicion washed over Jared—suspicion she might be doing the Good Samaritan bit for a Dom who couldn't dominate without his sub's overt consent. "I may want to fuck your ass."

Her nipples hardened noticeably at his bald declaration. "That would please me immeasurably." Those words slammed into him, got his heart to pounding, his mouth watering to taste those rosy nubs. So what if she was in it for a pity fuck? He wasn't about to question her motives, not when she was here and she was hot. The heady smell of her sex already filled his nostrils, and he'd barely touched her. His balls throbbed and his cock pressed painfully against his zippered fly. "Come then, I'll get us a private torture chamber." He wasn't ready to strip in front of between twenty and thirty strangers. Not yet. Maybe not ever.

\* \* \* \* \*

One on one. Ninia wasn't surprised Jared wanted to play their scene between just the two of them, but she found herself craving privacy too, needing to go into this one step at a time. Yes. She'd enjoyed group scenes with Earl, found it exciting to have strangers watching him play her body like a fine violin. It had aroused her when he'd allowed his fellow Doms to join him in their sex play, sometimes even to take whatever holes he wasn't using at the time. But this was different, a first time with a new Master. She sensed it was Jared's first scene since his injury, as well. When she heard the heavy door close with a thud, she took in a deep breath, felt the heat of Jared's dark eyes burning into her from behind.

"I'm going to unwrap my present now," he told her, his deep, mellow voice sending chills down her spine as he laid his hands over hers and splayed their fingers over her belly. "Help me."

In those two words she sensed his doubt. His vulnerability. His determination to give her what she wanted in spite of the emotional baggage obvious from the way he'd dressed to cover the evidence of his loss. And she wanted to heal him, give him back…

But then he pulled her close, stole her thoughts with pure sexual sensations. The heat of his body, the rasp of his leather chaps and jeans against the backs of her legs, the woodsy smell of a light cologne, the powerful aura of a Master surrounded her, reassured her, made her feel lightheaded as she glanced around the chamber he'd chosen.

Big enough for a group scene, the paneled room reminded her of a bedroom in the bordello in an old-West movie she'd once seen, with its roughly hewn four-poster bed, matching washstand, and a mirrored wardrobe conveniently placed beside the big bed. One of the wardrobe doors was ajar, showing off an array of toys that seemed somehow incongruous with the antique furniture. Her heart beat faster when she noticed a sturdy spanking horse centered on a red frieze carpet beside the bed and imagined Jared restraining her across it, using that cat o'nine to flick at her tender skin.

The room suited him. Suited them. Her hands moved beneath his, found where she'd tied the rope and loosened the knot. "Here, it's loose now, Master. Do you want me to unwrap it?"

"No. I want to see how it's done, because I intend to learn how to wrap the rope myself." Very slowly, gently, taking his time to free her from the silken rope, he bent and nuzzled her neck. His warm breath heated her, made her want him to hurry, take her, force her to unleash all the restraint put on her by a long-ago promise that could never be fulfilled.

Earl had bound her as surely as if he'd been the one to tie the *Karada* in the dressing room tonight. Now Jared was releasing her, symbolically. Releasing her so he could take her and make her his, for tonight. Maybe longer. She absorbed his heat, his strength…the desire that surrounded them as the rope slid gently off her body onto the floor.

He reached out, took her hand, led her to the bed and laid back the red brocade coverlet. "Stand here a minute." Limping now but looking no less powerful because of it, he moved to the washstand, grabbed a towel and came back to spread it on the edge of the bed. "Now sit down and spread your legs for me."

"Yes, Master." When he sat beside her and drew one of her legs over his thigh, she felt his erection and wished she dared to touch him there. But she didn't. It felt so good when he lathered up her pussy and began to shave her, following the razor with his fingers to be sure he'd made her completely smooth. Moisture gushed, slickened her flesh so his fingers glided over it. God, it had been so long. She needed to come, prayed he'd order her to do so. But he didn't. Her clit hardened, elongated, throbbed with anticipation as he worked the razor around her ass. "Oh, yesss."

"There, that's the way I like my pussy." He set the razor down then stroked along her slit, slipping one long finger up her pussy before moving back and working it gently up her ass. "So soft. So wet. So fucking tight. I'm going to have to stretch your rear so it can take my cock."

"Please, Master." Had he always been so considerate, or had the horrors he'd endured tempered his Dominance, made him go easy, shield his partner from the rough edges Earl had always exhibited not only in public D/s scenes but also when they'd been alone, like this?

She loved the way Jared caressed her with his gaze. "Relax. Your pulse is racing already and we've barely begun. I want you so hot you're screaming for me to let you come." Lifting her leg and setting it on the bed, he stood, looked at the selection of toys and chose a bright blue anal plug from a shelf in the wardrobe. A shadow of pain crossed his face when he shifted his weight to the right, and the nurse in her longed to have him sit, remove not only the jeans he now was unzipping to free his long, thick cock but also the prosthesis she was sure must have been hurting him.

The sub in her kept quiet, concentrated on the cold, wet sensation of the lubricated plug as he worked it into her ass…and the delicious sight of his huge, rigid sex, already glistening wet at its purple-veined tip, beckoning her touch. Her tongue. "Master, may I…"

He stepped up to her, gave silent permission. She leaned forward, tasted him, took his cock head in her mouth and swirled her tongue over the pulsating, velvety flesh. He caught her head between his hands, guided her to take him deeper. "Swallow it, honey. Take it all. Oh yeah, suck me, like that." His words dissolved into a moan when she bent her head back and took him deep. He tasted good. Clean, a little salty. When she reached and weighed his heavy seed sac in both hands, he leaned closer, encouraging her.

She liked the smooth feel of his balls and around his anus, wondered if he'd been thinking of her when he shaved all but the thick, trimmed nest of dark hair that surrounded his cock. She swallowed around his cock as she ran a finger slowly around his asshole.

His cock twitched against her throat, and he shuddered when she started to work that finger against his anal sphincter.

"Stop or you'll make me come," he ordered, stepping back and depriving her of his cock. "Get up and stretch out over the spanking horse. It's obvious you need some punishment."

Now he sounded like a Dom, certain of what he wanted and what he expected of her. She liked that, liked that for the moment he'd apparently forgotten everything but what they were doing...what he intended to do to bring her pleasure.

Completely naked other than for the butt plug that stretched her tight rear entrance, she was feeling especially vulnerable as she moved from the bed. A delicious shiver of anticipation tinged with fear surged through her as she bent over the padded device, resting her belly against the red leather-covered top. A shiver went through her when he came up behind her, bent, spread her legs and secured them to the closest sawhorse uprights with Velcro straps. Anticipating his next move, she gripped the uprights on the other side with both her hands.

"That's a good sub," he said when he came around and found her waiting for him to fasten the cuffs. "Is your naughty pussy ready to take some punishment?"

Her pussy was throbbing, the tissue swollen with arousal. Her own juices flowed over her denuded skin, heightening the feelings. More than that, her emotions peaked at the prospect of him driving out the guilt, leaving her with nothing but the ecstasy she'd hardly realized how much she'd missed over the lonely years since Earl... "Yesss, Master, I've been a bad, bad girl. Please whip your naughty slave." She felt his hands on her shoulders, moving lower, caressing her bare flesh with searching fingers until he reached her butt cheeks and massaged them in a circular motion. He bent, a little shakily she thought, and nipped at the sweet spot just below the hairline at the back of her neck. "Mmmm."

He stepped back, out of her line of vision. Her breath caught in her throat at the thought of having the cat o'nine peppering her skin with its metal-tipped tendrils—of having her Master provide her the punishment she needed to find release.

*Craccckkkkk.* She'd been anticipating the bite of Jared's whip against her naked flesh. Instead she felt only air rushing by when the whip missed her by less than an inch.

He chuckled. "Guess this is one skill that hasn't gotten rusty. Next one's for real. I can hardly wait to soothe your pretty bottom after I redden it with this."

The next crack preceded a sharp series of stings as the ends of the cat made contact with her tender flesh. Again. And once more, she experienced the sort of pleasure-pain she'd almost forgotten, sensation that had her pussy wet, wanting…

"So wet. I like that." Jared stroked along her damp, swollen pussy lips with his right hand. Then he set aside the whip and traced the burning ribbons where it had marked her ass cheeks, his touch incredibly gentle. Incredibly arousing. "We'll go slow. You're so damn soft…like silk. Does this feel good?"

It felt good, yes. And he looked good enough to eat, naked now but for his boots and chaps. Seeing his cock curving upward toward his flat belly, watching a vein on its underside throbbing rhythmically, made her mouth water. His balls had drawn up tight against his body, a dead giveaway to the height of his arousal. The taste of him was still fresh on her tongue…salty and sexy and… "Oh, yes." It had been so long, too long, since she'd felt a Master's touch. Too long since she'd paid a lover homage with her hands and mouth. "May I service you now, Master?"

"In good time." He seemed in no hurry, stroking her first with one hand and then the other, as though learning her by Braille. She held the position, hands and ankles restrained, loving the anticipation, enjoying the slow arousal, Jared's seeming fascination with the pulse points behind her knees, the exaggerated curve of her spine. When he bent and blew along the length of her newly shaved slit, the sensation triggered waves of tiny shocks she felt deep in her belly.

"Don't come," he warned, giving her a sharp slap on the backside with the flattened palm of his hand. "Not until I give you permission."

He wanted her more than he'd wanted water when he'd been lost in the desert, more than he feared she'd reject him when she saw his scars, the functional but ugly prosthesis his boots and chaps couldn't quite hide. No, wait a minute, she'd already seen those scars. She'd seen his naked stump with blood oozing from the spots where the goddamn metal fragments kept working their way out. He ran his palms along the length of her firm, slender thighs, was rewarded with a soft moan that sounded a lot like "Jared."

When he ringed her pink asshole with a finger and jostled the plug, she squirmed and whimpered. "You like that, don't you?"

"Oh, yesss." She drew out the word so it sounded like an ecstatic sigh. Realizing her dead husband must have taught her every kink in the book aroused him yet sent a tiny twinge of jealousy through his brain. *Come off it. You're no virgin, either, and the last thing you'd want would be one who'd have to get over screaming at your scars before she'd let you teach her.*

Bending, he unfastened her bonds, pausing on the way up to caress the firm flesh of her inner thighs. "Get up on the bed now. Lie on your back and spread your legs."

She lost no time complying, and he wished he had as much confidence in her motives as he did in her need to be fulfilled. "Like this, Master?" Her lips were moist, slightly open, begging to be kissed—or wrapped around his cock, sucking out his climax. In another time and place he'd have obliged her, stood motionless while she knelt at his feet, arms wrapped around his calves while she gave him head. But not tonight. Tonight he'd fuck her until she screamed for mercy, and then maybe he'd let her taste him coming in her mouth.

He moved between her outstretched legs. God, but she was wet and swollen, so tempting to his starved libido. So trusting, so ready to take whatever pleasure he chose to give. "Yeah. Just like that. Relax and don't move." As he'd done a hundred times before in another life, he lifted the silk scarves tied to each of the four posts on the bed and laid them across her wrists and ankles. He didn't tie them, instead relied on her obeying his order to stay still, flex her knees outward, let him in.

It suddenly hit him that being a Master wasn't all about physical compulsion, that much of being a Dom involved emotional control. Still, he couldn't get it out of his head… "Are you doing this because you feel sorry for a beat-up soldier?" he asked as he withdrew the plug from her ass.

She lay there for a minute, her expression reflecting hurt, amazement…and anger inappropriate for a sub to express toward her Master. Then she moved, her motion deliberate, sliding off the bed and onto her knees before him. "Don't you dare think that! Do you have any idea how long I've dreamed about you taking me? About you letting me taste you this way? When you were in the hospital, you dreamed. You commanded someone to her knees. When you did, I got wet." Cupping his aching balls in both her soft, warm hands, she bent and licked away the drop of lubrication in the slit of his cock. Then she looked up at him, the burning desire evident in her gaze. "I had Marshall send you the invitation…"

"How did you know I'd be into this lifestyle?" Right now he didn't care. Her hands were on his thighs, her pretty head resting against his belly as she looked up at him with those big blue eyes. But he had a feeling she needed to tell him, so he threaded his fingers through her hair and made her look him in the eye. "Tell me."

"When you were sleeping, you'd dream. And say things that made me know you're a Master. Lots of times you'd cry out in your sleep and I'd come stand by you. You'll never know how much I wanted to crawl into that bed with you, comfort you."

He bent and lifted her. He let her feel the strength of his arms when he held her tight. His mouth came down on hers, hard, and he tongue-fucked her the same insistent way he intended to fuck her wet, hot cunt. "Lie back down and spread your legs for me," he growled.

This time he knotted the silk ties, holding her helpless for his pleasure—and hers.

"Yesss, Master. Please fuck me."

"All in good time, my naughty little slave." Leaning over her, he took her mouth again, using his fingers to play with her tight little nipples. When she whimpered with pleasure, he raised up, giving the rosy nubs a farewell twist as he stood and moved to the wardrobe again.

As she moaned with her arousal, he squeezed lubricant onto his index and middle fingers before slowly working them past her tight anal sphincter, stretching her, readying her to take the larger plug he'd selected. Someday he'd fuck her ass, but not tonight, not until he'd stretched her enough so she could take his cock without pain. He withdrew his fingers, replacing them with the plug until its flared base rested against her tight, inviting rear entrance.

"I want you to wear this for me when you're home," he said when the last and largest of the three sections slipped inside her. "Imagine it's my cock in you, stretching you, fucking you." When she whimpered his name he added, "Soon enough, I will fuck your pretty ass." It didn't escape his lust-driven mind that he'd just assumed this was to be a long-term situation. That deep in the back of his mind lay a growing feeling that Ninia was the woman over whom he'd like to exert full ownership. That realization didn't make him pull back, the way it had when he'd thought it with countless women in his past.

Before, he'd been just passing through between assignments in different ones of the world's hotspots. Anbar Province. Afghanistan. Before that, Serbia and the Philippines. None of them places to take a woman. He hadn't had time or energy to think of home or commitment, or even taking a slave for much more than a few nights' pleasure. Now he might be battered, but he was free. No longer a willing slave to the Marine Corps but a free man. Free to take a lover other than the Corps. Free to fall in lust and love, to commit himself to his woman's pleasure.

She squirmed against her bonds. Her mouth was tight, as though she was trying not to cry out, not to beg him to ease her arousal. His balls tightened at the sight of her nipples, distended, tight, beckoning his hands and mouth. He dared not look at her cunt because, if he did, he was afraid he'd come on the spot.

No. He had more self-control than that. Staying on his feet, he stroked the length of her body, catching her nipples between his fingers and twisting them until she moaned. He soothed the welts the cat had made on her sides and her thighs, inhaling the sweet musk of her sex and pinching her impudent little clit that poked temptingly from her satiny labia. "Feel good, sweetheart?"

"Oh, yesss. Fuck me now, Master, please." She sounded tortured, as if forming her words took too much concentration. "God, I need to come."

So did Jared. He wasted no time shedding his boots and chaps and rolling on a condom. Moving onto the bed and settling on his knees between her legs, he rubbed his cock along her wet, hot slit, found her cunt and sank inside. "Oh, yeah. You feel fantastic. So hot and wet. So tight. I could fuck you all night long. Squeeze me, baby." She worked her inner muscles on him. His balls drew up, preparing…

Too soon. He didn't want it over with, not yet. Not until she wanted to come so much she'd scream with frustration when he told her no. Deliberately he slowed the pace, rocking in and out, first shallow then deep, grinding his pelvis against her satiny mound, resting his hands on her ribcage and tugging at her rigid nipples. He tried to ignore the incredibly erotic feelings, the persistent pressure from the plug through the thin layer of her flesh that separated her two welcoming holes.

Pressure built inside his balls, his cock twitched. "Come for me now!" he ordered, fucking her hard, closing his eyes and pounding into her G-spot until she arched her hips to his and screamed. Her cunt contracted around him like a vise, drawing out his own shuddering climax.

When he opened his eyes, he fully expected to find her gone, to discover she was only another torturous dream.

## Chapter Four

### ❧

But Ninia was beside Jared, straining against the ties that bound her. She wanted to touch him, feel the tremors that still rippled through his big body. Her heart still pounded in her chest as she fought to catch her breath.

"Thank you, Master," she said when he bent over her and began to loosen her bonds.

"Thank *you*, sweetheart." His grin was feral, the look in his eyes that of a sated male who'd just staked his claim. "Since you like Japanese rope bondage so much, we'll go watch this Master Chad demonstrate it if you wish. I'd be remiss if I didn't learn an art that so obviously brings you pleasure." Standing, he stepped back into his boots and strapped the black chaps low on his waist.

But Ninia had seen him hesitate before leaving his jeans on the chair beside the bed, and she sensed his reluctance to leave the safety of their private cocoon. "If you'd prefer it, I could show you how. Here. Now." Sensing that was what he wanted, she rose and stood before him.

"I'd like that. You have no idea how incredibly sexy you looked, bound that way." He gestured toward the pile of royal blue nylon rope he'd unwrapped. "I figure there must be seventy feet of rope here. Plenty to net you nicely."

"Sixty-five feet to be exact, Master. The wrapping's not as complicated as it looks."

His dark eyes glittered with barely concealed desire. "Show me."

"First, you fold the rope in half and put the loop around my neck."

He did it, his fingers brushing the spots just below her ears, sending shivers of delight along the sensitive nerve ends there. "Okay. Now I knot it, right?"

"Right. The first knot needs to be here." She reached up and showed him the spot, above the upper end of her breastbone. "Now make more knots every seven inches or so. Don't pull them tight now, that way you'll be able to adjust them later to the exact positions where you want them."

"Got it. Now the doubled rope goes between your legs, up your back, and…" He shot her an inquisitive look.

"Now you pull the ends of the rope through the loop around my neck. Careful. Don't pull it too tight."

"Never." He ran a finger around her neck, slowly checking to be sure there was enough slack. The gesture made her feel cherished—protected, as much as she could remember ever having felt under a Master's hand. "What next?"

"Next you thread the ends of the rope through the loop between the first and second knots. Run both ends to the back again, pull them through the first loop on the back, and back again to the front, into the loop between the second and third knots. Keep going until you get to the last loops at the bottom, and tie off the loose ends."

Jared took a step back, admired his work and grinned, as though he thought he'd performed some great feat. "How'd I do, my pretty submissive?"

"Very well, Master." Ninia presented her back. "You need to adjust the knots here so they're not right on my spine. Right or left, it doesn't matter, but when you tighten the net, the pressure on the spinal column gets painful—even dangerous—if the knots are on the spinal column."

He wasted no time moving the knots, meticulously settling them the way she suggested, stroking the skin around her, making her crazy with need. The delicious pressure of the rope on her tender flesh increased as Jared tightened her bonds. "Your safe word is 'nurse'", he whispered as he made one final adjustment. "On your knees, now. I want to feel your sweet mouth on my cock."

She wanted that too. Each knot of the *Karada* pressed against her throat and breasts when she went back on her knees. With every motion, her bonds reminded her of his power, her helplessness. He loomed large before her, his erection jutting proudly from the dark nest of curls between his thighs. A powerful phallic symbol, living, throbbing, framed once again in those black chaps that had the not-unpleasant smell of leather fresh from the tannery.

She stuck out her tongue, tasted the drop of lubrication at the tip of his smooth, plum-shaped cock head. "Oooh." Salty, slightly bitter, deliciously male. Her lips went slack, and she took him in her mouth. Tilted her head back and swallowed, consuming him, giving him head as pressure from the net reminded her of her enslavement and made her pussy ache for him to fuck her.

"You like sucking cock, I can tell. Jesus, your mouth feels like heaven." He knotted his fists in her hair, holding her steady to take the rhythmic thrusts of his hips against her lips. "Yeah. That's it, make me come if you can."

Yes. She liked it. Liked him. Liked the feeling of being alive again, of giving pleasure to another human being…a man who'd been through hell and survived to come home. "Jared," she murmured, though the word was lost but for the reverberations of sound that rippled through her throat, his cock and balls.

"Stop. Now." If she didn't, Jared was going to explode, and despite what he'd told her, he didn't want to. Not yet. Not until he took her every way, claimed every orifice. Not until he drove away the loneliness, the doubts, the fear that when he opened his eyes Ninja would be gone, another mirage sent from hell to tease and taunt him.

But right now she was real. Beautiful and beautifully submissive in the *Karada* bondage she'd taught him to apply, caught like a flitting butterfly within a net of her own design. Jared lifted her to her feet, loving her responsiveness, the fine sheen of perspiration that made her pale skin glisten. "Shall I open the curtain to the observation window?" he asked once he'd pulled down the coverlet and settled her on her back on the bed.

"Only if you wish to, Master Jared."

At the moment he didn't care if the whole fucking world saw his scars, not if having observers would enhance her pleasure. But he sensed her reluctance, imagined she might have played out similar scenes here with her late husband and might feel awkward if other members were to watch her putting his memory to rest. "We'll leave them closed this time."

He sat beside her and traced the blue net, soothing the small angry marks made where the knots abraded her tender skin, the light welts he'd put on her with the cat. "You're beautiful." And so responsive. Her nipples beaded at the mere brush of his fingertips, and when he pinched them, she let out a high-pitched whimper that spoke more of pleasure than pain. "I want you to have these pierced."

"Yes, Master." From her quick response he surmised she realized he wanted to own her long-term. It pleased him immeasurably that she didn't spit out her safe word and run for cover.

He bent his head, took a nipple in his mouth and sucked it, hard. When he did, he felt her hand in his hair, a caress more than an effort to hold him to her breast. Soothing yet incredibly arousing, it was a lover's touch however fleeting it might be. Her giving made him want to give back, show her pleasure beyond this D/s scene, beyond a night.

Unconfined but for the rope net, Ninia held a position of submission, arms outstretched, legs apart, open for his inspection and use. Jared stroked her inner thighs, assuring himself by touch as well as sight and sound that she was here and she was real, awaiting his pleasure.

When she stirred and lifted her hips in blatant invitation, he removed the butt plug, untied the *Karada* bondage he'd tied moments earlier and unwound the silken rope from her lush body. "I want your arms around me, your gorgeous legs wrapped around my waist when I take you."

He wanted her to want him. Not just as a convenient release from sexual tension, not only for whatever satisfaction a sub found by relinquishing control. He wanted her to desire Jared McTavish the man, with all the emotional baggage he carried, all his scars.

For a moment it seemed she hesitated, but then she smiled and laid a hand against his cheek. "It will be my pleasure, Master. My greatest pleasure."

So, with the curtains drawn in a private room at Boundless Pleasure, Jared had the most satisfying sex in his thirty-two years of living. Plain vanilla sex, more or less missionary position. No toys and no kink. Just him and Ninia wrapped in each other's arms, their bodies locked together in ecstasy.

Reality. No posturing, just a sharing like he'd never known before. *God, let it last. Let this be real.* For the first time in his life he wanted to fall in love, not just in lust.

\* \* \* \* \*

Later on, when he waited for a cab to take him home, he clutched the folded paper Ninia had given him along with a shy promise that if he'd join her at her place the next night, she'd fix him a home-cooked meal. When he recognized her address as being in the same apartment complex as his, he wondered… Could she have been the one who'd given him the show of his life last night? Time would tell.

## Chapter Five

Ninia hummed the next morning as she prepared the yogurt and granola she ate for breakfast. She could barely wait to be with Jared again. Every move she made, the plug he'd ordered her to wear brushed against the tender flesh of her anus, reminding her last night had been real. Very real.

Not that she needed a reminder. With his careful mastery, he'd managed to imprint himself on every cell of her body. Her nipples tingled, her pussy wept, and her skin remembered every skillfully laid welt, each knot in the *Karada* he'd tied a little clumsily but with incredible care for her well-being and pleasure.

She had an appointment at ten to follow his orders and have her nipples pierced. Crossing to the patio door where she'd exposed herself to him, she looked across the courtyard, hoping to get a glimpse of him. No luck. He was sleeping, she imagined, rolling her nipples between her thumbs and forefingers and wondering what kind of jewelry he'd want her to wear in them. She'd never thought of body piercings before—Earl hadn't cared for them on females even though he'd sported one of his own, a thick curved barbell that entered his cock on its underside and exited through the eye in its head. Now the idea of piercing her intimate flesh for Jared had her panties damp, her heart pounding with anticipation.

She'd get gold hoops, she thought, simple and elegant. Imagining him hooking a finger through them, twisting them until she moaned with the pleasure-pain of it, had her practically panting with anticipation. He'd want to use them to tug her until his lightly furred chest brushed her nipples. Then he'd bend and catch a ring with his teeth, tugging the captive nipple into his mouth. She could hardly wait until she got the piercings and healed. Imagining him looking at them, knowing she'd pierced them for him had her pussy swollen and wet with anticipation.

Oh, yes. She could barely wait to feel the sharp bite of the needle as it pressed through her nipples, experience the unfamiliar weight of the hoops hanging from that sensitive flesh. Fingering her hairless mound and recalling the care with which Jared had shaved her there last night, she decided she'd go one step farther and have her entire body waxed smooth. Jared would like that, she was certain. The rest of the day she'd spend preparing, not just for dinner but in every way she could think of that would turn her lover on. Her Master, if she had her way.

* * * * *

The sun was close to its zenith when Jared opened his eyes and looked out the window. For the first time since his injury, he'd slept a full eight hours. He grinned as the events at Boundless Pleasure last night flooded his memory—and let out a big sigh of relief when he reread the dinner invitation Ninia had handed him before sliding behind the wheel of her car and driving away late last night. After limping back from the parking lot to the door of the club where he'd waited for a cab, he'd read it. Her words, penned in neat, rounded letters had practically obliterated the pain that had kept trying to remind him he shouldn't have stayed on his feet so much.

Suddenly he felt as if he needed to get his life moving. As if he had a future worth looking forward to. He looked around the sparsely furnished apartment, realized it was time to move along. Time to go home and put the Special Forces behind him. Picking up the phone, he called his brother Brad and arranged to have someone go clean up the big log cabin his grandfather had left him on his part of the family's nine-thousand-acre ranch.

His stump hurt like hell, but he didn't care. If he was going to take Ninia home, he needed to buy a car or truck.

Somehow the idea of asking the dealer to equip the vehicle of his choice with hand controls didn't seem quite as embarrassing as it had been at first. He'd balked at the requirement soon after arriving in Cheyenne a few weeks earlier, after a hard-faced woman at the Wyoming Department of Motor Vehicles had insisted he'd have to have "handicapped assist" controls if he wanted to drive.

Several hours later, Jared was even sorer. He was also the proud owner of a shiny, black Honda Ridgeline pickup, and the dealer had assured him he'd have the console-mounted hand control installed on it within two days. Damn it, he'd never liked an automatic transmission, especially in country like this where snow was pretty much a constant seven or eight months of the year. Since the DMV required it, though, that's what he'd have to live with. What he'd be fucked if he'd do was hang out a handicap placard for everyone to see. He could make his way from a regular parking spot just like everybody who hadn't lost a limb. And nobody better dare try to tell him he couldn't.

* * * * *

After firing up the gas grill on the patio and setting out a pair of T-bone steaks to come to room temperature, Ninia scurried around her condo, dusting here, moving a photo of Earl off the mantel and settling it in the drawer of a side table. "You'd like Jared," she said, caressing the glass covering her husband's smiling face, certain as she looked at his silent image that he'd given his blessing last night in the club when she'd removed the chain he'd used to collar her and stored it figuratively into the spot in her heart where she kept her most cherished memories.

She was alive. And so was her new Master. She started a pot of coffee then remembered Jared had always asked for tea at the hospital and put the teapot on the stove. The activity helped her ignore the stinging in her newly pierced nipples every time the hoops swayed as she moved—and the growing arousal that had her anxious for Jared to arrive and put out the fire.

She'd been hot ever since she left the piercing parlor, and the body waxing she'd had done afterward had fanned the flame. A whole day preparing to serve her Master, down to a thorough internal cleansing done before her bath, had her focusing on her body and all the delicious things he'd do to her—even before she'd lubricated and reinserted the plug he'd ordered her to wear. Before she'd dried herself, taking frequent looks in the mirror to watch her new gold hoops dangling merrily from her sore, puckered nipples, to check her buttocks and see the slightly raised welts he'd given her. Finally she'd put on a midriff top and a skirt that barely covered her ass, and tied her hair back in a high ponytail that bared her newly waxed hairline for a lover's pleasure and her own. She could hardly wait to feel Jared's hot breath on that sensitive skin, the rasp of his teeth and the rough callused surface of his fingertips as he held her to him for a deep, hard kiss. Unable to resist, she reached up and stroked that strangely erogenous spot at the base of her skull until her nipples swelled against their new rings and her inner thighs grew wet.

Now all she had left to do was calm her frazzled nerves. And wait for Jared to show up for the dinner she'd promised. She watched him coming out of the glass-walled elevator across the way, noticed he was limping badly. His stump had to be hurting. He'd worn the prosthesis all night last night. She understood why—stupid male pride—but now he obviously was paying the price in pain. Damn it, he didn't even have his crutches!

His stump was going to be a bloody mass of pain. Making a detour to her bathroom, she grabbed a first aid kit and set it on the coffee table on her way to answering the front door.

When she opened the door he strode by her, slid open the patio door and looked out over the courtyard. Then he turned back, stared at her framed in the doorway, an intense look on his face. Seizing her and dragging her hard against him, momentarily driving any thoughts of nursing him from her head, he practically torched her with the intensity of his gaze. "It was you," he growled, laying his hands on her shoulders and holding her at arms' length. "My little temptress on the balcony. When I saw your address last night I wondered… God, I can't believe it. You're the one who gave me one hell of a show the other night."

She wouldn't even try to deny it. "I also was the one who got you the invitation to Boundless Pleasure. I don't know why I want a Master who's too stubborn to take care of his body so he can enjoy having me pleasure him, but I do. Come here."

Before she could stop him, he'd scooped her up in his arms. "My body's doing just fine. Aching to fuck you until you can't stand up, right after you feed me." He jostled the butt plug, shot her a self-satisfied grin. "It pleases me that you've followed my instruction." When he set her down, he was grinning, but she saw the pain in his dark, expressive eyes and realized what his act of bravado had cost him.

"Go sit down. On the couch. I saw how badly you were limping when made your way across the courtyard."

For a minute he stared at her, his expression transforming from desire to anger — or bitter disappointment. He looked as though he might walk out, but instead he moved to the couch. "Sorry, sweetheart. I'm not angry with you. It's this that disappoints me when it won't do what it's supposed to do." He gestured toward his leg. "Kind of hard, being a Dom when I can't get past the fact of this. But the soreness is nothing. Just a little swelling in the stump. Happens all the time."

"I imagine it does, especially when you don't use common sense. No, don't sit just yet. Let me get these pants off you."

His grin was absolutely feral — and a bit nasty. "Eager, are you?"

She wished she dared wipe that smirk off his handsome face. "Right now I'm eager to see how badly you've hurt yourself. Don't you know you don't have to pretend this didn't happen to you?" As she dragged his khakis down, she rested a hand on the socket of his prosthesis, then slid it up onto his scarred thigh. "Now sit."

"Hey, who's Master here?" His smile turned to a scowl, and he made a move to heave himself up off the couch. "I came for dinner. I can get TLC at the hospital when I go for my therapy."

Ninia kept on, slipping off his shoes and stripping him down to his plain white boxer briefs before looking up at him and issuing a challenge. "Right now we're nurse and patient, not Master and slave. Let's get this thing off and see what damage you've done."

"If you insist." He reached down to loosen the prosthesis, unapologetically brushing his fingers over her breast on the way. "Damn it, don't you understand I don't want my lover having to take care of me like this? I want to be a Master for you, not a pathetic cripple who needs tending."

So that was it. Ninia stopped what she was doing and looked him in the eye. "You don't get it. You don't see it, you dense cowboy. Being a Master has nothing to do with physical ability, although you've got plenty of that. It's something bone-deep, some quality I recognized in you the first time you came onto my ward." She paused, took a deep breath, formed the words in her head before saying them aloud. "You look at me, just look at me with those intense brown eyes, and I get wet. I want to get on my knees like this and take your cock in my mouth. I want to feel you taking me over. But I can't do that if you kill yourself."

"I'm not going to kill myself." As though daring her to argue, he slid the prosthesis off and peeled back the stump sock, revealing his swollen flesh and a couple of raw, red spots where the doctors had worked out more pieces of shrapnel a few days earlier.

She could barely control the fury that he'd treated himself this way. "If you're going to keep doing this to yourself, you might as well grab a gun and do it the easy way," she snarled, pointing at his inflamed leg. "How the hell did you stand to walk over here with your leg swollen like this? Why did you? All you'd have needed to do was look, and you'd have known you ought to have left the prosthesis off and used your crutches."

"Calm down, would you?"

"No. I won't calm down." She took some sterile antiseptic wipes from her first aid kit and started to cleanse the stump. "By not taking care of this, you're weakening yourself, destroying your own spirit by refusing to accept who you are. A wonderful, sexy Master who happens to be missing part of his leg." She thought of Earl, tried to stop the tears from spilling onto her cheeks. "I can't bear to lose another..."

He caught her face between his hands, wiped away the moisture she couldn't hold back. It was as if her tears had washed away his anger, left only a gentle caring in his eyes. "You won't, honey. You won't. It wouldn't look this bad if I hadn't spent the better part of the day tromping around car dealerships to find me a new truck." Bending his head, he took her mouth for a long, hard kiss. "Now do your worst so I can show you I'm very much alive."

"All right." She reached for the first aid kit and began working on his leg again. "Promise you'll take better care of yourself, okay?"

"Okay. Ouch, damn it! I'm into dishing out punishment, not taking it," Jared said while she dabbed more antiseptic on the raw wounds. "Easy there." She heard the apology in his tone, if not in the growled complaint he made.

No way was Ninia going to let him put that limb back on—not now, and probably not anytime before this time tomorrow, if then. "Well, you've done it, Master. You're here for at least twenty-four hours because you were too macho to bring along your crutches. There's no way I'll let you try to walk on this until it's had time to heal a bit. You sit here while I fix our steaks."

* * * * *

Jared tried to be pissed, but staying mad was impossible when Ninia had just hand-fed him the best meal he'd had since he couldn't remember when. She'd cooked his steak rare, the potatoes soft and buttery. His salad had been drenched in some delicious kind of dressing that had him scraping the last lettuce leaf off the bottom of his wooden salad bowl. The final course was a hot fudge sundae, complete with real whipped cream and a cherry on top.

It had taken him halfway through their dinner to get over the embarrassment of sitting there in his underwear, the swollen stump of his right leg hanging out for her to see every time she walked by. Now, as they topped the meal off with a pot of hot tea, he found himself wanting to appease an appetite of a different sort.

Come to think of it, she'd fed that appetite too, sashaying around in that short skirt that rode up every now and then, giving him a nice view of her baby-soft pussy…and a midriff-baring halter top with a tie at the neck that looked as though it would be a cinch to unfasten. He could hardly wait to visually inspect the brand-new nipple rings he'd seen outlined through the thin cloth. It had his cock rock-hard, knowing she'd gone right out and followed his order to pierce them. For him.

He wanted to take back the control she'd made him relinquish. Yeah. He didn't mind Ninia playing Nurse Domme once in a while—especially when his stump hurt like hell, the way it had before she insisted on taking his prosthesis off. But he needed to remind her who was Master. "Take off your top, sweetheart. I want to see your new nipple rings."

Smiling, she undid the halter and bared her breasts. "Hope you like plain gold hoops. You didn't specify."

"Oh, yeah. I like 'em. And I like looking at you and knowing you obeyed me without delay. He reached over, brushed his fingers very gently across first one bare breast and then the other. "I think once you're healed I'll hang a chain between them, tug on it whenever I want to grab your attention."

"Mmmm. Sounds kinky, Master."

"I like seeing your nipples red and swollen. Can hardly wait until the piercings heal so I can play with them."

"You could have used clamps. That way you wouldn't have had to wait for the piercings to heal." From the small frown lines that appeared at the edges of her lush mouth, he imagined her experience with the devices hadn't been altogether pleasant, and that made him want to reach beyond the grave and punch out the one who'd hurt her that way.

Very gently, he touched one of the rings. "I know. But I don't like using nipple clamps. It's too easy to get carried away and hurt your sub with them. Come here. Flip up that sexy little skirt and ride me. Ride me the way you rode that dildo out on your balcony."

"I was hoping you'd come when you saw me doing that."

He laughed as he drew down his underwear and freed his erection. "I did, sweetheart. But coming that way doesn't feel a tenth as good as it does coming inside your hot little cunt. Now reach in the pocket of my pants and get me a condom." When she did, he rolled it on then grasped her at the waist, lifted her and guided her down until he was buried inside her to his balls. "Oh, yeah. Nothing feels better to my cock than a hot, submissive pussy. Squeeze me."

She took his mouth, tongue-fucked him, ground her ass up and down, around and around, clamping hard on his cock with her inner muscles, milking him. Damn, he was going to come, and there wasn't a fucking thing he could do about it. "Come, baby. Come for your Master now."

When she dug her nails into his shoulders he slammed her down on his cock, absorbed her cries in his mouth as he let go, filling the condom with burst after burst of his hot come. "Sorry to have hurried it," he murmured against the pale mass of her hair. "Help me into your bed, and we'll start all over again."

\* \* \* \* \*

Jared lay in the dark. Without his prosthesis or crutches, he was nearly as helpless as he'd been when his lieutenant had found him in the desert, but he didn't care. Ninia was sleeping in his arms, her even breathing against his chest welcome proof that she was real—that the explosive lovemaking they'd shared was no illusion.

He raised his upper body up on one elbow, watched her as she slept. Yeah, he wanted her. He'd lusted after her from the minute he'd wakened in her ward and gazed into her big blue eyes. But he was feeling more than desire. More than lust.

Love? He hadn't thought much about that, hadn't considered what love meant although he'd had the vague feeling he'd know when that emotion came up and bit him in the butt. He guessed it had just bitten him. Hard.

For the first time in his life Jared was thinking collars and rings…a home on his part of the family ranch…and if they were lucky, a kid or two. Sure, the mental picture he drew lacked the adrenaline-raising excitement of rooting out insurgents who'd vowed to destroy everything he held dear, but he found he liked the idea. He tossed back the covers to feast his eyes on his lover, tried to look at his own damaged body without bitterness.

Actually he found he couldn't dredge up any rancor even when he deliberately stared at the empty spot where his lower leg should have been or at the angry-looking stump. How could he, when Ninia had told him in every way but words that she desired him just as he was? When she'd shown him she wanted everything he had to give, but would ask for nothing beyond his ability to provide.

"Master?"

Her voice, husky with sleep, seduced his heart, not just his sex. "Yes?"

"Please hold me. I'm cold."

"Here." He felt a slight tremor in her body when he pulled her up against his chest, experienced the incredible softness of skin she'd had waxed smooth because she'd thought he'd like it. He did. A lot. Not just her baby soft cunt and ass, but her legs and arms and even the back of her neck where he'd quickly learned the simplest touch of his hand or mouth could get her squirming and whining for him to let her come. "I want you to wear my collar." *My ring too*, but it was too soon for that. "Be my slave…my lover…my everything."

Reverently, he traced the marks where he'd put the rope around her neck last night. "Will you?"

She reached up, framed his cheeks between her hands. "Twenty-four, seven?"

"Yes." It surprised him to realize he wanted that, not merely a committed Dom/sub sexual relationship. "Every day, all day. And all night. Especially all night." Mindful of her new piercings, he drew her gently to him, burying his face in the fragrant mass of her loosened hair.

"I'd like that." Shifting, she opened her legs, making a place for his thigh against the moist heat of her swollen pussy. "Except…"

"I want you to quit your job. I can support you," he added, realizing she might think all he had to offer financially was a disability pension from the VA. "I want my own private duty nurse to keep me from doing something stupid and hurting myself again." He surprised himself by saying that, but he realized it was true. While he welcomed Ninia's sexual submissiveness, he also yearned for the sort of loving care she showed him earlier—the nurturing he once would have rejected as a sign of weakness, an admission of his own vulnerabilities. "And I want to give you everything you need, all the pleasure you want."

Jared found that was true too. While it undoubtedly would test his bruised self-confidence, he'd willingly risk a little embarrassment to provide her every kinky pleasure available to them in the BDSM clubs. After all, it was a master's duty to see to his slave's pleasure—and he found himself looking forward to arranging scenes that would fulfill her streak of voyeurism and more.

Ninia laid a hand between his legs, cupped his balls. "I'll be your slave. Gladly. So long as you promise you'll take care of these." She slid her hand up the length of his cock and gave it a squeeze, loving the way he seemed to be learning to cope emotionally with his disability. She wondered if she dared hope some of his acceptance had to do with them having become lovers.

Jared silenced her with a kiss, a deep, hard kiss that took her breath away. "On all fours, sweetheart. As soon as you'll let me up, I'll go shopping for your collar. Meanwhile, I'm going to get rid of this plug and claim your pretty ass."

Slowly, gently, he prepared her, first with one finger, then two. "Oh, yeah. I can hardly wait to take you here." Pausing, he put on a condom then lubricated it and her rear entrance. "I hope I don't lose my balance," he commented as he positioned himself on his knees behind her, his arms braced on his hands at her sides. "Tell me if this is too much. I don't want to hurt you."

All she wanted was his hot flesh buried in her aching body. And he obliged her. The pressure of his thick cock head against her rear entrance made her take a deep breath, relax her inner muscles when they tried to tense up. She loved the way he entered her so carefully, an inch at the time, stretching her…filling her…claiming the only part of her he hadn't already taken. It hurt, but then love often did, and on the way to pleasure was a sea of pain to travel. Ninia held her breath, and as she did the discomfort eased, leaving her with a warm glow…and an exquisite climax she'd never forget.

* * * * *

Time passed quickly, and almost before she realized it, July was gone. Ninia had worked out her notice at the hospital. Now Jared settled her in the passenger seat of his new truck, and she had nothing more to do than enjoy the smell of the beige leather seats and the luxurious feel of it against the backs of her legs—and wonder what kind of goodies he had stashed in the cooler on the backseat for their picnic lunch. Her buttocks stung deliciously, reminding her of her Master's skill with the long whip he'd used on her again last night at Boundless Pleasure, after they'd picked up the results of the lab tests he'd insisted they both get, for her protection. When she turned to look at him, he was frowning, his right hand resting on the state-of-the-art hand control mechanism he told her he'd reluctantly agreed to have installed because he failed to pass the dexterity test required for driving using his prosthesis on the accelerator and brake.

"You know, you can take the test again once your leg has completely healed," she said, sensing his disgust at the reminder of his disability.

"Yeah. But with this I can also drive if I decide not to wear the damn prosthesis some time." He wove expertly through traffic onto the on ramp to Interstate 80 and patted the knob on the hand control. "It's not so much that I mind having this thing. It's actually a pretty cool device I might have ordered on my own. It's just that being told I had to have it made me feel like a cripple. I so don't want to come off that way to people I care about."

"You could never make me think of you that way, my darling Master." Reaching around the device, which looked a lot like an oversize gear shift lever mounted on the console between the two seats, she laid her hand on his thigh, was rewarded with a smile. "Tell me where we're going," she said, curious since all he'd said was to take clothes for a few days in the mountains — and the cowgirl outfit she'd worn for him at the club last night. He'd gruffly ordered her to wear the butt plug so she'd keep her mind focused on the fucking they were going to enjoy once they got to where they were going. Just thinking of it made her pussy clench, her newly healed nipples swell against their rings.

"I'm going to show you where I grew up. Where I want us to live once I've finished up with getting therapy."

"You're from Laramie?" The highway they were cruising along with a convoy of semis and the occasional car or pickup truck was a nearly straight stretch of asphalt that stretched the fifty some-odd miles between the two southern Wyoming cities.

He paused, shot a grin her way. "Close, but not quite. Tie Siding. Ever heard of it?"

Ninia thought a minute, couldn't recall having heard of the unusually named place. "'Fraid not."

"I'm not surprised. All it is is a post office inside a beat-up flea market on Highway 287, about eight miles from the Colorado line. But it's where Grandpa got his mail. Where we'll get ours if we decide to move to the land he left me. About an hour's drive from Cheyenne on a good day, fifteen minutes max from Laramie except when it gets snowed in during the winter."

"I'll bet it's beautiful." Especially on this gorgeous summer day, when the sun was high in the sky and the trees along the road were dressed in green, from the light-green leaves of cottonwoods and various shrubs to the dark blue-greens of towering spruce trees. "Why did you decide to leave?"

"I wanted excitement. Danger." He paused, shook his head. "Got plenty of that, didn't I? Never mind, don't pay me any attention. It's a beautiful day, I've got my beautiful slave by my side, and I'm happy to be going home."

"Really?"

He moved his hand from the control, flipped back her skirt and gave her upper thigh a reassuring squeeze. "Really. I'll always miss the rush I got in the middle of a firefight. But I won't miss getting shot at. Did I tell you we're going to check out my brother's dungeon in Laramie?"

Ninia squirmed when Jared slid his fingers under her silk thong she wore to tweak her clit. "No." She doubted, even if she'd been drunk with lust the way he kept her most of the time, that she'd have forgotten a piece of information like that. "You told me you have a brother named Brad and a sister, Diana. Both older than you. But I don't remember you saying anything about him sharing our lifestyle."

Jared cleared his throat as he withdrew his hand. "They both do. There's a closed campground about a mile down this road. We'll get out of the truck and have some lunch, and I'll tell you more about the McTavish family."

*Roped*

# Chapter Six

## ೫

As he figured it would be, the campground was deserted except for some fat squirrels cavorting in the trees. The smells of evergreens and female musk swirled around him as he helped her out of the seat. "Look. I fixed up a spot so your backside won't get sore," he said when he set the cooler on the ground and opened the truck bed cover. The inflated air mattress he'd stowed inside looked mighty inviting, but…

"Sit there on the tailgate and let me feed you. I owe you one," he told her, surprised he was able to recall that first meal they'd shared without embarrassment.

Her smile hit him like a sledgehammer, and when she lowered her gaze to his crotch he could barely resist ordering her to lie down and spread her legs. But that wasn't in his plan. After all, they both had to eat, and he'd gone to the trouble of assembling a portable feast—nothing that required a fork or spoon. He'd envisioned feeding her strawberries and pineapple and thin slices of roast beef and ham, filling her in on his ranch and siblings as they ate.

But he wanted her now, didn't understand what had happened to the iron control he maintained over his own desires as well as hers. His cock throbbed painfully inside his jeans as she looked at him, oblivious to his plan to eat and talk now, fuck later.

The hell with eating. They could do that afterward. They had the place to themselves, Ninia was wet and ready, and Jared had the feeling she wouldn't have cared if the campground had been filled with a hundred gawking tourists. "I'll feed you later. Now lie back and spread your pretty legs. I'm hungry for your sweet pussy."

"Yes, Master." Stripping off her sopping thong, Ninia lay on the edge of the truck bed, legs held apart in silent invitation, a hungry look on her pretty face. For a minute Jared just looked, his cock swelling and pressing painfully against his jeans. Then he laid a hand over her incredibly soft, smooth mound, rubbed his thumb over her hard, swollen little clit. Her moan of pleasure fed his determination to bring her pleasure in every way.

"So soft. So beautiful. Such a sweet little slut, but it's all for me. Isn't it?" He'd learned she wasn't averse to threesomes, even to group scenes. But he'd found himself holding back, keeping her to himself when they'd joined scenes at Boundless Pleasure. "One of these days I'm going to…" He couldn't say it, couldn't promise her he'd share her with other Masters, wonder if it was his cock or someone else's making her scream with orgasmic delight.

Instead he bent his head, opened his mouth over her sex, licked and sucked her clit, lapping at the little bud until she came. Then he found her cunt, tongue fucked her there, took her whimpers of pleasure and clutched them in his mind like lifelines. When he straightened up, pulled her ass to the edge of the truck bed and freed his cock, he growled, "I'm gonna fuck you now. Hard and fast, the way you like it. And I'm not using a condom."

"Oh, yesss." When she lifted her hips to take him deep, he thrust forward. God, but she felt good, all wet heat and slick lubrication with nothing between them to blunt the feeling. A warm breeze played along his balls as he drove into her time after time, kissed his fingers where he dug them into the taut flesh of her buttocks. "May I please come, Master?"

"Not yet." He slowed the pace, lifted her to change the angle of his penetration. "Imagine it's not that plug you're wearing, but another cock sliding in and out of your ass while I'm fucking your wet, hot cunt. Put your fist in your mouth and pretend you're taking another one there. Make believe it's not squirrels watching, but a room full of Doms and subs doing each other and wishing they could join in and pleasure you."

Her cunt clamped down on him so hard it almost hurt. Yeah, his slave got off on group scenes. "When we go to Laramie, I'll set up a scene like that. But nobody else gets to put his cock here." Thrusting hard now, his balls banging against her satiny slit while he fucked her, he held back his own orgasm as long as he could. "Come now, honey," he ground out as he sank in as deep as he could and came, burst after burst jetting from his cock against the mouth of her womb as her flesh spasmed around him.

When he could move again he shoved his cock back in his jeans, zipped them…and bent to lick every last drop of the salty, slick fluid that glistened around her cunt while she trembled with the aftereffects of her climax. Then he sat on the air mattress beside her and took her hand.

"You know how hard it's going to be for me to share you? How I…" His words trailed off and he stroked the back of her hand with his thumb.

Ninia knew it. Knew Jared had held back during their scenes at Boundless Pleasure. She just didn't know whether it was because he wasn't into group scenes or voyeurism…or if it had to do with his reluctance to display his body to virtual strangers in a dungeon. "You don't have to, you know. You're all the Master I need." She sat up beside him, looked into his troubled gaze.

"No. I've seen the longing in your eyes when I've passed on chances to share you, even to open the curtains and let others watch. I'd be a lousy Master if I didn't give you everything you need. Come on, let's walk over to that scenic overlook and I'll tell you a little about my family."

The subject of ménage was obviously closed, at least for him. For her, too, although she shoved it gently to the back of her mind. Sliding down from the truck bed, she smoothed the wrinkled skirt of her sundress, offered him her hand and matched her pace with his. Once they reached the rail that fenced off a deep sandstone gorge, Jared stopped and gestured toward a plateau on the other side. "This looks pretty much like home. Like the place on the outskirts of Laramie where we all grew up."

He paused, as though remembering Ninia had grown up an orphan and not wanting to hurt her with too much reminiscing about the joys of having parents and siblings. It stung her more, having her Master holding back from sharing the anchors of place and people that had made him the man he was. "Go on, please. Tell me about your skinned knees, your first pony. Your fights with Diana and Brad, and the spankings you got from Mom and Dad. After all, I bored you with stories of how I shuffled from one foster home to another, never finding a real home."

Leaning his backside against the rail, Jared rested his bad leg on his left boot. Then he looked at Ninia and shrugged. "I don't remember Dad all that well. He died when I was just five years old. An accident out at Grandpa's ranch, or so we were told. After that, Mom pretty much fell apart. She moved us into town, and she died when I was ten. Diana was only eighteen at the time, but she took over, practically raised Brad and me. We all finished school in Laramie. Brad went on the rodeo circuit as soon as he finished. After I graduated and went away to college, Diana moved out to her share of Grandpa's ranch. Guess all that responsibility made her want some peace and quiet—while having her watch over us like hawks sent Brad and me out seeking excitement. And learning sexual dominance was a turn-on to us both."

The picture Ninia got as Jared looked back on his childhood was one of three hardheaded kids, anchored on each other, all determined to find satisfaction in ways they'd been denied when they were children.

"Come on, let's see this piece of Wyoming you call home." It didn't matter what had shaped Jared or why he felt as he did. She put her hand in his and let his warmth surround her as they made their way back to the truck.

*****

The rugged foothills of the Rockies rose in the distance, a panorama of sandstone boulders and gnarly shrubs surrounding them in every direction from the large, old log cabin at the end of a winding road through the property Jared had inherited. Fields stretched out for what seemed like miles, fallow fields dotted with massive cottonwood trees like the one that shaded the cabin. Jared sat on the porch, a step above her, toying with Ninia's hair and pointing out places where he'd played as a child when he and his siblings had visited. "We lived in Laramie because Mom wasn't very much for the great outdoors, especially after Dad got killed in that freak accident up in the high pasture."

That was too bad, Ninia thought, because her Master obviously felt at home in these rugged surroundings. She liked them too—the sense of peace, the silence broken by a rustling breeze or the squawk of a bird on some branch of the sprawling tree. She imagined living here with Jared, bringing up children far away from the city and its temptations. "I love it here." *I love you.* She'd say it, but he hadn't uttered the words and it wasn't a slave's place to put her Master on the spot.

"I'm glad. Lift your hair for me." When she did, he reached in his shirt pocket and drew out a thick, gold collar set with a large, faceted topaz. Reaching around her, he held it for her inspection then settled it around her neck. "It looks like a piece of jewelry, but it's not. Once I close the clasp, it won't come off unless somebody saws it in two."

He paused, his hands still at the back of her neck. "You still want me as your Master? If not, you'd better tell me now."

"Yes. I still want you." How could he think otherwise? Couldn't he tell the only thing she wanted was to belong to him, body and soul, claim him as her Master in front of God and everybody on this earth? "I want to wear your collar so everyone will know I'm yours."

The gold felt smooth, cool. Its weight was a welcome reminder that she, like it, was the treasured property of her beloved master. She reached up, touched the precious stone above the leash hook, liked the way its weight made the front of the collar settle at the base of her throat. "Fasten it, Master, please." She wanted to hear the finality of the metal being joined, to know she belonged to the solemn man who'd stolen her heart long before claiming her body and soul. "I want more than anything to be your slave."

"And I want to be your Master." She felt his warm breath against the sweet spot on the back of her neck just below her hairline, trembled when he bared his teeth and nipped her there. "I want you to come when you hear my collar snap closed."

The feel of his knuckles as he fumbled with the locking mechanism was as arousing as if he'd been tonguing her clit, and the power of his suggestion had her growing wet between her legs. The warm breeze carried her scent and his, heady and arousing as it swirled around them. Her pussy clenched, the flesh apparently as eager as she to relinquish control…to entrust everything—her sexual satisfaction, her well-being, even her life—to Jared McTavish. To her Master.

The collar closed around her neck, its sound metallic. Final. Ninia's belly tightened. Her pierced nipples hardened and her clit began to throb. Her pussy started to spasm, and her ass contracted around the plug she wore at her Master's command. When she started to shake all over, he wrapped her in his arms. "I'll take care of you, sweetheart. Always."

\* \* \* \* \*

The inside of the cabin was much as Jared remembered it, and a lot like the private chamber he'd taken that first night at Boundless Pleasure. He and his new slave had shared a picnic supper on the porch then come inside, where he'd built a small fire to ward off the chill that always came in the mountains after nightfall. After they'd come inside he'd stripped down and ordered Ninia to shed her clothes, and it was his duty to see she didn't catch a cold. The firelight cast a glow over her beautiful body and made her collar and nipple rings sparkle in the near darkness. "Come here, my sweet slave," he said, motioning for her to join him on the red leather-covered couch in front of the fire.

She'd given him the riding crop earlier. Now he balanced its leather-wrapped handle on one palm, considered how the braided leather could easily bruise her tender skin. "Why is it you get pleasure from being hurt?" He'd often wondered but had never cared enough before to delve that deeply into the heads of the subs he'd pleasured.

"I'm a bad girl who needs to be punished." She stared at the fire, her fingers moving along the smooth gold surface of her collar, as if she was considering his question—and the answer she'd glibly given. "Seriously, I'm not sure. It's hard for me to let go of control. Always has been, even when I was a child. *Karada* bondage, the touch of those metal tips on your cat o'nine…wearing a plug or dildo at my Master's command. All these things remind me I'm helpless to your will. That I'm not responsible for the pleasure you make me feel."

"Does wearing this make you feel out of control?" He ran his finger under her collar, deliberately reminding her she'd accepted permanent sexual slavery. Twice. "Did wearing his collar make it feel safe for you to let go?"

"Yes, Master."

"You're one of the strongest women I've ever run across, strong enough to stand up to some of the meanest, nastiest soldiers on earth. Hell, you stood up to me when you thought I was being stupid about this." He rapped on the socket of his prosthesis. "Take this off me and come straddle my lap."

When she did, he didn't feel the sense of helplessness that usually followed when he went without the limb somewhere other than in bed, and he knew that was because she was there. Because he trusted her the way he'd never trusted any woman, the way he'd trusted the other members of his Force Recon team to protect his back, same as he'd done his damnedest to protect theirs. "Ride me. Milk my cock with your hot, wet cunt. Do it well and I'll try out my present on your delicious ass cheeks." When she clamped down those strong inner muscles he felt the plug in her ass, imagined it was another man's cock pleasuring her. "Open your mouth," he growled, and when she did he plundered it with his tongue. She sucked it hard, as if it were yet another cock filling the last of her holes. Grasping the crop in his left hand, he laid a light blow, then another. Her cunt clenched around his straining flesh as she took him deep.

When he came in long bursts that seemed to go on forever, she shattered in his arms, her incredibly soft skin slick with sweat. He wrenched his mouth away from hers. "Come, baby, come with me. It's okay. God, but I love you, just the way you are." It didn't matter. If she wanted a ménage, he'd arrange one even if it meant stowing his own insecurities.

A Master's job was to take care of all of his slave's sexual needs, he reminded himself later that night when he spoke with Brad, told his brother how he wanted the dungeon's observation room set up the following night so he could pleasure Ninia.

"Tomorrow night we're going to play a scene at Roped and Lassoed," he told her later, stroking her naked body as they lay in bed in the light of a bright, golden moon. "You'll be the star attraction…to me and the others I've invited to watch and share my precious slave. You won't have a hole left empty, or an inch of your sweet body left untouched by hungry eyes. Hands." He stroked her cheek then inserted a finger in her mouth. "You've been dreaming about ménage. Don't deny it."

She wriggled her ass cheeks against his erection, sucked his finger and stroked it with her tongue. "Mmmm."

Jared couldn't resist her blatant invitation. Rolling her onto her back, he rose on his knees and joined their bodies. "That's it, sweetheart. Wrap those pretty legs around my waist and squeeze my cock. Love me." *I want more than your lust, more than your submission.*

"I do." Her arms went around his shoulders, holding him close, dragging him down on her until they couldn't get any closer. Her cunt throbbed around his cock, milking him, holding him in her as though she'd never let him go. It felt good. So fucking good, this closeness he'd never yearned for before. And when he came in her, she gave him the words he needed to hear, words that let him set aside the fear she'd find him lacking compared with the ones he'd recruited to enhance her pleasure.

"I love you, Master. Only you."

* * * * *

*God, but I love you*. The words he'd said last night still echoed in her ears, warming her heart. She'd said the words too, but in the heat of passion. She wanted to say them now, when her mind was clear.

"I love you." Ninia bent and nuzzled Jared's neck while he finished off his second cup of tea. When he turned and shot her an intense look, she tried to distract him before he had time to question her simple declaration. "What's on for today?" she asked.

"A visit to the bedroom if you don't stop that," he growled, capturing her chin in his hand and giving her a long, hard kiss.

"Is that a threat or a promise, Master?"

"A promise. But later. By the way, sweetheart, I love you, too."

"Mmmm, I just thought you might. But tell me, what are we going to do today?"

"I want to show you around the ranch. After all, you're a city girl, and you've got a right to see what I've got in store for you. You ride me like a champ," he said, a sexy grin on his handsome face. "But I'm wondering. Can you ride a horse?"

"I haven't, not for a long time, Master. But I can probably manage to hang onto the saddle horn if the horse is tame."

"We'll take the truck, then." He gave in too quickly, she thought. Then she figured he probably wasn't all that anxious to take his own first ride since his injury and have to watch out for a novice like her. "Come on."

"Okay." He'd come a long way in a short time toward accepting his physical limitations. She was glad, because she'd have hated to spoil the moment by pointing out that he shouldn't have even been thinking about riding a horse again until he had some sessions with his physical therapist on how to compensate for the lack of weight balance the amputation had created.

"Since we'll be driving most of the time, I think I'll take off my leg and use crutches. I'm not anxious to get the stump sore."

That last remark had her speechless. Jared never went out without the prosthesis, and he rarely consented to using his crutches in public no matter how sore and swollen the stump became. "Uh—"

"We're going into Laramie tonight to play. I figure I'll need to be in top form then, or you may toss me over for one of the cowboy Doms."

"Oh." Unable to come up with a good reply to that, she watched him roll up his jeans and pop off the artificial limb. He was about to roll down the jeans when she found her voice. "If you leave it uncovered, the air will help heal the sore spots."

It surprised her that he did just that, leaving his jeans rolled up over his knee and letting the stump hang out as they drove around the ranch. A very impressive ranch, she thought when he showed her high pastures dotted with what seemed like thousands of red cows with white faces. And dozens of oil wells. "That's where the money comes from," he said when he noticed her staring at the pumping equipment that dotted the boulder-strewn fields with about the same frequency as huge, green cottonwoods where the cows seemed to congregate under the trees' wide canopies. "Diana says the cattle operation barely breaks even."

She hoped Jared's sister would like her as they neared a rustic stone ranch house near what must have been the opposite side of the ranch from Jared's log cabin. "You said Diana is into our lifestyle too?" she asked, fingering the collar no one in the BDSM community could possibly mistake for a plain old necklace.

His frown wasn't something Ninia could have missed. "Yes. She's a sub." He paused, his expression darkening further. "The collar she wears is leather, and most of the time it's attached to a leash. Don't be surprised if she's got a shaved head. Brad said she told him she'd done something yesterday that pissed Gareth off, and that's usually how he punishes her." He paused, as though deciding whether he should say more. "Gareth Bender isn't the sort of Dom Brad or I think much of, but as long as Diana's happy…"

He stopped the truck and turned to her. "With any kind of luck he'll be out with those wranglers we saw chasing mustangs in the canyon. Diana had to raise Brad and me when Mom sort of fell apart. Guess Diana had so much of having to be strong that she wanted to be under the total control of somebody else. Now Brad and I are different. Between Mom and Diana, we never had the chance to act on our own, so I guess that's why when we grew up we wanted to exert a little of the discipline we got onto our lovers." He paused, reached in the backseat, grabbed his prosthesis and put it on.

"I'm glad. Glad you want me to be your slave. If you ever want to, you can shave my head. Earl did it once, or rather he took me to a barbershop around the corner from Boundless

Pleasure and had the barber do it. But it wasn't a punishment. He wanted to see if my scalp was as sensitive as this sweet spot just below my hairline on my neck." She fingered the spot, got wet when she recalled the rush she'd gotten as she'd felt the clippers buzz off her hair. She'd practically come when the barber applied a hot towel then brushed fragrant hot lather over her head. The best part had been the razor, the sound of it mowing down the short bristles the clippers had left—and later, feeling Earl's rough fingers against her scalp, holding her bald head to his crotch while she serviced him.

"Was it?" Jared stroked the back of her neck, sent shivers all the way down her spine. "You don't need to answer, I can feel it in the way you tremble when I touch you here, smell your arousal. Do you want me to shave you sometime?"

"Would you?" In spite of his expertise as a sexual Dominant, Ninia thought of Jared as being essentially conservative, not the type who'd want his slave parading around making such an obvious statement about their lifestyle.

"If it gives you pleasure, sure. If I can wear an artificial leg in public, you can certainly wear a wig if it turns you on to have me shave you bald and play with your bare scalp." He grinned then drew her to him for a hard, hot kiss. "We can explore this fantasy of yours, but later. We'd better get on down to Diana's house or we'll miss our lunch. My sister may be a complete submissive to Gareth, but she's not to me or Brad. I learned how to use the cat o'nine just to keep her and her hickory switch at bay."

*****

Damn it, Jared hadn't been able to shake the feeling Diana wasn't happy, but she hadn't been willing to talk about it. She hadn't talked about much of anything for that matter. That wasn't like his sister. Neither was the way she'd refused to meet his gaze, or her failure to joke about her recently shaved head or the welts no one could miss noticing on her arms and legs.

When he and Ninia stepped through the swinging doors of Roped and Lassoed, Brad's dungeon on the highway outside Laramie, Jared was still fuming. Normally he'd have stopped downstairs where cowboys dropped in for a beer and burgers after work, and exchanged pleasantries with guys he'd grown up with. Not tonight, though. Barely acknowledging the chorus of friendly greetings, he herded Ninia past the dungeon master and up the stairs to the second floor. "Go on, get changed for our scene," he told her gruffly, gesturing toward the dressing room.

She put a hand on his arm, a strangely soothing gesture he couldn't shake off. Then she pressed her lips against his throat. "Please, Master. When Diana's ready for help, she'll know she can count on her brother. "

"And how do you know that?"

"Because there's no one I'd trust more with my safety and well-being. " When she reached up and stroked his cheek he caught her hand and brought it to his lips. She was good for him, better than he deserved.

"Wait, sweetheart, I want you to meet Brad." No matter how steamed he was over the abuse he was certain Diana must have been enduring, he'd promised Ninia this scene. Where had his manners gone, shunting off the woman he loved? "Then I want you to go change into that cowgirl outfit that sends my libido through the roof. I've been thinking about you in those short shorts and boots all afternoon."

Standing back to let her precede him through Brad's open office door, Jared took a couple of deep breaths to keep his anger in abeyance. "Ninia, this is my brother. Brad, meet Ninia. Notice the collar before you get any ideas," he said, trying to sound jovial.

"Hey, Ninia. Jared tells me you're into rope bondage. Welcome to Roped and Lassoed. My baby brother has arranged one hell of a scene for you tonight." When Brad kissed her hand and shot her the sort of grin Jared had seen make the most reluctant subs melt, Jared had to restrain himself from stepping between them.

"Yes, he told me. He also told me I need to go change, so I'll say goodbye for now." As if she knew seeing her interacting with other men—even his brother—made Jared feel uneasy, she went up on tiptoe and laid a quick kiss on his lips before lowering her gaze and backing out of the room.

"Women's dressing room's the third door at the end of the hall," Brad called out. Then he turned to Jared. "What's wrong?"

"Diana's what's wrong. Son-of-a-bitch Gareth's hurting her." Jared clenched his fists so hard the nails bit into his palms. "She's too fucking stubborn to admit it."

Brad rubbed the bridge of his nose as though hearing that information had suddenly given him a headache. "You know she likes it rough."

"Yeah? Ninia likes to feel the sting of the cat. And she gave me a flogger to use on her. But I whip her for her pleasure, not to hurt her." It had been all Jared could do not to scoop up his sister and drag her away from Gareth when he'd noticed the deep marks on her arms and legs.

"Bastard broke her nose last year when you were in Iraq," Brad said, his fists clenched at his sides. "I sent the sheriff out to drag him off to jail, but she insisted it was an accident, part of one of their scenes."

"We've got to get her away from him whether she wants us to or not. Do you do it, or shall I?"

Brad shrugged. "I've tried. Nothing will stick as long as Diana's there, saying Gareth has never done anything to hurt her."

"Are you saying the only way we can help her is have her committed for some treatment?" The idea of forcibly putting away the woman who'd always been there for him and Brad stuck in Jared's gut. "I'd hate doing it, after all she did for us when we were kids."

"If we don't do something, he's likely to kill her one of these days. Bastard." Brad met Jared's gaze, his expression uncharacteristically serious. "Maybe if we go together and try to talk some sense into her…"

Yeah, that might work. Meanwhile Jared had his own slave, and he'd promised her an evening of unlimited pleasure. "By now Ninia will be wondering where I've gone. Feel free to observe, if you'd like. She's into showing off for an audience." A picture came to Jared's mind of Ninia standing on her balcony in Cheyenne, pleasuring herself for his arousal before they'd connected with each other the following night. His anger faded, replaced by lust that had his heart pumping, his balls drawing up with anticipation, his cock hardening painfully against his zipper.

## Chapter Seven

When Ninia stepped into the observation chamber wearing her cowgirl outfit and Jared's collar, her hair secured in a knot atop her head as Jared had ordered, there he was, waiting. He wore the same chaps and boots he'd had on that first time at Boundless Pleasure, only without the jeans. Already wet with anticipation, she looked at him and his hard cock curving almost to his navel, and every nerve in her body started tingling with arousal. "Do you trust me?" he asked, that rough, deep voice as much an aphrodisiac as seeing him, remembering what he'd told her he'd be doing to her tonight.

"Yes, Master, I trust you," she said, her gaze meeting his before she went to her knees before him, her eyes downcast as a good slave's must always be. "May I service you now?"

He grasped his cock, held it to her lips. "Kiss me."

He tasted a little salty, a little sweet, that delicious drop of lubrication nestled in the tight slit of his cock head. She'd have sucked the plumlike head of him but he quickly pulled back.

His motion a little clumsy, as though her kiss had cost him some self control, he bent, drew her to her feet and fastened a padded blindfold over her eyes. "They say if you can't see, you feel more. And if you can't touch or speak, you respond more fully to your Master's touch. His orders. Open your mouth."

When she did he kissed her hard then inserted a leather-wrapped ring gag and secured it in her open mouth. Its straps pushed against the back of her head, reminding her of the erogenous zones she'd discovered there long ago and making her long for Jared to let her experience that pleasure again. "I'm taking your clothes off now. So you can service me and my friends," he whispered, once more thrusting his tongue into the center of the gag as he slid off her skimpy garments, his big hands ever so gentle on her body. "God but you're beautiful naked." He hooked his forefingers through her nipple rings and twisted them. "It's time for the chain. It pleases me that you've healed so well. Hold still."

She'd never been blindfolded before, but he was right. Not being able to see or speak enhanced the sensations when he tugged on her nipple rings, as the weight of the chain pulled gently on them, as a small object centered on the chain bounced against her ribcage. She squirmed, and that unordered motion earned her a hard jerk on the chain that sent rivulets of pleasure-pain radiating through her breasts.

"No coming until I say so. What I'm doing now is putting you in a sling. Don't worry, it's sturdy enough to hold a slave three times your size." The sling smelled of oiled leather, felt soft as he worked her arms into sleeves. "Be still now while I thread the front of it through your nipple chain."

He talked her through each step, his gravelly whisper as arousing as the feel of the sling pressing her flesh at the shoulders, waist, arms and thighs, reminding her of her helplessness, showing her she was completely subject to his will. His hot breath against her throat sent a shiver of desire along her nerves, and when he laid an open-mouthed kiss just below the collar he'd given her, it was all she could do to follow his orders…to let the sexual tension build inside her until he granted her permission for release.

She heard a door open, felt a cool breeze. "My friends will hoist you up. They're eager to taste you too." Jared spoke into her open mouth then bathed it with his tongue. "Very soon you'll take all three of our cocks. I know you'll like that, my precious slave. You'll like Eli's fat pierced one, it's just the right size for your mouth. John's is long, not too thick. Perfect to fill your tight little ass. They'll both wear condoms, because I want you protected." He paused a minute, and she felt his hot breath against her lips. "Your cunt is mine." He moved away, and she felt herself being lifted, turned, hoisted into the air.

Her ass was slightly higher than her head, and her forehead rested on the padded device that kept her head held back. Her arms were confined close to her sides while her legs were swung wide apart, her cunt and ass open for the invasion. She tensed, waiting, felt nothing for a moment then the sensation of being stroked on her cheek by a feather…on her back and ass cheeks with the talons of a light flogger…on her inner thighs with somebody's hands. Not Jared's callused ones but softer hands with slender, long fingers that brushed her clit and cunt lips with every practiced, arousing movement.

The flogger stilled. So did the feather and the hands that had been teasing her pussy. One hissing stroke, then two, then three had her wanting to cry out with the pleasure-pain of the cat o'nine's metal tipped strands. Jared. No one could wield the cat the way he did, making each strike almost a caress. When he stopped she wished she could beg for more.

Then a huge cock—Jared's she was sure—slid between the edges of the ring gag, filled her mouth. When she swallowed, she felt his cock head fill her throat. Then she felt another cock, Eli's, she guessed, because it was pierced. The smooth surface of a ring brushed against the skin of one cheek. It felt warm, smooth as it rubbed along one corner of her mouth. The third man—John, she recalled—joined the others, using his rigid cock head to stroke her other cheek. Its warm, damp head pressed against her stretched lips…against Jared's hot flesh that moved ever so slowly in and out of her mouth. Jared's flesh stretched her throat painfully, yet she wanted to serve him, needed to take them all because that was his command.

And because every cell in her body ached for the triple invasion, the punishment from the cat and flogger that would make wanting this okay. For the mind-shattering release that would be her prize for serving her Master and his friends.

The heat of the three Masters, the heady mix of their male musks filled her senses, made her wish she could talk and beg them to take her, to leave no hole unbreached.

"Soon now, sweetheart." As if he felt her need, he knotted his fist in her ponytail, held her head steady while he moved deeper, breached her throat with the blunt head of his cock. "That's it, relax." She swallowed reflexively, breathed through her nose that now pressed firmly against the base of her Master's cock. Hands explored her back, soothing the little stings that would be the least bit red and angry by now, carefully laid marks made moments ago by her loving Master. Other hands played with her exposed nipples, flicking them, tugging at her Master's rings.

When the three stopped, she felt lost, but only for a moment as the sound of condom wrappers being torn open filled the silent room. The pierced cock, now encased in a condom, moved into her mouth. The man who'd been stroking her other cheek moved to the end of the sling, resumed stroking her thighs, then moved in close and smeared something cold and slick around her rear entrance. When he breached her anal sphincter with a heavily lubricated finger, he spoke, his voice smoother, but not as deep as Jared's. "Relax and enjoy this. I'm gonna fuck your ass. Your Master says you like it. Oh yeah, baby, you're tight."

Warmth emanated from beneath her. Jared. His heat as he stretched out on the adjustable table beneath the sling made her want to angle her body down, find his hot cock and impale herself on it, had her panting for more. For the depth of sexual fulfillment only he could bring her. He grasped her waist, held her steady, positioning his cock just within her outer lips as that other cock pressed lightly against her rear hole.

"Now," he growled as he found her pussy and thrust home. Eli framed her cheeks in his hands and moved in and out of her mouth while John slowly reamed her ass and her Master claimed her pussy. And her heart. They both belonged to him.

The others were mere adjuncts, tools Jared had brought to force her ultimate arousal. To fulfill the need he sensed in her to be punished for her desires so she could finally soar free. Three men fucking her, yet only one commanding her pleasure. Pressure built inside her. Every small welt stung deliciously. Eli's pierced cock tickled her throat. Chad's stretched her rear, his rhythm in tandem with her Master's as he slid balls deep in her swollen cunt then withdrew, only to claim her again. Faster. Harder.

Her flesh burned when she sensed hot eyes burning into her, witnessing her ultimate surrender, watching her service her Master and his two friends. Seeing the sheen of sweat on her body and theirs, knowing how much she needed to come, how hard she was struggling not to.

"Soon, my darling little slut," Jared growled from beneath her as he reached up and laid an open-palmed slap smartly against one ass cheek. "I feel John fucking your ass. Feel your naughty pussy starting to spasm around my cock."

*Please, Master, let me come.* The sensations bombarded her, made her tremble in her captivity. Her passion-overloaded brain registered it wasn't the others she begged for release even though they too were contributing to this arousal that was becoming too painful for her to bear. She held on, silently begging Jared. Only her beloved Master.

"You may come. Now." His command was little more than a series of grunts as his cock began to twitch inside her, as each of the Doms plunged deep. As hot spurts of Jared's climax bathed her spasming pussy, concentrating the feelings there. Around him. Only him. He was all she needed—all she wanted. Chad and Eli might as well have been animated sex toys.

*It was Earl, not me, who'd thrived on the group scenes I thought I'd been missing.*

But Jared was her Master now. Ninia barely managed to wait until he'd freed her and removed the blindfold and gag to say the words she somehow knew he'd been waiting to hear.

"I love you, Master. Only you. I don't need what we just had to find fulfillment."

The look on his face was priceless. One she'd remember the rest of her life. When he held up the chain he'd put between her nipple rings, she saw the weight—a large, perfect diamond set in gleaming gold.

"Marry me," he said, a huge grin on his face. "If I have anything to say about it, you'll never want for anything again. In bed or elsewhere."

# Epilogue
## *The following year, at Roped and Lassoed BDSM Club, Laramie, Wyoming*

ಸಿ

"I never knew you to be so possessive," Brad commented as he and Jared changed from the costumes they'd worn for a group scene at Roped and Lassoed. "Don't blame you, though. Your wife's one mighty hot chick to have a gimp for a Master."

Jared popped off his prosthesis and wiped out the socket. "Gimp, hell. Gotta change the suspension sleeve. I always sweat when Ninia and I demonstrate the art of karada. Tell you the truth, I'm scared shitless every time we do it that I'll get something wrong and hurt her."

It struck Jared that before Ninia, he'd have been ready to fight if anybody had said anything to him about his injuries, except for when the comments had sent him into a blue funk of self-pity. Now, though, he could not only laugh at good friends' ribbing, but also laugh off more thoughtless comments made by strangers—and actually mean it. "Seriously, it feels good to be home."

"Never thought I'd hear you say that, little brother. Of everybody we went to school with, you were the one who couldn't wait to get out and conquer the world."

Brad was right. Jared had yearned for excitement, exotic places and the adrenaline rush that came from risking his neck for a cause. Until Ninia. "Now I consider myself lucky to be able to conquer my wife."

He loved her and loved living on the ranch. Together he and Ninia had built a home and planned the dude ranch operation they'd be opening in the spring. Meanwhile, winter in Wyoming offered plenty of opportunities to cuddle before a fire...

Just last week he'd fulfilled his wife's fantasy and taken her hair, but only after they'd flown down to Denver, gotten her a short haircut and had a wig made from most of her blonde locks. The wig covered her baldness nicely—and he had to say he found massaging her satiny scalp while she was servicing him orally almost as erotic an experience as she apparently enjoyed when he clipped and shaved her every other day. Only time it bothered him seeing her bald was when he thought of Diana and the way her ass of an almost-ex husband had often shaved her head for punishment before he and Brad had taken the reins and had Gareth sentenced to three-to-five for spouse abuse.

So far, no one had even noticed Ninia was wearing a wig. It looked exactly like her own hair, a hell of a lot more real than his prosthesis. But Jared didn't care. Life was great, as long as he had her and she had him—and they had a warm fire, a soft bed and the everlasting dose of hot passion that had brought them to this. "Gotta go, man. Ninia will be waiting. I'll go over to Diana's next week and see how she's doing, now that she's finished with her therapy."

"Come back. My dungeon is your dungeon. You're always welcome. Both of you."

"Thanks." Whistling, Jared made his way outside the dressing room...to Ninia.

It had been a long time, a blessedly long time since he'd had the dream that used to plague him. Instead, all his fantasies now were about his wife—and when he reached for her, she was always there for him. No more mirages, just a flesh-and-blood woman Jared loved with all his heart, who loved him in return.

*The End*

# HITCHED
ಞ

# Trademarks Acknowledgement

༄

The author acknowledges the trademarked status and trademark owners of the following wordmarks mentioned in this work of fiction:

Arctic Cat: Arctic Cat Inc.

Bath Bed & Beyond: Bath Bed & Beyond Procurement Co. Inc.

Bearcat: Arctco, Inc.

Beechcraft: Hawker Beechcraft Corporation

Cessna: The Cessna Aircraft Company

Gore-Tex: W. L. Gore & Associates, Inc.

Velcro: Velcro Industries B.V.

## Prologue

☙

Damn. The rigors of a rough rodeo season had left him aching enough that he had little doubt he'd turned thirty-five this year. Brad McTavish shifted positions, managed not to wince when he stretched his legs out on the sofa and tried to focus on the crackling fire. Yeah, he hurt, but the physical aches and pains weren't what had him feeling down.

It was more this sense that life was rushing by all around him while everything about his own life stayed the same. It was almost as if he were on a roller coaster, bumping and sliding, churning his guts over and over before depositing him in the exact same place each time the ride was over.

Brad might as well own up to it. He was bored. Bored with running Roped and Lassoed, Laramie's only BDSM dungeon. Bored with chasing a young boy's dreams that drove him onto the rodeo circuit every summer. Fuck, he'd even gotten tired of looking out this wall of windows at his land, watching the pumpjacks' rhythmic up-down motion as they kept money flowing into his bank account. Just like every year since he could remember, fat red and white cattle munched hay in the pasture closest to the house, having been moved from the high grazing fields in anticipation of an early freeze. Meeting Keely in the observation room at the club every Tuesday and Friday night and giving her the sex fix she seemed to need, pleasurable though it was, wasn't satisfying him anymore, either.

He could always fly down to Denver. Get some new sex toys for the dungeon, maybe even trade his ten-year-old Cessna for a newer one. Or he could go get a tattoo or another piercing. Too bad he didn't cotton much to needles. He remembered how he'd practically jumped out of his skin when he had his cock pierced years ago, even though he'd been practically dead drunk at the time. *Nope, no tattoo in this guy's future. Besides, no new toy or body art's likely to cure you of this blue funk.*

Those were all things he'd have done ten years ago. Things that now held very little appeal. *Face it, Brad. You've gone and grown up, despite all your best efforts not to. You want more out of life than fun and games and new toys. You want Keely.*

But how was he going to convince Keely he was more than the club Dom always on hand when she needed a friendly fuck? Like everyone else in Laramie, she still thought of him as that wild twenty-some-odd guy every adventurous girl wanted to take on in a scene at the dungeon. None of them, Keely included, wanted anything that smacked of "long-term relationship" with the likes of him.

He sighed. Yep, that was the heart of it. Keely, the five-foot-two redhead who liked her loving rough and took to dungeon scenes. She was the main cause of his black-ass attitude.

Why the fuck was she so eager to be his submissive when she came to the club yet totally stubborn about extending their relationship out into the real world? When Brad thought about her attitude of not mixing sex with friendship or risking putting out emotional ties, it made him feel sort of like a paid stud—and he didn't like that. Not at all.

He ought to dump Keely and find a woman who wouldn't mind devoting her life to meeting his every need, the way his brother Jared's wife Ninia did for him. And who allowed him to reciprocate, loving and cherishing her with everything he had. Brad closed his eyes and imagined himself here with his own sex slave. She'd be kneeling at his feet, naked, resting her cheek on his knee while she waited for his order. Trouble was, the woman in his mental picture had Keely's face. Keely's hot body and the sassy smile she shot him on the rare occasions when their paths crossed on the streets of Laramie.

And that scene he'd just envisioned wasn't likely to happen. Only time Keely got down on her knees was in the dungeon, when the pose was part of a BDSM scene.

# Chapter One
*Two weeks later*

※

In his office at Roped and Lassoed, Brad watched a trail of steam thin and disperse over his coffee mug. What with the way the wind was blowing outside, he imagined it would be a damn slow day.

Falling Star, the Native American woman who kept them all in line, stuck her head through the door. "Everything's all ready. Dressing rooms are clean. I even scrubbed down the showers. All the furniture's wiped down and sanitized, and the supply cabinets are filled up." She wrinkled her nose as if put off by the "supplies" that included condoms, handcuffs, ball gags and more. "You boys be good, and watch the weather. My old bones tell me bad storm's brewing out in the mountains."

Brad grinned. Star had gone from scowling to smiling in the three years she'd been keeping Roped and Lassoed in order. "Thanks, Star. Is John here yet?" If he weren't, Brad would have to step in if any horny members needed a Dom on the early shift—and he wasn't keen on making it with anybody but Keely.

"Yeah, boss, he's hard at work already. With that little redhead gal."

Any doubts Brad may have had about the evolution of his feelings for Keely into something more evaporated at Star's casually uttered words. He saw red and suddenly knew exactly how a bull calf must feel when the cinch strap is drawn cruelly over his testicles.

"Drive carefully," he said, dismissing Star lest he take his rage out on her. Once he was alone, he exploded out of the chair, tore off his clothes and put on the leather chaps and vest he wore for scenes.

Out of breath by the time he changed, Brad stomped into the dungeon, fists clenched. It pissed hell out of him that Keely had gotten to Roped and Lassoed early and was in the middle of a scene with John, Brad's day manager. Hell, he'd half expected her to stay home today since it looked like a nasty storm might soon be blowing in from the west.

When he saw her writhing, gagged and blindfolded on a St. Andrew's Cross while his buddy applied the cat -o'-nine, he wanted to drag the whip out of John's hand and use it to stripe his back until it bled.

He must have gotten the love bug bad. He'd never before felt possessive toward a sub, not the way he did now about Keely. "John! Drop the whip. You're out of here."

"But, Boss, I was just doing my job." The other Dom's reasonable tone only served to further incense Brad.

"Out. I don't like other men playing with what's mine." Not that Keely would consider herself his, but that didn't matter. Still he had the grace to realize John had only been doing his job. "Hey, buddy, it's not your fault. Now beat it before I put welts on your skinny ass that make what you did to Keely look like love taps."

"Okay. Didn't mean to encroach on your territory. But she never said a word. Have fun, you two," John said as he beat tracks out the door.

Brad circled the cross, looking at every welt, each sign of submission she'd endured at the hands of another Dom. It made no sense, this feeling of betrayal. He'd hired John to see to the needs of subs who came into Roped and Lassoed without their Masters. So why did he feel she'd been violated? Why did he have this sour taste in his mouth, as if he might be about to retch up whatever kind of doughnut it was that he'd wolfed down with his coffee?

Moving forward and taking the flat of his hand to Keely's reddened bottom, Brad winced at the feel of welts that cut deep into her pale, creamy skin. Welts put there by somebody other than himself. "It's me, Brad. Maybe you should have waited. Hold on now, I'm going to set you loose so you can pay the price—other than the sore bottom which is going to remind you trying out a new Dom was a bad, bad idea."

She strained against the Velcro fasteners as he loosened them. Muffled sounds from her mouth made him pause and get rid of the large ball gag so she could talk. "Pay what kind of price, Master?"

For the first time it bothered him, having her use the generic "master" that could refer to any male Dom controlling her at any moment. "What's my name?"

As soon as he got the blindfold off her, she shot him a puzzled look before lowering her gaze the way a good sub should. "Brad McTavish. Master Brad McTavish. Why did you throw Master John out?"

"His shift was over." That was true, even if it wasn't the reason Brad had gone ballistic and put a quick end to the scene that had been in progress. Quickly, he finished untying her. "Come here. We're going to start again, from scratch."

At Brad's silent order, Keely went on her knees in front of the new fucking machine, a motorized device he'd doubted when he bought it that anybody would like. The subs, male and female alike, had proven him wrong. A shiny stainless steel base, securely bolted to the floor, held a vertical arm and an adjustable piston-like horizontal bar with a two-prong extension that held the brand-new dildo and butt plug of the Dom's choice ready to penetrate his willing sub. The sight of her folding her hands together over her flat belly, a classically submissive pose, made Brad desperate to know Keely's submissiveness was meant for him and him alone.

He stepped in front of her and dug his fingers through her soft auburn curls, breathing in the sweet, somehow innocent smell of her shampoo and conditioner. Her warm breath tickled his cock, tempted him to flex his hips and deliver the punishment she so obviously wanted. "On all fours now. That's right, now back up against the machine and raise your pretty red ass just a little more." With a flick of the machine's remote control switch, he positioned the twin dildos and set them to moving, slowly, in and out, as she thrust her hips back and forth in time with the machine's sensuous, slightly circular motions. "Tell me, slave, who's your Master now?"

"You are, Master Brad." And he was, for now. Keely leaned forward, ran her tongue over his rigid cock head. He tasted so good, clean and just a little salty. "May I…"

"You want to suck my cock?"

"Please, Master." She braced herself when he finished adjusting the angle of the double-headed dildo to fit her pussy and ass now that she'd arched her back to give herself access to his cock. Carefully, he set it in motion again. "Please let me taste your long, thick cock. I want to feel it deep in my throat while I run my hands over your tight ass."

It had been so long since she'd chosen another Master to get her off, but she'd been desperate. Brad kept pushing them to be more, and she just couldn't. So she'd thought she'd try another, just to see if she could make the same magic happen, and it had been a dismal frustration. Until Brad had come in like a furious warrior, and she'd practically climaxed just to see him. She was in serious trouble. Had a perverse part of her wanted to see how Brad would react to her submitting to another Dom?

He moved closer, took her hands and laid them over his velvety-smooth scrotum. "I want you to play with my balls this time. Take them in your mouth and roll your tongue over them while you jack me with these pretty hands. Do you really think, as naughty as you've been, that you deserve to suck my cock?"

"No, Master. I've been naughty. Very naughty." When she pushed her hips back against the machine, it started moving deeper and faster, making her mindless with uncontrolled arousal. It was Brad's huge pierced cock with the barbell's two captive beads that she really wanted pressing against the stretched walls of her pussy while the fucking machine did its job on her rear hole, but this punishment had her aching for more. She swirled her tongue over his balls, loving the way they moved and shifted inside their baby-smooth sac.

"Oh yeah, don't stop. That feels incredible." His deep mesmerizing voice swirled around her brain as she kept on, sucking first one and then the other large, oval testicle while the fucking machine kept bringing her to the edge of a climax she dared not release. "Stop now. I'll give you ten seconds to get up and climb onto the table in the center of the room."

Keely's pussy and ass still vibrated even after she'd lifted herself off the fucking machine and perched on the edge of the table. Every nerve in her body screamed with arousal, with burning lust that only seemed to ignite with this Dom. What would be her punishment? Would he deny her his beautiful cock, send her away unfulfilled and regretting even more that they couldn't have more together than these few stolen hours every week at Roped and Lassoed?

When he joined her, he had a flogger in his hand. Not the leather one with metal balls on each strand, but a soft one. "I know you want to be punished. I don't know why. There is no way I'm going to put any more welts on your beautiful body." With that he dragged the silky ends over her breasts. "Feels good, doesn't it?"

She managed to let out an ecstatic whimper at the strangely tender punishment he was inflicting. She didn't want kindness, she wanted to come. And she dared not let that happen unless her Master gave her permission. The sharp nip of his gleaming white teeth on her nipple gave her the push that let her know she had no choice, that Brad was her Master and she had no option but to surrender.

"Enough of this, my pretty slave. I'm going to fuck you now, and you can come any time you want to." He laid her flat on the table, knelt between her legs and rolled on a ribbed condom. Slowly, deliberately, he slid his swollen cock into her hot, wet pussy while he bent his head and drew first one nipple and then the other into his mouth. Faster, harder, he plunged into her. With every stroke, she felt not only his rigid flesh but also the twin bites of the beads that secured the bar they held in place just behind his cock head.

When he lifted his upper body and changed the angle of his thrusts, she saw his powerful muscles bulge. A vein in his neck throbbed, and he was breathing hard. Didn't he know he couldn't just give her *permission* to come? He had to *order* it. She dared not give in, think of him as a partner, not just a Dom who could make her lose her inhibitions for the moment.

"Damn it, I told you to come." He slammed into her harder, almost as if he desperately needed her to let go. "Do it now, or you're really going to face some punishment."

Keely felt it coming, that warm glow that spread through her body like a caressing touch of pure sensation. The congested feeling in her pussy as it contracted around her Master's rock-hard cock, the sensation of heat building, building…and finally exploding in a fiery climax as he thrust one more time and clutched her to his chest as if he'd never let her go.

He held her there for a long time, his pounding heart beating in time with hers. Two bodies drenched with sweat, in the aftermath of a mind-blowing climax. Finally he raised his head from her shoulder and looked her in the eye.

"You're mine. Only mine. Whenever you come to this club, I'm the only Dom you're even going to look at. Guess I'll have to be satisfied with that for now, but what I really want is to take this thing to the next step." The look on his face made it clear he'd staked his claim.

But she couldn't accept it, couldn't risk losing herself entirely. She wouldn't take a chance that her neighbors would fail to notice if she were seen with this man who was notorious for his sexual exploits. Not to mention that he was way, way out of her league socially and financially, so much that the few who didn't see her as a sex freak like her mom would shun her as a social-climbing gold digger.

She tried to quell the tears that wanted to explode inside her head then forced herself to meet his gaze as if they were equals. "It's not going any farther. It can't."

"It can and will. Eventually. I'll give you time to work through your crazy hang-ups. But not too much time. Get up now and run for cover, my sweet slave, before I decide to show you now how fully I own you."

As soon as he slid off the table, Keely got up and bolted for the door. He owned her body, that was for certain, but she dared not risk handing him her soul.

* * * * *

*You're gonna lose him, Keely girl.* Keely shivered as she stood there naked in the dressing room at Roped and Lassoed, her blood still soaring through her body in the wake of the intense scene she'd just enjoyed with the Dom who brought her wildest fantasies to life. She had to admit the other Doms who'd pleasured her, no matter how skilled they were, couldn't hold a candle to Master Brad.

Determined not to worry about what might happen in the future, Keely slipped on her jeans, boots and sweater. She had to get out of there lest her determination waver. Shrugging on her sheepskin-lined jacket, she pulled the hood up over her head and made her way downstairs, moving quickly past the swinging door that led to the saloon where half the locals came to enjoy some beer and man-talk. It wouldn't do for any of the customers at the farm implement store where she worked to see her leaving Roped and Lassoed.

Too bad it was such a poorly kept secret Brad had started a BDSM club ten years ago above this roadhouse on the old highway that snaked through the hills between Laramie and Tie Siding. Even worse, almost everybody in Laramie knew Brad was so much into scandalous, kinky sex that he occasionally acted as a club Dom and dipped his wick not only into the few female club members, but—rumor had it—also some of the men.

Actually those rumors were whispered with a good bit of care, as if nobody was anxious to get back to the McTavishes that he or she had originated the rumors.

It didn't help Brad's reputation that he went off every summer, chasing the elusive all-around national rodeo championship, risking his neck to prove he could master even a Brahma bull. Keely shouldn't care. After all, it wasn't as if she was in love. At least she didn't think she was.

Damn it, she wouldn't let herself get tied up emotionally by the Master who'd enslaved her libido. No way. No matter how much he tempted her to get to know the man behind the leather chaps and vest, to learn when and how he'd gotten the various scars that dotted his perfectly sculpted body. She'd wanted to ask him if the one on his inner thigh—a new addition she guessed he'd gotten this summer on the rodeo circuit—still hurt. And she often wondered when and where and why he'd gotten that Ampellang piercing, and if he ever took out the burnished gold barbell he wore through his thick cock head for dungeon scenes. But she'd never asked. If she had, she'd have had to concede she had an interest in her sometimes-master that transcended lust. She wasn't about to admit to herself that their relationship might become any more than strictly sexual.

For a long time Keely had realized vanilla sex didn't cut it for her. Just like her mother. After struggling with memories of a hero Dom—her dad—and villain Vince, she'd finally decided to take care of her needs this way, twice a week at Roped and Lassoed. She wouldn't allow any more than that. And she could rationalize to her guilty conscience that what she was doing was keeping her sexual cravings down to a manageable roar. No way would she risk losing her self-control. No matter how much she wanted those scenes to continue, to have them finally end with her cradled in Brad McTavish's strong arms. To feel totally protected in his keeping. Maybe it was the fact that Brad made her want to make their relationship far more than it was — than it could ever be — that frightened her beyond reason.

* * * * *

Outside, Keely felt fast-falling snowflakes stinging her cheeks. A frigid Wyoming wind invaded her jacket, swirling over her sensitized flesh through her unlined jeans. Shivering, she made her way toward her ancient pickup. She had to get home in a hurry, or she'd be stuck on the road for God only knew how long.

She should have stayed home, ignored the impulse that had driven her to brave the storm. Three hours ago it had only been a lazy snowfall coming down from a sky still glowing as the sun was setting on the western horizon. Nothing to indicate a blizzard might come of it in such a short time. There was nothing lazy about the hordes of snowflakes that obscured her vision now, or the fierce wind that whipped around her. It came close to catching her up as though she was as light as one of the fallen snowflakes. The wind was forming treacherous drifts like this one that had practically buried her truck.

Maybe. Just maybe she should go back inside, not try to leave until the storm let up. But no, she didn't dare let down her guard. As much as she would like to spend a whole night in Brad's arms, to kneel at his feet and suck his cock before a roaring fire while he tunneled his fingers in her hair and forced her to take him deeper, she mustn't give in. Not even now, while her knees trembled and her pussy still twitched with aftershocks from an orgasm that seemed to go on and on and on.

Especially not now.

And especially when the snow had started to swirl all around her so much she could hardly see to fit the key into the door lock. She had to get home fast, or she wouldn't be going anywhere except into the nearest ditch. That was if the truck decided to start, not just wheeze and sputter into a screeching, silent heap right there in the parking lot the way she imagined it might.

\* \* \* \* \*

"Snow's coming down mighty fast, boss. Can't hardly see your hands in front of your face. Looks like we may be in for the first real blizzard of the year. Doubt if anybody gets here who isn't already inside. Sure looks worse outside than what the weatherman predicted."

His night manager Eli Thompson's gravelly voice was easy to place even when Brad had his sweater halfway over his head, blocking his vision. "Looks bad, does it?"

"Mighty bad, winds whippin' around the snow. Wouldn't be surprised if it buried whatever cars are still in the parking lot before too long."

Oh, shit. If Brad didn't miss his guess, Keely would already have hightailed it out. His cock twitched at the memory of what they'd been doing over the last two hours. *Why do you always have to run out the minute a scene's over?* He jerked his sweater all the way down and wrestled open the small window in the men's dressing room. There she was, climbing into that worn-out wreck of a truck that he'd have consigned to the junkyard at least ten years ago. Stubborn little bitch! He pictured her freezing her ass off, stranded in one of the deep ditches bordering the highway into Laramie. "Gotta run. Try to stop her."

Shrugging into his Gore-Tex jacket but not taking time to zip it, Brad took the stairs three at a time and sprinted across the icy lot. He grabbed the driver's side door as Keely was trying to start the balky engine, and flung it open. "What the fuck do you think you're doing? Got a death wish?"

"Close the door. Can't you see I'm trying to get home before this storm rolls in?"

"Looks to me like it's already rolled. You're not going anywhere in this rust bucket, even if you can manage to start it."

"Hey, the Master-slave scene's over. Get out of my way." She jerked on the door, but he easily maintained control. Reaching into his jeans pocket, he used the remote control to start his own truck on the other side of the parking lot and turn on the heater.

He grabbed Keely around her narrow waist and lifted her onto the ground, slamming the creaky door behind her. "Well, Keely girl, I've decided it's time to start a new one. Come on, unless you want to get laid right here in the snow." Determined that she wasn't going to get away so easily now, Brad scooped her up in his arms and strode across the lot.

"What are you doing? Where do you think you're taking me?" She punctuated the words with sharp jabs to his chest that might've hurt if it hadn't been for his several layers of winter clothes.

"Here. Get in. Sorry it's cold in here, but you didn't give me much time to start the truck and get it warm."

He tossed her into the cab of a huge red truck and strapped her in. Jerking up the hood of his jacket, he stomped around to the driver's side. Somehow when he crawled in behind the wheel, the air inside seemed to grow warmer just from his presence. Keely shivered when Brad cupped her chin with his icy calloused fingers and made her look into his dark, mesmerizing eyes.

"I'm taking you home with me. It's closer than downtown Laramie, not to mention a much less treacherous drive. If you weren't such a priss about folks seeing you come out of here in the morning we'd just go back upstairs." He paused, shot her the grin that had a way of turning her resistance into jelly. "Relax and think about the hot cocoa and grilled cheese sandwiches I'm going to make you before I tie you to my bed and make you come until you forget all about why it is you're so damn determined not to be seen with me."

Keely could've screamed, and maybe someone would have charged out of the saloon and rescued her if they'd been able to hear her yelling over the raging wind. But for a moment she was taken aback. She'd thought Brad had accepted at face value her very rational explanation of wanting to keep her BDSM life private and confined to the club. She'd assumed the typical conservative reasons for secrecy made sense to him. She could've insisted Brad take her to her place in Laramie, storm or no storm, and she knew instinctively he'd do it. Dom or not, Brad McTavish wouldn't do anything to her that she didn't want.

And there it was again, that niggling sense that maybe, just maybe Brad had more of her dad than Vince in him. Of course she could be only deluding herself, hoping that was the case so she could indulge her repressed desire to learn who he was and how he lived in real time, outside the fantasy world of the dungeon. Could she manage her wayward libido long enough to sample his loving on his own turf without losing perspective?

The temptation was now here, right in front of her, and it was almost as if the storm was conspiring with him, blowing away her choices. Of course every submissive knew how even the illusion of having her choices taken away could ratchet up desire. The battle lost, she lowered her gaze and spoke. "I-I don't mind. Not really. I know you'd never hurt me."

"Hurt you? No, baby, I'll never hurt you, not unless you need a little pain to get off." Brad tilted her head and joined their lips.

He'd never done that before. She'd never allowed it. She must have been crazy all these months, because this simple kiss conveyed more than lust. It spoke of tenderness that touched her deep inside.

He ran his tongue along the seam of her lips, asking entrance. Not demanding it. Keely opened to him, stroked his tongue with hers, felt his warm breath mingle with hers in the dark solitude of his truck's cozy interior. All of a sudden the chill left her bones, replaced by a warm glow that began in her belly and snaked its way through her body. Yeah. She was still afraid of taking their purely sexual relationship to a new level, but not so afraid that she could tell him no. "Please take me home with you," she murmured against his lips when he released her.

"Oh, yeah." He slid over and put the truck in gear then patted the space beside him. "Curl up here and let me keep you warm. But don't think I'm about to forget you need a good old-fashioned spanking for even thinking about taking off by yourself. Look out the window, watch the snow. Feel the wind rattling the windows. And thank God this truck has four-wheel drive and new snow tires, and that it's only a couple of miles to my place."

"Yes, Master." Keely stared out the window, watching the wiper blades send melted snow flying as they made their way out of the parking lot and onto the highway. Brad drove the big, new pickup truck like a pro—the way he drove her to mindless climaxes in every encounter they'd shared at the dungeon. "Your transportation's a far cry from mine."

He turned into a winding country road that led up a steep rise. Though she braced herself for feeling the truck slipping and sliding, instead she listened to the motor's growl become fiercer. The oversize tires dug in, crunching through the newly fallen snow to get to the frozen ground below. Soon Brad drew to a stop inside the garage of a breathtakingly beautiful contemporary house, all angles and expanses of sparkling glass and rough-hewn cedar.

After turning off the motor, Brad came around and opened her door. "I need something rugged and reliable to get myself home on nights like these. You do too," he added, his smile morphing into a scowl. "Come on, let's go inside and get warm."

## Chapter Two

"Make yourself at home," Brad said, helping Keely take off her jacket and hanging it beside his on a rack outside the door from the garage. "Fire or food first?"

Keely's teeth were chattering so hard she had trouble speaking. "Fire, please," she said, her voice as shaky as her heartbeat. Now that she'd given in to temptation, no amount of rationalizing could make her believe she'd done the only thing she could have, even considering the rotten weather that had come on so suddenly. The warmth of Brad's big hand at her waist as he ushered her into the biggest living room she'd ever seen should have made her quit shaking. Instead, she kept on trembling even after he'd started the kindling with some sort of giant lighter.

The warm overhead lights he turned on bathed the room in a cheery glow. "Be right back, Keely girl. Relax and let the fire thaw you out while I fix something to warm your innards." He bent, framed her face between his hands and kissed her, a gesture more tender than sexual.

Was this the stern Master who regularly subjected her to his will? He looked the same, had the same seductive smile, the same woodsy cologne she'd learned to recognize from across the dungeon. But this—this gentle reassurance, this kind, respectful treatment—soothed her trepidations more than any overt action could have done.

Keely sighed as it came to her that he'd touched her many times, many ways. He'd taken her pussy and stimulated her ass. He'd ordered her to service him orally. She'd squirmed under his lips when he sucked her nipples and teased her clit with his tongue. But the simple brushing of his lips on hers...he'd never done that until tonight. And these two brief kisses somehow seemed more intimate than anything they'd ever played out in a scene back at the dungeon.

It boded ill for her resolution to keep their relationship strictly sexual, especially here in the warmth of his home, before a crackling fire that was slowly letting her absorb its heat. The chill in her bones began to dissipate even though the storm raged outside. The scene looked almost like a Christmas card, with snow on the ground in billowing drifts and huge evergreens tipped with a thick coating of snow and ice.

She looked away from the windows, focusing instead on the casual yet elegant lines of the towering peak of the ceiling, the cheerful whistling of a teapot she traced to a spot just past a circular staircase. A mouthwatering smell of melting cheese and hot cocoa reminded her of sleepy winter days when she'd been a little girl, before her dad died.

Sitting there, Keely let her thoughts wander back years. She'd often seen her mom and dad at home, enjoying each other and a stormy night. They'd been happy, and so had she. Had Mom been so desperately lonely after the love of her life had died that she'd grasped at anyone—even Vince—who had made her feel a tenth of the way she'd felt with Daddy? Like the home she remembered from her earliest years, Brad's house had similar homey touches.

She'd expected he'd have a showplace, not a home, but the effects were totally masculine. Oversize, earth-toned leather furniture, inviting stacks of pillows and expansive spaces hinted that he valued casual living. Framed photos looked down from their spots on a wide mantel made of native stone. Not what she'd expected at all when she'd allowed herself to imagine Brad in his personal space. She saw no hints that he was a sexual Dominant...at least down here. She glanced up the staircase, wondered if he had his private dungeon tucked up there where no casual guest would see it.

Suddenly Brad appeared in the doorway where all those good smells were coming from. "The bedrooms are up there.

Three of them. And an exercise room. I'll show you after we eat." He set a tray on the table, set out plates, mugs and napkins. "Come on, sit beside me. I won't bite."

*Much.* The man had a snake charmer's ability with her even when they weren't playing a scene. She couldn't resist joining him at the rough-hewn table then letting him seat her. The clean citrusy smell of his cologne mingled with aromas of melted cheese and hot cocoa. Homey smells. Not the smells she desperately wanted to associate with him—musk and sweat and sex, and the distinctive odor of those leather chaps and vest he always wore during their scenes at the club on Tuesdays and Thursdays. "I didn't know you could cook."

"So how did you think I manage to keep my strength up for the games we've been playing?" He lifted an eyebrow, giving him a devilish look before spoiling it by taking a monstrous bite from a sandwich and snaking his tongue out to catch a wayward strand of melted cheese.

"The saloon downstairs? Or maybe a housekeeper in a Parisian maid's outfit ruling over your kitchen here?" She knew as soon as she said it that she sounded jealous as hell, but she couldn't call back the words.

He set his cocoa down and shot her a self-satisfied grin. "Well, you're half right. I grab plenty of burgers and barbecued ribs at the saloon on days when I'm holding down the fort at Roped and Lassoed. As for the housekeeper, she comes to clean in jeans and sweatshirts and leaves as soon as she's finished. Once in a while she brings me a jar of the chili or soup she's made for her husband and kids. I don't need a woman living in unless she's my lover...my 24/7 slave ready and willing to satisfy all my needs, not just fill my growling stomach with food."

"You know that wouldn't be me." The way butterflies were flitting around her stomach, Keely guessed they were as scared as she was.

"It wouldn't? Somehow I have no trouble picturing you here, settling down, letting me take care of you. Wearing a frilly apron and nothing else while you see to my body's needs so I'll stay in shape to take care of yours." If that last chauvinist word picture hadn't been accompanied by a wicked, teasing grin, she'd have had her hackles up, but as it was, all she wanted to do was reach over and wipe the whipped cream froth from the cocoa off his smiling lips.

His expression turned serious. "How about it, Keely girl? God only knows how long we'll be stuck here in this blizzard. We've played scenes together that left us both wrung out to dry. Are you game to take the next logical step, learn a little more about what makes us tick…and find out whether the sexual magic's still there without the BDSM trappings? When it's just us and the storm outside, no one to watch or ask to join us in a ménage?"

"I'd like to, but—"

"You're afraid." Brad took her hand and brought it to his lips. "I'm never going to hurt you, sweetheart. Come on, tell me why it scares you so to think about you and me becoming us out in the real world, when you obviously enjoy the hell out of what we do at the club."

"I'm scared." Keely found it hard to find the words to tell him why. "I'm afraid of turning over complete control to any man, or…" Did it really matter what everybody thought of her? "I've known a good while now that you're looking for more. Dinner dates, weekends out here. Trips to Denver. Stuff like that." Since he'd come back from the rodeo circuit this fall, he'd kept dropping hints about making their Master-slave relationship permanent and binding. "I want to keep our relationship the way it is."

"Why? I don't have leprosy or anything. Are you ashamed to be seen with me?" Brad tilted her chin, made her meet his dark gaze.

Should she tell him? She guessed he deserved that much. "You're a Dom. Everybody knows you run Roped and Lassoed. If we're seen together they'll know. And they'll talk," she blurted. She was so afraid she'd lose him. "They'll whisper about our lifestyle…and the fact that you're filthy rich and I'm not."

He snorted. "So fucking what? I can't help being rich any more than you can help it that you're not. Besides, we are into the BDSM lifestyle. I like the games we play that make you crazy, and I'm pretty damn sure you do, too." His tense expression morphed into a grin. "Filthy rich or not, I'm hardly at the top of any mama's list of eligible fish they'd like to hook for their daughters. You said yourself that you didn't want your neighbors knowing you were hanging out with Laramie's bad boy, keeper of the local BDSM dungeon."

Keely knew that if she didn't give a little more she was going to lose the only Master she'd ever found who could always sweep away her sexual quirks and bring her to mindless climax. She didn't need him to tell her that. But she had to maintain her pride. The self-respect she'd worked so hard to earn after having grown up the way she did.

How to say this without sounding like a whining ninny? She didn't know, but she had to try. Holding his gaze, she managed to find her voice again. "I can't do the 24/7 Master-slave thing. Ever since I graduated from high school and went out on my own, I've had to avoid giving people things to talk about."

Brad reached up, rubbed a tear that was making its way down her cheek. "What sort of things? If some sonofabitch at the club has said a word about you…about us…I'll take care of him before he knows what hit him."

Covering his hand with hers, Keely spoke again. "No, it's not that. It's—other things—things from when I was a kid and lived with Mom and Vince."

He curled his fingers around her palm, drew it to his lips. "I need you to spell it out for me, sweetheart. Make me understand."

"The last thing I ever want is a full-time Master/slave relationship. It will never work for me because I grew up watching my mom become a walking doormat for Vince. He became her Master after Daddy died."

"Who says that's what I want?" Brad sounded a bit put off.

"Well, you are a Dom. You're into Dominance and submission games."

"Being a Dom doesn't necessarily mean I want to take the games out of the bedroom into our everyday lives. Is that what this Vince did? Did you get teased about it when you were a teenager?"

Could he mean he didn't expect a relationship like his brother had with his wife? "You don't want to humiliate me in public the way Jared does with Ninia?"

"What I want is to bring you pleasure." His deep voice poured over her, made her pussy twitch and her skin rise up in goose bumps. "Jared feels the same way about Ninia, and she needs the full-time BDSM lifestyle to satisfy her. Different strokes…"

"Submission's fine in the bedroom, or at the dungeon. I'm not about to turn control of my entire life over to any man, though." Sometimes Keely wished she hadn't been born a sexual submissive, able only to reach orgasm in the context of a D/s scene. Then she wouldn't be torn between wanting more with Brad and being terrified of taking a chance.

"What if I only want to be the Master of your sex life? Would that work?"

*Yes. No.* Keely wasn't sure she could take the whispers about her taking up with Laramie's best-known bad boy, or the sly accusations that she was a money-grubbing gold digger for the county's richest bachelor. She broke visual contact with Brad and forced herself to recall the humiliation and taunts she'd lived with through her teen years. "Brad, please. I'll tell you a story, one I probably should have shared with you when I first came and joined Roped and Lassoed."

"Okay, tell me. It's not going to make any difference, and I'm gonna do my damnedest to shoot down your arguments." He leaned back in the chair, sipped his cocoa and settled his gaze straight into her eyes.

"My mom's a sexual submissive. Like me. After Daddy died she needed a new Master, so she took up with Vince. He gets off on humiliating her in public. When I was in high school he sometimes made her walk with him holding a leash he'd attached to a thick leather collar with a big silver padlock holding on the leash. My friends saw them, and they made my life hell on earth, so bad I got out the minute I graduated from high school. The taunts followed me for years, until some of the kids grew up and found better things to do than humiliate me.

"It's still happening sometimes. Last week one of Mom's neighbors told me Vince was ordering Mom to go around the house naked except for that collar, and sometimes to answer the door that way. At least she hasn't spread her news all over town. I went to visit and found the neighbor hadn't been lying."

"This Vince sounds like a psychopath, not too different from the asshole who married my sister. Jared and I finally talked Diana into pressing charges on him for spousal abuse and assault, but not until he'd nearly killed her." Setting down his mug, Brad rested his chin on his hands. "Do you seriously believe I'd ever hurt you that way?"

Keely didn't know. When she thought about the situation with her mother, she wondered sometimes if her mom felt the same all-encompassing sense of helpless, delicious surrender as she felt when she was under Brad's command. "I don't want to end up like my mom. Daddy wasn't like Vince. I don't think you are, but I can't be sure."

"What was your dad like?"

"He was very loving. He never showed his Dominant nature even at home, unless it was in their bedroom behind closed doors. Until I was twelve or thirteen years old, I never realized Dad was Mom's Master. He never made her flaunt her collar or do demeaning things."

"What makes you think I would?" Brad's voice was low, his tone dead serious.

"Damn it, I just don't know." Taunts rolled through Keely's head, years old yet still hurtful. *Take a look at your mom. Bet he has to keep the bitch on a leash so she won't stray.* Keely clenched her fists, refused to listen to the chorus of even worse invectives that were trying to escape that deeply guarded corner of her memories. "I just know no one will ever say things like that about me. Ever. Not even if I have to go the rest of my life without being forced to the brink of orgasm and held there, only to be granted release when the pressure becomes too much to bear."

"You don't need to deny yourself the pleasure of submitting. And you don't need to be afraid I'd ever put you in position for anybody to talk shit about you. You know, sweetheart, one of the benefits of being on top of the local economic heap is that folks don't dare sling too many arrows at the McTavishes. Or at anybody we love. They may think I'm Laramie's perennial bad boy, but they *know* I can extract a good bit of retribution if I get too pissed."

Brad loved her? The expression in his eyes was fierce, yet deep emotion shimmered behind the mutant anger. "I want…"

"Let go, sweet girl. Trust me to take care of you. Know anybody who dares say a word about you will figure out pretty quickly that they'd better keep their big mouths shut."

God, how she longed to do just that, hand herself over to Brad with the complete confidence that he'd protect her as well as giving her the kind of kinky sex it took to turn her on.

Keely understood her mom's need to be punished and humiliated in order to unleash the strong sexual feelings only a strong Dom could force past her inhibitions. She experienced that need and its satisfaction, too, in the dungeon with Brad, opening up a compartment of her deeply buried psyche that could only break free under the sting of the lash. There was something appalling yet arousing, knowing eager eyes in the observation room were looking down on her performing for her Master, seeing her pussy swollen and wet, her every orifice breached for his pleasure. And her own.

* * * * *

So Keely didn't want her vanilla neighbors to know the owner of the infamous Roped and Lassoed turned her every way but loose. And scars from taunts about her mom's hardcore submissive lifestyle were still raw now, ten years or more after they'd been uttered. She was also worried she'd be talked about for latching onto Laramie's richest bachelor.

Yeah right, he might have knocked off her argument about him having too much money to get serious with a girl of modest means. But he'd fortified her first objection by pointing out he wasn't every good conservative mama's idea of an ideal catch. Yeah. He'd been a pretty reckless, crazy guy for a good many years, and it was going to take some doing for him to show a new leaf and overcome his own past.

But he'd realized somewhere along the way that Keely was worth it to him. God, this deciding all of a sudden to become a grownup could be a pain in the ass. As he glanced at Keely, a shaft of unexpected humor twisted his lips. Yeah, he still wanted to dominate his lovers, but his focus had narrowed. He wanted one sub in particular, one who would keep him satisfied longer than a new machine for the dungeon…a kinky scene…even still being aboard a bucking bronc when the whistle blew. He had the feeling that being with Keely would keep him satisfied forever.

Brad glanced outside, saw no evidence that the blizzard was going to pass by anytime soon. He had time. Time to let her work out her own demons, tamp down the fear that kept her holding him at arm's length now that they finally were alone. He got up and held his hands out to Keely. "Come on, sweetheart, let's go to bed. That spanking I promised you can wait 'til next week at the dungeon."

"B-but—"

"But nothing. There's nothing I'd like more than to take you to my bed and snuggle with you while the snow swirls over the skylight in the ceiling. Oh yeah, there is something. I'd love to sample every inch of your sweet, soft skin, twine my fingers in your silky hair. Shit, I'd give a month of my life to fuck you until we both collapse from the pure pleasure of it all. But that's not what you want right now, so you're going to sleep by yourself in one of the guestrooms."

"If you want me, Master…"

He sure as hell wanted her, but not this way. Not with her playing the role of sex slave. Not when she could look back and tell herself he'd forced her to submit. That this was just another scene played out on slightly different turf than in one of the dungeon's observation rooms. "If you want me, my room's the second door on the right. The door will be open." His balls ached, as though they were punishing him for deliberately denying himself satisfaction, but he opened the door to the room where his sister had slept when she came home from the rehab facility, and swung it open. "You'll find some of Diana—my sister's—clothes and stuff in here. Feel free to use anything you need. This door locks, in case you're afraid I'll join you during the night."

Before he could change his mind and drag her to his bed, he slid his lips across hers once more then strode down the hall. "Sweet dreams, Keely girl."

Sweet dreams? What a joke. Every nerve in Keely's body tingled in unison, screaming for the satisfaction she was denying herself. And Brad. Part of her wanted to leave this beautiful room and take the pleasure she knew she'd find in his embrace. But she couldn't. If she did, she might never leave, and a full-time D/s relationship would never fit in with the conventional lifestyle she wanted to pursue.

Yes, Brad was right when he'd told her earlier that such relationships could work. Keely had watched his brother Jared do a scene with his wife Ninia. She'd envied the woman the devotion she saw in Jared's eyes as he slowly, deliberately tied the Japanese rope bondage. She envied Ninia the sublime pleasure of having her Master perform an art obviously less familiar to him than the cat-o'-nine he wielded with such skill. Keely couldn't deny the envy had come with a twist of sorrow, for the scene had triggered long-suppressed memories of her mom and dad.

Brad had whispered in her ear that his brother had learned the complicated *Karada* bondage only because it gave Ninia such pleasure. Tonight he'd confided that Jared took pains to fulfill Ninia's every sexual fantasy, even when it meant allowing her to act out fetishes he didn't completely share. And that he took pains to exercise discretion when handling the nonsexual things like going out to the grocery store, to church—anywhere they'd be around others who didn't share their lifestyle.

But Jared and Ninia were different. Ninia had no local ties, and Jared had come home a wounded warrior. A hero despite his known status as a sexual Dominant.

Brad was the bad boy personified, a man apparently not caring what his neighbors thought, an anti-hero who did what he wanted, when he wanted, and damn the consequences. Keely herself was no Ninia. While she admired the beautiful gold collar Ninia wore locked around her slender neck, Keely had no desire to wear a collar or become publicly known as Brad's full-time sex slave.

Briefly Keely checked out the room, her gaze stopping to admire the clean lines of the headboard and chests. The natural-finished wood picked up one of the colors in an earth-toned Oriental rug. She stepped to the bed and drew back a goose-down comforter. God, but the pale green sheets felt soft, softer than any she'd ever touched at Bed Bath and Beyond in Cheyenne. Still fighting the urge to join Brad in his bed, she stepped into a large bathroom, found a new toothbrush and toothpaste and looked longingly at the large clawfooted tub. Maybe...

She tore off her clothes and stared at her reflection on the mirrored wall. Minus the utilitarian jeans and sweatshirt, she thought she looked like she might actually fit in this luxurious room. Before she could lose her nerve, she stepped into the tub and turned on the water. *Heaven.* Fragrant bubbles surfaced all around her, soothing tired muscles while sensitizing every inch of her skin. Only when the water began turning lukewarm did she drag herself out and let a thirsty terrycloth robe catch the remnants of her bath.

Warm. Fragrant. More luxurious than any bed had a right to be, it beckoned Keely, but not nearly as much as Brad's room down the hall. But she wasn't about to give in, not unless she could manage to overcome the obstacles in her head. If she did, and it didn't work out, she'd be devastated.

More important, so would Brad. And she couldn't bear the thought of hurting the Master who'd brought her sexual fantasies to life. He was a kind man, a little wild for sure, but when she got to thinking about it, she realized he'd been settling down some these past couple of years. Yes, he still went on the rodeo circuit, but he was quieter about it once he came home...almost as if he were just going through the motions.

Maybe...maybe she could come to believe he truly wanted more, that his determination to take their BDSM relationship to the next plateau wasn't just a passing phase. That might be part of her fear, too, that she might stick her neck out, give him her heart when he wasn't really in for the long haul.

She wouldn't think about that now. Not when the sheets proved to be every bit as soft as they looked, like warm silk against her sensitized skin. When she pulled the comforter over her, she found it surprisingly light, incredibly warm. Not sleepy, she stared out the window at growing snowdrifts, at the silhouettes of cowboys fighting against the wind, dragging reluctant cows and calves into the huge, sturdy barn.

The sound of the wind echoed in Keely's ears. Falling even harder now, the snow practically obliterated her view out the window. She wouldn't have been able to see anything if not for a strong, bright light that penetrated the snow and gave her an off-and-on view of the activity below. She shivered, despite the warmth of the room. Temperatures had to have been dropping fast, to have brought the ranch hands out from the comfort of their bunkhouse to bring all the cattle inside.

Was Brad out there? Keely imagined him chattering in the cold wind, seeing to his livestock. She sat up, dragging the comforter around her like an Indian blanket, and looked harder for the man whose close proximity was keeping her from sleeping through the storm.

The falling snow, glowing through strong beams from spotlights aimed toward the barnyard, made it difficult to see, but Keely was fairly certain the tall cowboy dragging a reluctant animal into the barn was Brad. Did he need more help getting all the cattle to safety? She started to get up and dress but stopped when she heard muffled footsteps in the hall. "Brad?"

The doorknob turned and he peered inside. "You ought to be asleep, not staring out the window at the snow. Damn it, I should have remembered these spotlights light up this whole side of the house as well as the barnyard. Sorry we disturbed your beauty sleep."

"You were out there, getting those cows into the barn." She didn't need to ask. The full-body shivering and flushed cheeks framed in a heavy flannel cap with earflaps securely fastened told the story. "Come here, you need to warm up."

"No, you come here. You'll never get any sleep on this side of the house with all that light outside. The hands will be out there off and on all night, making sure there are no calves buried under the snow. You sleep with me. Nothing will happen unless you want it to." When he held out a gloved hand, Keely untangled herself from the covers and headed for the door.

*What am I doing*? At the moment she didn't care that she'd promised to keep Brad a sometimes sex scene partner and nothing more. She hadn't wanted to see how he lived, to know he'd furnished a special room for when his older sister had spent weekends away from the rehab center. Keely hadn't wanted to find out his kindness extended to the cattle she'd assumed he'd leave to the ranch hands to take care of. Seeing this side of him, his sense of responsibility toward the livestock, was eroding her determination to keep the motivation for their relationship strictly lust. Trying to hold back as much as she could, she still held out her own hand and took those last two steps into Brad's icy embrace. "Brrrr. You need to get out of those cold, wet clothes."

"And into a hot shower. Come on, I'll tuck you into bed first."

\* \* \* \* \*

The lingering taste of her lips stayed with Brad as he showered, letting the hot needles of water drive away the worst of the chill from out of doors. He had a feeling Keely's body warmth would do the job a damn sight better. Just thinking about her in his bed, waiting, had his pulse racing, his cock getting hard.

He tamped down the lust. This was about getting to know Keely, showing her he was more than the club Dom always ready to take her on a hot, wild ride. After all, fortunately timed blizzards like this one didn't come along every day.

Dragging the towel across his chest, he wondered if he should shave again. After all it wasn't that Keely hadn't seen him close to naked, lots of times. Or that she didn't know he shaved his body hair. But that wasn't the point. He didn't want to scratch her pretty face, and he intended to do a lot of sampling of her sweet lips, so he grabbed his electric razor and mowed down the five o'clock shadow. His chest and belly felt smooth enough when he ran his hand down his body. The waxing he'd endured yesterday had apparently done its job. Except for the small tuft of pubic hair above his cock, he was smooth as a baby's ass all over. All for the sake of fitting the stereotypical image of a club Dom.

Taking a towel and wrapping it around his hips, he crossed the room then dropped the towel and slid into bed beautifully, powerfully naked.

When Keely rolled over and put her hand on his thigh, his balls tightened. The sweet smell of her damp hair filled his nostrils, and her soft breath tickled his collarbone. Then she shifted, tossing one long leg over his thigh. One move and he'd have his cock nestled in her soft, neatly trimmed pussy hair. The next step would be to roll her on her back and fuck her until she begged him to make her come.

"Oh, Master. You feel so good. Please, Master, take me."

"Not Master, not now. Tonight I'm just Brad, the guy who wants to make love with you, for real. No whips or chains, no having you service me. Tell me what you want, Keely." He used her name deliberately because names had no place in the dungeon. There it was Masters and slaves, cocks and cunts, mouths and assholes, once in a while a mental whistle at well put together tits and ass. Here was different.

Here in his house, his bed, he wanted to celebrate that he'd found more in Keely than a sexual submissive who needed her pleasure punctuated with pain and occasional humiliation. When they'd talked earlier, he'd discovered a woman with fears and hope, a woman he hoped was beginning to see him as a man and not just the Dom decked out in leather who could wield a cat-o'-nine or flogger to ensure her pleasure through pain. "Come on, tell me what I can do to make you happy."

"I want to please you. But I don't know how." She traced the line of his jaw then rubbed her thumb along his lower lip, her touch tentative yet incredibly arousing.

"You're doing fine so far." Shifting his hips, he settled against her. "I love the feel of your breasts against me. Of your heart beating next to mine. I like the way your pussy hair tickles my cock when we're lying here like this."

"Would you please, please…" Her voice was hesitant, but the way she writhed against him made it obvious what she wanted.

"Tell me what you want, baby. I need to hear the words, not just feel you getting me so horny it's all I can do to hold back."

"Damn you, I want you to fuck me. Now, before I burst inside."

"And I want you to fuck me. Take what you want, I'm not stopping you and I sure as hell am ready." That was an understatement. His cock was about to explode, being so close yet so far away from her hot, wet cunt.

He couldn't help but feel her tremble as she moved over and straddled him. Her expression reminded him of how the doe he'd almost hit out on the highway a few weeks back had looked when she'd stared into his headlights, certain she was about to die yet hoping for his mercy. It was then he realized he loved Keely, whatever love was.

Somehow he seemed more intimidating lying beneath her, his huge rigid cock probing gently at her pussy, than he ever had cracking the whip over her in one of their dungeon scenes. That was it. This wasn't a scene. This was Keely and Brad, on new territory, mingling emotions with desire. It scared her half to death.

He had to have known she was terrified, because he reached up and cupped her cheeks. "It's all right, baby. Come down here and give me a kiss."

She did, as if she had no choice. Maybe she didn't. She bent, running her fingers through his dark, silky hair as she joined their lips and tasted him. The fresh smell of mouthwash and aftershave reminded her once more that this was no scene. Like it or not, Keely had crossed a line she said she never would. She was making love to Brad, not serving her temporary Master.

Tentatively, she licked his lips, and when he opened to her she plunged her tongue inside. Their tongues tangled, each seeking the other. And what she felt wasn't just lust. He conveyed warmth, affection, all the things that terrified her about giving in to this undeniable attraction. She'd been fighting those deep emotions now for months, since the first time she'd walked into the dungeon and submitted to Brad as her Master.

Tonight she had no will to fight anymore. The incredible feelings swept her away like a strong wave beating on a windswept shore.

Everywhere their bodies touched, she burned. His hands, calloused but oh-so gentle, slid up and down her back, the way she imagined he'd someday comfort his child. Soft swirls of arousal started in her belly, making their way slowly through her body as he raised his hips and joined their bodies, never breaking the intimacy of the kiss.

She wanted to touch him, not just to feel the heat of his cock in her pussy, the slight abrasion of his clean-shaven chin and upper lip on her face. His thrusts, measured yet deep, made her wish she could keep him there forever. Only half aware of her actions, she tightened her inner muscles, caressing and milking his long, thick shaft.

He groaned. His muscles tightened as if he were fighting for control. The veins in his neck bulged, but he kept up the motion until she cried out with her climax.

While the aftershocks were still going through her, he lifted her away.

"You didn't come." Somehow that made Keely feel she'd cheated him, and that made her lift her hands, wipe the sweat off his brow.

"No condoms in the house. I didn't dare come inside you, maybe force you into a relationship you haven't quite accepted." The words came out harsh, guttural, as he obviously tried to slow his racing heartbeat.

"No condoms? You? I can hardly believe it."

"Believe it or not, you're the first woman I've ever had in my house except my sister and the woman who keeps the place clean. The first I've ever had here that would have given me reason to stock some protection."

His confession shocked her, but what surprised her more was her own realization that she'd gladly have taken his seed. Her traitorous body still wanted that ultimate mating that carried too much risk. A lifetime of responsibility. "Thank you for being a lot more responsible than I was," she said, dragging her hand down his body until she curled her fingers around his still-pulsating erection.

He smiled, a wry upturning of those sensuous lips she'd sampled moments earlier. "Not that I'd mind you having my kid, but I'm not sure if you're ready to make the kind of commitment I want before we start our family."

Was she? Keely didn't say. Things were apparently moving too fast for her. She swallowed, as if she were trying to stave off the tears that wanted to erupt. But it did no good. She had that deer-in-the-headlights look in her eyes again, and it made him feel incredibly protective.

"Don't cry, sweetheart. Relax. We've got time. The way the weather looks outside, neither of us is going to be going anywhere for the next few days. I'm going to go take care of this little problem myself. Don't trust myself not to give in to the temptation to come inside you, bare skin to bare skin. But you're not ready, I can tell."

## Chapter Three

When he finished taking care of his painful hard-on in the bathroom and putting on flannel PJ bottoms, he went back to bed to find Keely sound asleep. He slid in beside her and gathered her in his arms.

She wasn't the sort of sub his brother had married. It was understandable, considering the fact she'd grown up watching her mother fall completely under the control of a cruel Master. Yeah, she liked kinky sex, needed to give up control in the context of dungeon scenes. He had a sneaking suspicion she couldn't come without a certain amount of force or at the very least coercion. But she wasn't likely to go down on her knees and give him head while he watched TV, at least not unless it was her own idea. He didn't imagine she'd take to cooking dinner in the nude either, for that matter. It seemed his pretty sub was mighty concerned about what other people thought of her.

Did that bother him? A few weeks ago Brad would have said yes. Now he wasn't so sure. Spending time tonight with Keely, he'd seen a whole new side of her. A strong side, a caring one not just for him but for the damned stupid cattle they'd had so much trouble forcing into the barn so they wouldn't freeze.

His little brother had lucked into one of the few true slaves. Not that Brad resented Jared. If any Dom had needed a woman like Ninia, Jared had after losing his military career, part of one leg and a good bit of his self-confidence.

But Brad was beginning to think he could do just fine with a woman who needed him to take the lead in bed but wanted to be his equal in all the other aspects of their lives.

Keely. Now all he had to do was talk her out of her doubts about him.

There wasn't much he could do to stop the gossips from whispering about what they thought went on at Roped and Lassoed, or what part he took in acting out scenes there. What he needed to do was persuade Keely it didn't matter, that no one cared what a bunch of old biddies thought. Yes, he'd been a wild rich kid interested only in kinky sex and rodeo, but now he was thirty-five years old, grown up and ready to take on responsibility for a family. Hell, he already took responsibility for his family. Since Diana had gone to rehab more than two years ago, he'd taken care of her part of the family ranching business. He was still doing most of the work of running their cattle operation, even though Diana had come home almost a year ago. If Brad said so himself, he'd handled it all pretty well, between running the dungeon and spending the summer on the rodeo circuit. He even kept an eye on Jared and Ninia, made sure as much as he could that Jared didn't overdo it trying to disprove his disability.

All he had to do was show Keely this responsible adult side of him, prove he loved her and that he wanted her the way she was. He had the feeling it wouldn't be nearly as easy as convincing her he didn't give a damn whether she was dirt poor or a millionaire.

He lay there for a long time, looking up through the skylight at the storm raging outside. It showed no sign of letting up anytime soon.

\* \* \* \* \*

Keely woke up, snuggled closer to the warm muscular body behind her. Brad had put on PJs, she realized when the soft fabric nudged her bottom. It felt good, being close enough to feel his heart beat, listen to the up-and-down cadence of his breathing.

*What time is it?* She opened her eyes and glanced at the clock on the bedside table. *Oh no! I've got to get to work.* She started to roll over but was held firmly by the arm draped over her waist. "Brad, I have to go."

"Take a look outside, sweetheart. No one's going anywhere now. Not to mention, I doubt your boss will open the store, even if he can manage to get to it." He propped himself up on one elbow and looked out the window. "Power lines are down. You can use my cell phone to call whoever needs to know you're okay."

She picked up the phone and dialed her work number. "Hey, this electric plug for the charger is working. And the bathroom light is on. What…" There was no answer at the store, so she left a message that she wouldn't be in and handed the phone to Brad.

He grinned. "Don't get all bent out of shape. The electricity in the house is coming from a generator. It's not safe this far out not to have backup power. Here, let's see what they're saying on TV about what this blizzard is doing up in Laramie." He flipped on the TV, came up with nothing but a crackling screen. Swearing under his breath about the satellite being out of commission, he got out of bed and disappeared into a walk-in closet. "Here, these sweats will be awful big on you, but at least they'll keep you warm for now. We can go downstairs and rustle up something to eat before I go check on the animals. If you want to come outside with me, you can raid Diana's closet. I'm pretty sure she left some cold-weather gear when she moved back to her house."

"That's all right, I'm sure my own clothes have dried off by now."

He doubted the blue jeans and that short sheepskin-lined jacket she had on last night would do much to keep her warm outside in this mess, but he didn't want to raise her hackles. He was learning fast that Keely had an extra-large dose of pride.

*****

Keely was beginning to view Brad differently every minute she spent with him on the ranch. No way could she keep on seeing him as only a club Dom, a man without a face who had no interests other than giving and taking physical pleasure. Watching him seek the source of a mournful, frightened sound beneath the snow until he found a bedraggled, practically frozen calf and lifted it in his arms, she realized there was much more to her kinky lover than met the eye.

Most of the gossips in Laramie thought Brad was the same old playboy, hiding his goodness under the brash exterior of a carefree rodeo cowboy, a Dom who had no qualms about doing whatever he needed to do, to run Roped and Lassoed. But they hadn't seen Brad up close and personal the way she had, the man who cared for his family and his animals, accepted responsibility for friends and family when they needed help. It came to Keely that Brad ran Roped and Lassoed as much to meet the needs of others in the lifestyle as to satisfy his own Dominant nature. He'd taken over and managed Diana's as well as his own huge land holdings while she was in rehab. And how could she keep herself from falling in love with a man who'd tromp through hip-deep snow to rescue one small, stubborn calf?

"Come on inside the barn before you freeze out there," he yelled over the shrill sound off the wind as he moved toward the barn door. It wasn't an order, but Keely found herself wanting to obey, and not just because she was getting chilled despite the fact she was wearing several layers of cold-weather clothes. Inside, she grabbed a towel off one of the stall rails and went down on her knees to wipe down the shivering baby.

Brad found another towel and knelt beside her. "Do it a little harder, sweetheart. He's got a tough little hide, and we need to get him warm before he runs off to find his mother." He looked over at her and smiled. "I'm surprised you didn't want to stay in the house out of the cold, but I'm glad you came out with me. You never told me you knew your way around barns and stables."

Putting a little more muscle into rubbing the calf's side, Keely considered how long it had been since she lived with her parents on a small ranch outside Laramie. "I've always loved the outdoors, and being around cattle and horses. But my close-up experience came when I was real young, before Daddy died."

"Doesn't matter about experience. What matters is that you care about animals as well as people." The calf was getting restless by now, but they both kept on rubbing him until he bolted. "Guess the little guy's thawed out enough now. What say we—"

Brad's phone rang, and he snatched it out of his pocket. "Damn it, Jared, I told you to be careful. What the hell are you doing in the stable? Never mind. It doesn't matter. I'll be right over, assuming one of the snowmobiles will start."

He hung up and turned to Keely. "Jared hurt his good leg. Fool doesn't want Ninia to find out. Want to take a ride on a snowmobile?"

"Sure." Right now she'd go anywhere with Brad, even if it did mean letting yet another group of people know she was actually "seeing" him. Besides, she enjoyed cross-country skiing, and she imagined snowmobiling would be just as much fun. "Then let's go. Thank God the snow seems to have stopped falling for now."

He looked at her from head to toe. "We're not going anywhere until we get you into some clothes that will keep you warm. I'm not going to have you freeze on me. Go back in the house and find some of Diana's ski gear. I'm going to go start the snowmobile."

Keely shivered as she stripped down and slithered into a pair of silk long johns. She was almost afraid to step into Brad's sister's red and black Gore-Tex ski overalls and turtleneck sweater. Just these two garments had to have cost more than Keely made in a month. The matching Gore-Tex jacket, also black with red trim, would have kept her starving for at least another month, maybe longer. What if she damaged these things?

Brad would replace them, she knew. He'd probably think nothing of it, but it would make her feel like crap. Never mind, she told herself. She'd be very, very careful with the borrowed outfit. Pulling her own scuffed roper boots back on over thick wool socks, she picked up the heavy gloves she'd found in the pocket of the overalls and put them on. As Keely hurried downstairs she heard the roar of a powerful motor running outside the garage.

"Put on this helmet and climb on, sweetheart. If we ride double, we'll stay warmer." She wasted no time straddling the black leather seat behind Brad, because the sudden burst of cold air was freezing her nose and sending shivers all the way down her well insulated body. "Ready?"

"I'm ready—oh, wait a minute, I've got to pull my scarf up over my face. It's okay now, let's go."

Blanketed in heavy snow, the scenes they passed by looked as if they belonged on a picture postcard. Keely understood why all of the McTavish siblings had chosen to make their homes on this breathtakingly beautiful, rugged land. The sleds on the Arctic Cat snowmobile dug in to the newly fallen snow, shooting out excess snow and carving a path for them. She hadn't seen this model before, even though the farm implements store ordered in an Arctic Cat from time to time and had the company's catalogs for the few of their customers who could afford the pricey toys. If she wasn't mistaken, this was one of the Bearcat models, undoubtedly the top of that line. As they sped down the drive on the way to the highway, she grabbed Brad around the waist and held on tight.

"Scared?" he yelled over the roar of the engine. "Once we pass the highway we're nearly there."

She wasn't, really, even though she thought she'd been holding her breath for the last two miles, ever since they'd begun the roller-coaster ride down the frozen road. She hadn't even been able to see the tread marks they'd left last night with his truck. "Not scared, just out of breath. I trust you to take care of me. I didn't know part of the ranch was across the highway." A long ribbon of undisturbed snow marked where the highway had been last night, and beyond that she saw a house and outbuildings in the distance. When they got there, Brad paused and looked both ways.

"Never can tell when some fool's gonna try to turn his pickup into a sled," he commented once it became obvious that no one was driving along the road, at least for the moment. "Great-Granddad made a bunch of money when the state decided to put Highway 287 right across his land. Good thing Jared drew the part on the other side, since it's pretty much ideal for the dude ranch he and Ninia opened up there to occupy themselves in the summer. There's a good-sized stream on the western border that the guests seem to like paddling around in. Wouldn't catch me in that water on purpose, because it's snowmelt-off coming down from the mountain by way of Dirty Woman Draw. Even in the heat of summer, it's freezing cold."

"I don't think I'd like to swim there, either, if it's as cold as you say."

"Trust me, it's that cold."

Once they crossed the highway, Brad headed not for the old log cabin with cheery smoke snaking out of the chimney, but for the stable some fifty yards or so farther from the highway. Keely sensed his urgency, said a silent prayer that Brad's brother wasn't seriously hurt as he pulled up in front of the stable door and shut off the Bearcat.

\* \* \* \* \*

"So what the hell have you done to yourself?" Brad asked, letting go of Keely's hand and kneeling beside his brother.

Jared's smile looked forced. "Somebody knocked over a bucket of water in here last night, and I took a spill on the ice it turned into while I was trying to hook a bale of hay from up in the rafters. Tell me I haven't broken my leg. If I have, my wife will kill me."

Brad doubted that, but he understood why Jared would worry. Ninia was fiercely protective of her Master—especially when it came to him not always acknowledging the physical limitations put on him because of his injuries in Iraq. "Can you straighten it out, or is it stuck that way?" The angle of the leg didn't look good, but if Jared could move it...

When Jared tried to move his injured leg, it straightened some but not that much. It had to have hurt like hell, because Brad saw the skin around his brother's lips turning chalky white. "Okay, having you try to move it probably isn't a great idea. Where does it hurt the worst?" When Jared pointed to a spot on the outside of his left thigh, Brad turned to Keely. "Get down here and help me shove his pants down far enough that we can see what's going on."

Brad liked the way she wasted no time going on her knees on the other side of Jared, working fasteners loose and gently sliding his pants down, not flinching at all when she encountered the straps that helped Jared hold his prosthesis in place when he was exerting himself more than he should. "Do you want me to pull down his long johns?" she asked while Brad was working the pants past Jared's butt on the left side.

"Sure. Jared won't mind, will you?"

"Just find out what the hell's the matter. It's not as if Keely hasn't seen me naked at the dungeon. I just want you to patch me up so I can get my miserable ass back to the house before Ninia rips me a new one." Jared lay back and closed his eyes while Brad and Keely kept working his clothes down. He yelped when Brad tugged the pants and underwear over the spot where he'd told them it hurt. "What the hell?"

Brad bent, trying to get a good look in the dim light. The first thing he saw was a nice neat hole that went through both bloody layers of Jared's clothes, right above a nasty-looking laceration that was still bleeding profusely. "Looks to me like you fell right on the grappling hook you were using to pull down hay. It doesn't look like you broke any bones, but I doubt you're going to be walking anytime soon with the mess that hook made out of the muscles inside your thigh. What the hell were you doing? Don't you hire enough hands to take care of your horses and cattle?"

"Would you leave your animals to the ranch hands in a storm like this?"

"No, I wouldn't, but…" How the hell could Brad point out the differences between Jared's physical abilities and his own without fracturing his brother's still shaky self-confidence? He was about to say more when Keely laid a hand on his forearm and smiled.

"Of course you wouldn't. Instead of worrying about what you might not ought to have done, we need to figure out how to get you back to the house so Ninia can take care of this. It's more than either Brad or I can handle." Keely got up and went into the tack room. When she came out, she had a roll of gauze, some adhesive tape and a box of four-by-four sponges. Brad had to admit his woman had common sense as well as the tact he lacked. "I saw some ointment and stuff in there. Do you think we should use it?"

Brad followed her gaze to the gaping wound on Jared's leg. "Let's bandage him up now to slow the bleeding, and get him to the house so Ninia can take care of him." He hoped she could handle whatever needed to be done in the way of emergency care, because it would be nearly impossible for them to get Jared to a hospital in Laramie or Cheyenne. Taking a handful of four-by-fours, Brad laid them over the wound and exerted pressure with the heel of his hand. "This seems to be slowing the bleeding. Let's wrap the gauze around his leg as tight as we can and figure a way to get him on the Bearcat."

Jared let out a disgusted growl. "Help me up and I'll walk to the damned snowmobile," he told Brad. "You said the leg's not broken. I'll be damned if I'll let you carry me into the house and scare Ninia half to death."

When Brad was trying to figure out how to tell his brother he wasn't about to take on Ninia's fury if he did what Jared asked, Keely took Jared's hand and looked him in the eye. "Please, Jared. I don't want your wife to be angry at me."

"It's me she's going to be screaming mad at. Brad, take it easy with the pressure you're putting on that pad."

Brad loosened the gauze wrap until blood started seeping to the surface again. He tightened it up again until the bleeding stopped. "Better? Can't make it much looser than this unless you want to risk bleeding out."

"It's okay. Help me up now." Jared sat up and held out his hands. "No, before you do, toss some hay in those last two stalls and fill up the horses' feeders. I'd finished up with all the others before I slipped on that goddamn ice."

"I can do that." Without waiting for instructions, she got a rake and started loosening the bale Jared had apparently dragged down from the rafters. "About how much?"

"Go ahead and fill the feeders. God knows whether I'll be able to get out here for the next few days," Jared told her.

Keely never ceased to surprise Brad with her eagerness to help. It gave him a warm feeling inside, even now, when his hands were freezing without his heavy gloves. "Thanks, sweetheart."

Securing the grappling hook onto the rail of an empty stall, he tried to figure the best way he could get his brother up without injuring him further. "Jared, sit up if you can."

Jared did. "Lift me up and let me put some of my weight on the stall rail. That way you can get under my shoulder and be my left leg until we get outside to your snowmobile."

Although Brad didn't think it was a good idea for Jared to stand up, he couldn't see any other way that they could get him out to the snowmobile. As soon as Keely finished filling the feeders, she came back and seemed to size up the situation. "Get on Jared's right side and steady him," he told her.

Brad squatted and caught Jared by the shoulders, pulling up until he was able to grab on to the stall railing. "You okay like that?"

Jared nodded, but it was obvious he was in pain. "Let's hurry and get me out to that snowmobile."

The snow was coming down again, flakes floating slowly to the already heavily blanketed ground. At least the wind had died down for the moment. With Keely driving the snowmobile while Brad held on to Jared, they made a slow journey the fifty yards or so between the stable and Jared's cabin.

* * * * *

An hour later, after Ninia had Brad help get Jared to their bedroom and patched up his hurt leg, Brad and Keely relaxed in front of the fire in the bedroom fireplace. They'd be here quite a while, until their outdoor storm gear dried. Keely didn't mind. She'd thought they'd never get warm again after the long snowmobile ride from Brad's place, but now she was feeling toasty warm in one of the spa robes Ninia had found for them.

Ninia and Jared wore similar robes. Keely had visualized them sleeping in a room equipped with fucking tables, machines and at least one restraining device, but she was wrong. Nothing readily visible in the massive bedroom hinted its owner was a Dominant, that is unless she counted those red silk scarves hanging from each bedpost on the king-size bed.

Keely smiled at Jared, whom Ninia had settled comfortably on the bed, his upper body propped up by a stack of pillows. Minus his prosthesis and the black leather chaps and vest he'd worn in the dungeon exhibition she'd seen, Jared hardly projected the image of absolute power, complete control. When Ninia perched cross-legged beside him and held his hand, Jared smiled at her.

The obvious devotion the other couple shared made Keely wish she dared enjoy a similar sort of relationship with Brad. Until Jared ordered Ninia to shed her shoulder-length blonde wig, revealing less than a quarter-inch of pale stubble. When Keely would have let out a yelp, Brad pinched her ass and hissed, "Shhh. Don't let them know you're shocked."

"Yes, Master."

Keely could barely hear Ninia's whispered apology for having failed to shave her head completely smooth this morning. "Would it please you if I went in and shaved now?"

*Not in a million years, Master.* No way would Keely walk around bald as a cueball because some man told her to. But Ninia seemed okay with it, even eager.

"Not now. If you're very good, I'll shave you myself. Later. Right now I want to enjoy the silky feeling of this baby fuzz." Jared bent and drew his tongue across the nape of his slave's neck then traced around her earlobe before dipping inside the ear and tongue-fucking it while Ninia whimpered in apparent delight. "Join us," he said to Keely and Brad, a broad grin on his rugged face.

Could she? Could Brad? The memory of watching the couple demonstrating *Karada* bondage at the dungeon titillated Keely. Brad squeezed her hand. "Watch all you want, they're into exhibitionism. Are you?"

Keely wasn't sure, even though her nipples had tightened and she longed for Brad's touch. She couldn't help seeing the love in Jared's eyes as he caressed Ninia's scalp, or the possessive way he stroked beneath the engraved gold collar with its tiny ring above the large topaz center stone that nestled in the hollow of her throat.

A slave collar, with a ring to attach a leash. Not just a piece of jewelry but an unmistakable symbol that Ninia had given herself to her Master. Irrevocably. Keely imagined the emotions that must have gone through Ninia when Jared put it on her, the finality of the sound of the collar closing permanently, binding her to her Master for all eternity. The collar was beautiful, not an ugly black leather one with spikes and a heavy padlock like the one her mother wore. No one who wasn't into the BDSM lifestyle would recognize Ninia's collar as anything other than a unique necklace she wore all the time.

But it was still a collar. A symbol of his total possession, her total submission. A sign that Ninia belonged to Jared, as obvious to those in the BDSM lifestyle as the large, elegant set of rings she wore on her left hand was to those in the vanilla world.

When Jared straightened, he rubbed his palm in a circular motion over the crown of Ninia's head. Keely watched Ninia shudder as though her Master's gentle touch aroused her almost beyond control. "Take off your clothes and suck my cock like a good slave."

Keely turned to meet Brad's hot gaze. "I guess I must be ready. Feel how hot I am." Taking his hand, she drew it first to her lips then settled it between her legs. As soon as he slipped a finger up her pussy, she started to pant.

"You're wet, too. Undress for me." Brad undid the tie on her robe and spread it open then stood and took off his boxer shorts. "Well?"

The sight of his hard, muscular chest made her ignore the voice in her head that said sex play should be between one man, one woman unless you were inside Roped and Lassoed or some other BDSM club. Still she hesitated.

"Come on, now. It's not like we're about to switch partners. Not here, not now. Watch Ninia and Jared. Focus on them while I take care of you. By the way, I grabbed some of Jared's condoms in case we need them once we go home."

"Look. Ninia's got pierced nipples. Imagine the feeling when Jared tugs on the chain between them. Have you ever thought about—"

"No!" Keely said it so emphatically, Brad knew she'd thought about it, just as she most likely had pictured how it would feel if she shaved off the curly mop insulating her scalp from his sensual touch. Not that he entertained the idea that she'd ever shave it off, or let him do it. And not that he could imagine himself wanting her to do it. Different strokes…

"You know you do." He pulled her down on his lap and dug his fingers between strands of her hair. "You wonder whether having rings jingling from your nipples would keep you wet all the time, wanting sex with the Master who had them put there."

Keely shot a questioning look Brad's way. "Does having that bar through your cock keep you horny all the time?"

"It did when I first got the piercing, and each time I switched to thicker gauge jewelry—that is, after the swelling and pain went down. But now it's almost like another part of me."

"Then why not take it out?"

He bit her earlobe, hard. "Because you seem to like the way it feels inside your sweet pussy. And because it adds to my pleasure when you play with it with your tongue."

"Oh."

He loved it when she couldn't think of a proper comeback. "The Ampellang's not going anywhere, baby. Not as long as it gives you pleasure."

She sighed as she watched Ninia kneel between Jared's legs and go down on his large, impressive and unpierced cock. Deep, fast, her shaved head bobbed up and down until Brad was so hard it was all he could do to stop himself from grabbing Keely and fucking her mouth, her cunt…

He fished a condom out of a deep pocket in his robe, ripped it open and peeled it carefully over his cock. "Have you ever been fucked in the ass?" he asked, shifting her so her rear hole was within easy reach.

"Not except by the machine at the dungeon." He thought he felt her tremble, hoped it was with excitement, not fear, as he smeared the contents of a tube of lubricant as far up her anal passage as the applicator nozzle could reach, and over his sheathed erection.

Slipping her robe off, he squeezed her breasts then set her on his lap. His sheathed sex twitched when it came in contact with the crack of her taut, inviting ass. "I want you to watch Ninia and Jared. Meanwhile I'm gonna introduce your tight rear end to its personal fucking machine." With that Brad lifted Keely, rolling her swollen nipples between his thumbs and forefingers as he slowly lowered her backside onto his rampant erection.

Fuck but her ass was tight. If it hadn't been for the condom, he figured he'd have come as soon as he worked his way past her anal sphincter and seated himself balls-deep in her rear hole. As it was he had to fight to maintain control. "Be still, baby. Watch Ninia and Jared. See how they're both damp with sweat. Tell me what you're seeing, what turns you on." Brad reached around and tugged on Keely's nipples, his motion rhythmic—in time with the way Jared twisted his wrist, jiggling the chain between his wife's breasts while he used the other hand to force her bare head up and down on his cock. Ninia's cheeks rose and fell as though they'd choreographed the motion, perfected it as only long-time lovers could. "Come on, don't be shy."

Keely wiggled her butt, and Brad punished her by pushing two fingers in her cunt and rubbing his thumb over her throbbing clit. "Oh yes, Master. Hurt me. Hurt me the way Jared's hurting Ninia."

"Like this, my sweet slave?" Tensing his thigh muscles, Brad pushed himself deeper into her ass. He finger-fucked her cunt until she screamed and a stream of hot pussy juices pooled in his palm. "Not very obedient, are you? I didn't give you permission to come."

"I'm sorry, Master." Keely spoke so softly he could hardly hear her, but her excited yelp reverberated around the large room. Obviously it wasn't only his fucking that had pushed her over the edge, he decided when he looked over at the bed and noticed Ninia now straddled his brother's face while she deep-throated him.

Ninia's practically bald head bobbed up and down while Jared's strained up off the pillows so he could tongue-fuck her bald cunt. He dug his fingers into her plump buttocks. Controlling her the way Brad longed to control Keely and bring her to ever-deepening orgasms. How could Keely not have tumbled over the edge when she was watching Jared's show while Brad was fucking her ass, stimulating every highly erogenous spot on her delectable body?

"You're forgiven, this time. Down on your knees now and close your eyes. Don't say a word, and don't move. I'll make your punishment light, but you're gonna come again when I say it's time." While Keely positioned herself on all fours in front of the fireplace, Brad peeled off the condom and replaced it with another one. Good thing he'd spotted one of Jared's floggers in the bathroom closet, he thought, eyeing the faint marks John had left on Keely's tender skin last night at the dungeon. He raised the small whip and started to inflict the pain she seemed to need then changed his mind.

Keely's skin was creamy smooth and redhead-pale, with a few freckles he could hardly distinguish from the slight bruises on her back and buttocks. They fascinated him, and he couldn't resist running the metal-tipped silk ribbons of the flogger along the length of her spine, watching her muscles twitch despite his order for her not to move. "Be still." He set the flogger aside and went on his knees behind her submissively raised butt. "I'm going to take you in the pussy, doggy-style. You're not to come until I tell you to."

The musky smells of sex surrounded them. Jared's terse order for Ninia to ride him reminded Brad that two pairs of ears could hear every command he voiced to Keely. It didn't bother him—he'd been in the dungeon business too long not to have experienced public sex, even ménages—but it brought home the fact that when he was with Keely he didn't need a scene. For the first time he realized he'd be just as happy to have her for himself, claim the intimacy that two people in love would sometimes want to have…their most physical moments between just the two of them.

Right now he saw that Keely's cunt lips glistened with the dampness of arousal. His own cock ached for release. He grabbed her butt cheeks and positioned her, stopping to caress the taut twin mounds before pulling her cunt in line with his cock and thrusting home. "Be a good slave now. Squeeze my cock. Imagine me claiming you like this in front of everybody in the dungeon one Saturday night." Her tensing beneath him hinted she wasn't all that much into voyeurism, at least right now. "Come on, fuck me now. Jared and Ninia are so tied up with each other, they wouldn't notice if a hundred other couples were fucking each other on their bedroom floor."

"Mmmm." Apparently Keely was taking to heart his order not to speak. Her cunt spoke clearly enough, though, squeezing and releasing his cock with every thrust, coaxing out the orgasm he'd been fighting for what seemed like hours.

He fucked her hard, feeling the mouth of her womb on his cock head with each inward motion. His balls bounced against her hot, wet outer lips. The slapping sounds of flesh on flesh surrounded them. He had to come. Couldn't wait much longer.

Leaning over her, he thrust two fingers into Keely's mouth, felt her begin to suckle him. "Now, baby. Feel me coming into your hot, wet cunt and let go all that pent-up energy. Scream if you want to. It's okay."

"God, yes, Master Brad. Oh yes, I'm coming. Hurts so good." She sucked hard on his fingers then bit down on them when her climax began.

He lost it. Letting out a scream, he started to come. Felt so good. So fucking good. Burying himself deep inside her, he held her there until she stopped trembling. Then he rolled onto his back, taking her with him while the strongest orgasm he'd ever had kept on going, leaving him sweating and sexually drained.

It was the best fuck he could recall ever having.

## Chapter Four

By the time Brad pulled the Bearcat into the garage beside his big red truck, snow had started falling again and the wind had practically blown them off the pathway. There'd be no getting home tonight for Keely.

That didn't bother her nearly as much as it had last night, before she'd learned a lot more about Brad than that he was a skilled Dom she dared not see outside the dungeon. She followed him into the house, eager despite her lingering reservations to learn more, see if she might actually trust him enough to give him her full-time submission. At least when they were at home alone.

"Hmmm. Smells like the bunkhouse cook brought us over some of his famous chili and cornbread," he said once she stepped inside and started peeling off Diana's ski togs. "Shall we have some before we go upstairs?"

Part of Keely wanted to skip the food and go upstairs, but then her stomach gave a very unladylike growl. She grinned. "Guess that means I think we should try some of that chili first."

"Good. Sit over there at the table and I'll serve it up. Hope you like it hot."

"Yes. Just so long as it doesn't burn my throat so much I won't be able to suck you off." The picture of Ninia servicing Jared that way had kept Keely's pussy wet all the way home. It had also cemented the image of Jared's slave with her shaved head and pussy, and that pair of good-sized nipple rings with a gold chain dangling between them.

"Jared won't let her go out without a wig." Brad rubbed his nose through Keely's hair while setting two glasses and a carton of milk onto the table.

He must have been psychic. "How did you know I was thinking about your brother and his wife?"

Brad looked back at her from the stove, where he was ladling soup into two huge mugs. "Because I thought the same thing when I first found out about their fetishes. And I talked to Jared about it." Setting the mugs, a pan of cornbread and the butter dish from the refrigerator onto a tray, he brought it all to the table and took a seat across from Keely. "Eat up."

Keely observed the steam coming off her soup mug. Too hot. "Why does he make her shave her head?" The pussy she could understand, lots of submissive women shaved their pubes for their Masters' pleasure. If Brad wanted her to, she'd shave her pussy every day. She might even consent to having her nipples pierced, though she wasn't at all sure about hanging a chain between them. But her head?

"Jared isn't the one who wants her to keep her head shaved. But it's apparently a turn-on for Ninia. Before Jared she'd had a Master who trained her to expect and want the darker sides of bondage and submission. He was another military guy. He died in Afghanistan several years before she met Jared, but he left her with a real taste for voyeurism, ménages, public humiliation—and *Karada* bondage. Jared's a Dom, never doubt that. But if not for his slave's need for kink, he'd satisfy his need to dominate with an occasional club scene, a few good sex toys and a cat-o'-nine."

"You're saying he humiliates her because she wants it?" Keely tested the chili again, smiled. "I think the chili's cool enough to eat now. Ooh, it's delicious."

Brad grinned and lifted his mug. "Mmmm. Charley does know how to make chili." He buttered a slice of cornbread and devoured it in four bites. "Did you know the job of a Master is to bring pleasure to his slave, no matter what it takes?"

Keely had never thought of it quite that way, but she guessed Brad was right. "Are you a good Master?"

"I hope so." He took her hand and brought it to his lips. "I aim to please you, that's for sure."

Keely met his gaze then stared out at the snow blowing outside the expanse of windows in the large, cozy kitchen. "I never thought before today that there could be anything erotic about having a shaved head. When my mother is shaved, it's because Vince is punishing her for something."

"I saw that kind of punishment, too, when Diana was with her bastard ex-husband. From what you've told me about your stepfather, he sounds a lot like Gareth. By the time I got enough evidence on him to get him tossed in jail, he'd practically destroyed my sister. She spent nearly a year in rehab, getting him out of her system. She couldn't give up the lifestyle, so she made a switch."

"Your sister's a Domme?" Keely had trouble picturing a woman obviously as submissive as Ninia or more so, suddenly switching, that is unless she'd taken so much abuse for so long that she wanted to turn the tables.

"That's one I have a hard time believing, but she swears she is. Even takes a turn at the dungeon once a week, servicing two male subs who seem to thrive on pain. Makes no sense to me, getting off on having your balls walked on with a woman's stiletto heels or wearing a cock cage that jabs spikes into you if you dare to get a hard-on." Brad shook his head then reached over and stroked Keely's forearm. "Come on, enough of this. Even thinking about what my sister does to her submissives makes my cock start to shrivel up. Not a good thing if we're going to spend the next few days riding out the storm, seeing if we can make this work. Let's go to bed."

\* \* \* \* \*

Keely lay on the black leather recliner across from a matching sofa, naked except for one of Brad's dress shirts she'd left open in front. No need for modesty. He'd claimed her pussy, her mouth, even her tight rear passage that had never felt a man's pulsating shaft before today. He'd kissed and nibbled every square inch of her body, and while they'd relaxed in the sunken hot tub he'd set her on its marble edge and made her pussy as soft and smooth as a baby's butt.

He'd ordered her to shave him too, maintaining that iron control of his while she clipped then shaved off every last bit of his dark pubic curls. Funny she hadn't noticed before that he'd already shaved his cock and balls not too long ago. After she was done, she'd just had to sample his long, thick cock, verify that it and his balls were as velvety soft as they looked. She'd even traced around his baby-smooth asshole with one finger. Amazingly he hadn't punished her.

Finally he emerged from the bathroom, beautifully naked, his face freshly shaved. He took her breath, his cock swollen, his smooth balls pulled taut against his body, powerful muscles rippling beneath the surface of smooth, tanned skin. Hairless skin or close to it, whether by nature or frequent waxing. Keely didn't care. She wanted nothing more than to go on her knees and service her magnificent Master, but he stretched out over her, claiming her mouth in a warm, wet kiss that sent powerful waves of need to every cell of her body. As he tongue-fucked her, she felt him slip a hand between them and attach nipple clips to first one and then the other already aroused nub of flesh. The bite of the clips hurt, but he flailed the tips with his fingers, pulling away and sliding down her body. When he cupped her breasts and pulled them together so he could lick both constricted nipples at once, the pain began to dull, replaced by a glow of desire as her tortured nipples swelled in their restraints and poked at his questing lips.

"I love seeing your nipples like this, all red and swollen and ready to catch between my teeth. I want you to have them pierced for me so they'll be like this all the time without causing you pain," he said, his words sending a shiver all the way to her needy pussy. With that he gently removed the clips and sucked the pain away, leaving her frantic—frantic to have him burst the climactic bubble that already had her aching…throbbing in every hole he might choose to fill.

"Please, Master Brad, I need you to fuck me." She reached up and dragged her hand down the length of his chest and belly, stopping when she curled her fingers around the throbbing length of his smooth, hot sex, using one thumb to sample a drop of creamy lubrication she saw glistening in the slit at its tip. "Why do you keep this shaved?"

He laughed. "I can tell you want my cock, baby. And I want to fuck you so much I'm aching." Cupping her newly bald pussy, he slipped one finger in her cunt, another just past her anal sphincter. "I don't like scratching your sweet cunt with a lot of coarse pubic hair, any more than I like having anything between me and your soft, sexy little body, dulling the sensations."

"You have your body hair waxed?"

"I've kept it that way ever since I first serviced a shy, redheaded sub at Roped and Lassoed and scraped her incredibly soft skin with my wiry chest hair. I'd have kept my groin waxed, too, but it hurt like hell so I started shaving my cock and balls but leaving the rest of the pubes so she wouldn't think I was too kinky for her." Brad looked up at her then bent and drew his tongue along her swollen slit. "Baby, that sub was you."

His serious tone left no doubt he'd wanted to please her a lot more than he'd ever indicated at the club. For some reason that pushed Keely closer to the edge of being his full-time sub than any of the arguments he'd given her before.

Not to mention that what he was doing to her had her ready to come. He kept licking her clit, nibbling at her hairless outer lips, delving his tongue deep into her weeping pussy then inserting a large dildo where his mouth had been. "I hope you like your cunt bare, because I intend to keep it that way."

"Oh yes." Keely liked it, basked in the pure eroticism of his bare flesh caressing hers, the titillating feeling, knowing there'd be nothing between them dulling the sensation of two lovers becoming one. "Please fuck me now," she begged, knowing she was drenching him with pussy juices that bathed them both. "I'm—"

When he raised his head, his cheeks and lips glistened with her juices. "No need to be embarrassed, baby. I love it when you get hot for me. Stand up and I'll fuck you like you've never been fucked before. In my own personal dungeon. I've been waiting for the right woman to initiate it with me."

Her heart beat faster when she saw him open a mirrored door that led not into a closet as she'd thought, but a small yet imaginatively equipped torture chamber. Creamy walls held a black iron St. Andrew's Cross as well as strategically placed stainless steel handcuffs and leg irons with what looked like soft, faux fur padding. A small, stainless steel table with stirrups and a thick leather pad was centered on the floor, whose red plush carpeting felt springy against her bare feet. Along the other wall was a recessed cabinet whose glass doors revealed all sorts of toys that made her pussy twitch with anticipation. And the ceiling boasted a bevel-edged mirror centered above the table.

*He said he'd never used this room before.* "This is your first time here? Really?"

"Really. You're the first person besides the contractor to see this room. The first sub I ever wanted to bring into my home. My heart. Come here and climb up on my fucking table. You're gonna give me head while I eat your delicious cunt. Then, maybe, if you're good, I'll take out this dildo and fuck you for real. I grabbed some more condoms from Jared before we left his place."

When he rolled one of the condoms over a large bright blue butt plug, her mouth went slack. The idea of him taking all her holes at once had more pussy juices trickling around the dildo, along her slit and down her thighs. Eager for the triple invasion, desperate to take his big cock in her mouth and suck him dry, she bent over the foot of the table and spread her legs. "Please don't make me wait," she begged, hating the plaintive sound of her voice yet yearning for the punishment her instinctive act should cost her.

He took up a soft flogger and snapped it in the air. "Climb up on the table and put your feet in the stirrups. Don't try to anticipate my wishes again. I'm not the least bit shy about telling you what I want."

When she lay back on the padded table and situated her bare feet in the icy stirrups, she felt him snap the flogger over her belly, experienced the mild stings from those metal beads while she heard a snap and sensed he'd dropped the hinged lower section of the table, fully exposing her sopping pussy to his gaze, and to the flogger whose beads now pummeled her bald mound.

"Oooh." She loved the feeling of helplessness, made more so when he bound her knees and ankles to the padded bottoms of the stirrups that held her open for his pleasure and her own. Then he worked the butt plug up her ass until its flared head rested provocatively against her wide-open, incredibly sensitive rear entrance.

Her pussy clenched when he set the dildo to vibrating and moved to the end of the table. She wanted him to own her, strip her of every inhibition she'd ever had, force her to come and come until she couldn't come any more. Holding her breath, she savored the feeling of helplessness, made more intense when he planted one knee in the padded sling to the left of her head and straddled her face, settling his other knee in the matching sling on her right.

"I want you to suck my cock now." The heat in his deep voice was nothing compared to the feeling of his muscular thighs scalding her cheeks, his throbbing cock nudging her mouth then finding a home between her eager lips. "That's it. Take me deep. Swallow me. Blow me until I'm wrung dry."

The musky yet clean scent of him surrounded her.

"Easy now, I'm gonna raise your sweet cunt so I can fuck you right." Then she felt her ass rising as he pushed a button and raised the table. "There. I want to see you play with your nipples while I'm taking care of your sweet pussy. Pinch them until they're tight little nubs while you give me head. Oh God, lick me. Yeah, like that," he rasped out when she ran her tongue up the underside of his rock-hard cock then extended it to taste his balls that pressed so enticingly against her stretched lips. "Take a look at the ceiling. Watch. Tell me seeing us like this doesn't excite you."

She couldn't talk around his pulsating cock, but she couldn't help looking in the mirror above them, watching her own flesh tense, observing how he'd bent over her, and squirming when he turned up the speed on the two vibrating objects in her cunt and ass while grabbing her clit between his teeth and flailing it with his tongue. Compelled by the escalating feelings inside her, she tugged at her nipples, rubbed them against the smooth, muscular plane of Brad's lower belly. And she swallowed, lodging the head of his big cock in her throat, breathing slowly through her nose and tickling his satiny balls as she milked him, taking him deeper down her throat with every delicious swallow.

Her pussy clenched against the dildo. She wished it were his cock instead, but she couldn't imagine losing the incredible sensation of being possessed, filled, driven toward a climax she'd never been able to achieve with vanilla sex or sessions with other Doms. She dragged her nails up his chest, struggled to hold back her climax until he gave permission.

When he pulled out she cried out. She'd failed him, failed to suck him dry. His rock-hard, glistening penis held her gaze, almost made her fail to realize he'd stuffed her mouth again, this time with a firm ball gag. "Keep pretending it's my cock you're loving with your pretty mouth," he ordered as he secured the gag with straps he tightened around her head. "And keep watching. I can tell it turns you on."

Would he fuck her pussy or her ass? Not that Keely cared much at this point. Every cell in her body screamed for release of the intense pressure that kept building up as he moved to the end of the table and slipped on a condom. The vibrating anal plug stayed in, its rhythmic motion keeping her lust at a fever pitch, but he slowly retrieved the dildo from her swollen cunt. "I'm wearing a condom. Blink twice if you want me to take it off and fuck you bareback."

Did she? She knew he was clean and so was she. Everyone who came to Roped and Lassoed had to submit monthly reports from their doctors certifying them free of all kinds of venereal disease, from the fairly benign ones to HIV. It was the wrong time of the month for her to get pregnant. The thought of risking that didn't scare her nearly as much as it might have two days ago.

"Don't you want to feel it all, skin on skin, no barriers?" He stepped closer, so close she felt the heat of him, the pulse of life beneath the rubber barrier. "I could order you to take it off me, you know."

But he wouldn't. He'd leave it up to her. Keely trusted him, far more than she'd ever dreamed she might trust a Master. She looked down at him and blinked twice, then watched him peel the condom off and toss it aside.

"I'll take care of you, my own sweet baby. Not just now but always." The smooth, creamy feel of his cock head against her cunt fueled her flames. His, too, she could tell as he let go his restraint and sank into her all the way, until his cock slammed against the mouth of her womb and his balls rested tightly against her shaved pussy. "I'll never let you grow hair down here again," he told her, and she nodded vigorously. She'd never again deny herself—or him—the incredible sensation of mating, nothing between them. "And the only thing I'll be using condoms for is fucking your delicious little ass. I think we'll keep the butt plug, though. I love the way it feels when you're vibrating around my balls. When my cock can feel the pulsating sensations in your wet, hot cunt."

His thrusts grew harder, faster. She tightened her vaginal walls around him, loving the intense feeling of the rounded ends of the bar he wore in his piercing as they pressed against her. They scraped deliciously on her insides when he moved. More than anything she yearned to feel him come inside her, fill her with the long, hot spurts of milky fluid she'd felt before only when she'd serviced him with her mouth.

She had to come. She dared not do it without her Master's order, so she clenched her muscles and tried to focus on the intent look in his dark eyes, the smoothness of his wide chest, the coppery nubs of his small nipples. When those delicious sights couldn't distract her she closed her eyes, only to feel his calloused fingers settle on her already distended nipples. He plucked them hard then bent and drew one fully into his mouth, lapping at it with his tongue until she was about to explode.

"Now, my sweet submissive. Come with me this time." He slammed into her once more, balls-deep. Her last bit of self-control flew away, and she clamped down her inner muscles on his cock. The first hot, wet spurt surprised her with its intensity, triggered the most incredible orgasm she'd ever experienced. It only got better as he released burst after burst of his essence deep in her spasming pussy.

He'd never felt so satisfied. So tender toward a woman as he did toward Keely. Gently Brad released her from her bonds and carried her to the bed. "You're going to marry me," he said as he tucked her in and crawled in bed beside her. "I want to sleep with you like this every night, love you for the rest of our lives. I'll never force you to do anything you're afraid of."

Keely glanced up at him, tears in her eyes. "What if I want you to? I was afraid of shaving my pussy until you showed me what I was missing. The idea of making love in front of others or watching others have sex in front of me was pretty disturbing until I saw how beautiful sex could be between two people who're obviously in love. I don't think I'll ever encourage you to shave my head, but the idea doesn't turn me off as much as it did when Jared made Ninia take off her wig and show off her baldness." Her voice trailed off, as if she might be imagining how it would feel to have him rub his hands over her naked scalp.

"I could always say I wanted to come all over your bare head," he said, repeating an experience often related by other Doms who visited Roped and Lassoed and once proven when the biggest braggart of the bunch brought his collared slave with him, shaved her bald and masturbated onto her scalp, massaging his seed into her skin until it shone. "Does that pique your curiosity?"

She wrinkled her nose. "Not really. If you want, you can come on my head, hair and all."

"Fair enough." Wrung out as he was, he still felt his cock coming to life at the idea of coming in her short, auburn curls and using his hands to massage it through her hair. "Seriously, I don't share Ninia's fetish. Neither does Jared, but he loves her so much he keeps her head shaved because he knows it gives her pleasure." He paused then shot her a grin. "Tell you what, sweetheart, I've never seen my little brother as embarrassed as he was when she insisted on them meeting me for dinner in Denver the night she first went bald. She'd had on a Muslim-style headscarf because the wigmaker had kept the hair he'd cut off her to make a wig. One of Jared's conditions was that she never step outside their house without one, but she'd talked him into letting her cover her head with the scarf until the wigs were ready."

Keely couldn't help guessing what had happened to embarrass Jared. "Are you trying to tell me the scarf slipped off in the restaurant?"

"Worse. She went in the restroom and took it off. Then she sauntered over to our table, just like there wasn't anything wrong with showing off her shiny bald pate in front of everybody there." Raising himself up on one elbow, Brad ran his fingers through Keely's unruly mop. "I like you just like this. Whatever hair fetish I may have is satisfied when we both have smoothly shaved pubes. And waxed-off body hair everywhere else."

She laid a hand on his chest, circling a nipple with her finger as she smiled up at him. "I can't afford a waxing job like this."

"You can once we get married." Brad knew he'd have to go easy, sweep away her pride and lingering feelings of inadequacy so gently she wouldn't realize what he was doing. "While we're snowed in, though, we can treat ourselves to blade shaves all over. Every day." Very gently he ruffled the pale hairs on her forearms, stopping when he saw her smile go away.

She wrinkled her nose. "Will you make me wear your collar?"

"No decent Master would ever let his slave's neck go unadorned. But don't worry. I'll pick you out a pretty one set with your favorite precious stones. No black leather or chain links. No one but you and I will know it's on for keeps, and I'm the only one who'll know how to take it off you. I'm not planning ever to snap a leash on onto it. I promise."

"Does Jared ever put Ninia on a leash?"

"I've only known of him to do it one time, and that was the time she sat down beside him with her shaved head on display. He only made her wear it until they got back to their hotel." Brad hadn't blamed his brother, considering the way Ninia had disobeyed his order to deserve that punishment.

Keely grinned. "Oh, I can see how that might have made Jared pretty angry."

"Yeah. I've got the feeling you won't find the need for showing off your kinks to anybody but me, so I'll save myself the extra bucks Jared paid for that gold chain he calls a leash." Brad traced a line around the base of her neck then lifted her left hand. "You'll wear my rings here, too. I won't have anybody, our BDSM friends or vanilla-type guys who might see you on the street, not be able to tell on sight that you're taken."

She reached up, her fingertips tracing the veins that stood out on his hand from all the years of holding on to cinch straps wrapped around the middles of nasty-tempered bulls and broncs. Her touch had him hot, hard and very much aware he wanted her for a lifetime. When she spoke, her soft breath tickled his wrist. "All right. I just don't ever want everybody knowing about the collar. About its significance, anyhow. I can't take more of the teasing I endured when I was a kid."

"Fair enough. Now come snuggle up and keep me warm. We're gonna need our strength until the weather breaks." With any kind of luck the storm would keep them snowbound for at least three more days. Brad intended to make the most of this time, seduce Keely so completely she'd never backslide from the promises she'd made.

\* \* \* \* \*

It took a week for the road department to clear two avalanches that had blocked Highway 287 in both directions. A week of seeing to the cattle and horses, preparing food and clean outerwear for the ranch hands. Charley helped with those things while Brad kept the wranglers busy outside from sunup until noon when he and the hands came in the kitchen and put down the fuel that kept their bodies going. The rest of Brad's days belonged to Keely, and she loved it. Loved him as much as she constantly lusted after him.

"Come on now. You can give me a bath, warm me up. I've got some news." Cupping her buttocks, Brad lifted her and ground his fully clothed but obviously aroused cock into her mound that never had been so sensitive before he'd shaved it.

She purred, tucking her head into the hollow above his collarbone and wondering what today might bring.

As if she were the most precious bundle he'd ever held, he undressed her and laid her out on a hot, thirsty towel he'd placed on the shower floor. Her squirming while he spread foam from the hot lather machine on her from neck to toe earned her a sharp slap. Needles of hot arousal radiated from where his hand fell on her thigh, once, then twice, then once more before he knelt beside her and ran a new razor over her legs, her cunt, even over the practically hairless expanse of her belly and rib cage. "Raise your arms," he told her after shaving her aching breasts, and when she obeyed he scraped away the little underarm stubble that had grown back since this time yesterday. Then he shaved her arms before moving back to her trunk and carefully denuding her neck and throat. "Roll over so I can take care of those fine, silky hairs on your back," he told her while inserting a new blade into the razor.

She shuddered when Brad lifted her hair and shaved the skin just below her hairline. It felt so good, made her so horny she almost begged him to shave it all off, let her feel for herself the erotic sensations Ninia must experience when Jared shaved her first in one direction and then in the other, reducing her head to a shiny, smooth scalp stretched taut against her perfectly rounded skull. Keely bit her lip to keep from saying the words she knew Brad didn't want to hear. Then her breath caught in her throat when she felt him take the blade higher. Not much higher but enough that she felt the slightly longer curls just above her hairline slide down her back, a breeze from a forced air vent chilling the newly bare skin.

Brad was raising her hairline in the back. Not enough that anybody might notice, but just enough to make her pussy cream at the prospect of him stroking that highly sensitive strip of skin, blowing on it, running his tongue over the smooth surface until she came in a shivering mass of sensation while he shot spurt after fiery spurt of his hot, slippery seed into her hungry pussy. "Hold still, I'm about to do your back."

It felt incredible, this feeling of almost total nakedness that came over her as he shaved the fine fuzz off her back before paying particular attention to her buttocks and ass crack. She almost came when he inserted two fingers up her rear hole and scissored them back and forth, stretching her for what she hoped would be his next step in their afternoon play. He took them out but replaced them with the anal plug he often had her wear all day. "That's to keep my naughty sweetheart hot while I finish you off," he whispered in her ear, blowing his breath on the newly shaved skin. "And while you take care of me."

The motion of her hair bouncing against her raised hairline felt incredibly erotic. She barely noticed Brad spreading her legs until he'd shaved her again from ass to cunt, taking short strokes to ensure that no stray hairs had popped up to mar her smoothness. "There, you're done."

She shaved him neck to toe, just as thoroughly as he'd shaved her, taking special care not to nick his beautiful cock and balls. When she finished and turned on the showerheads, she knelt and started to take him in her mouth.

But he pulled her away and onto her feet. "Come on, I've got a surprise for you," he said, wrapping them both in a thirsty bath sheet and dragging her along to the recliner beside the fireplace.

"Well?" Curious, she let him drag her down until she impaled herself on his cock. Unusual. Their previous afternoon lovemaking had been everything but conventional yet no more erotic than now, as she felt him throbbing against the walls of her pussy. "I love surprises."

As if he knew it would drive her crazy, he cradled her head in both hands, settling his thumbs over each side of what used to be her hairline and rubbing in a circular motion. "They've cleared the highway. You've got two choices. I can take you back to pick up your truck and you'll never see me again, or…"

His words panicked her. "Or what?" she croaked, not able to draw away, yet not certain now that what they'd lived here during the storm hadn't all been a figment of her fertile imagination.

"Or you can come with me to Denver and we'll get married. Right now."

"Oh, yesss," she hissed as she tightened her pussy around his cock and milked out his seed. "Shouldn't you ask your family to come?" Keely didn't need witnesses. Brad was all she needed to make her life complete.

"They'll be pissed if I don't," he said, frowning at the prospect of having to delay his plans. "Don't you want to invite your mom and Vince, too?"

"They're my past. You're my future." Keely felt a load drop from her shoulders when Brad didn't push it. The only kind of BDSM relationships she ever wanted to see were ones like theirs…like Jared and Ninia's. Relationships based on mutual love and the Doms' need to ensure their submissives' pleasure, whatever that might entail. "If you want to do it in Denver, why not ask Jared and Ninia—and your sister—to join us?"

He grinned. "I'll call Jared now. His Beechcraft's newer and bigger than my Cessna. He bought it last summer to ferry his dude ranch guests to and from the airport in Denver. If he's in shape to fly it now, with his gimpy leg, we're a go. Diana will jump at the chance to show off her new sub, I'm sure. She says he's no sissy boy but he lets her take control of their relationship."

He talked with Jared a few minutes then set the phone down and kissed Keely deep and hard, until both of them were out of breath. "He says he's fine as long as I sit up front as copilot. He and Ninia are calling Diana now. We'd better dress and get going if we're gonna get off the ground before the wind kicks up again."

"Dress?"

"As in, wear clothes. Grab something of Diana's. She won't mind since she never bothered to pick up the things I got for her when she was here on furloughs from rehab. Her taste's a lot different, now that she's made the switch to Domme. You can shop for your wedding stuff while I'm picking out your collar and rings."

## Chapter Five

The penthouse suite Brad had booked consumed half the top floor of a downtown hotel. Keely shuddered at the thought of what this place must cost. She'd never have dared even to inquire about rates for these accommodations.

Glittering chandeliers, plush carpeting, and gleaming Victorian-style furniture spoke of years gone by, of gentlemen in top hats and ladies sporting outlandish hats. Setting the clothes she'd bought onto the king-size bed in one of the three sumptuously decorated bedrooms, she looked around, imagining herself dropping to her knees, stroking the length of her lover's smooth, muscular legs, taking his cock in her mouth, rolling the Ampellang jewelry he wore around in its tight hole. At his command she'd grasp her ankles and brace herself for his first delicious thrust inside her. Imagining him fucking her ass while he worked a dildo in and out of her pussy had her sweating, longing for him to come and make her come in the many ways he'd shown her while they'd ridden out the storm.

Sounds of sex bombarded her from all around, traveling through walls that couldn't quite seal off Ninia's whimpers or Jared's shout of triumph when he came. From Diana's room came muffled sounds of a cat-o'-nine grazing her rancher lover's flesh.

Certain it would be hours before Brad returned from the jeweler with those scary, obvious symbols of his possession, Keely unpacked the sex toys they'd brought and inserted the plug in her butt, fiddling with the remote until the vibrations felt just right, not so strong as to hurt her yet strong enough that they reverberated through her body, driving her to a fever pitch of need.

Grabbing the dildo, she worked it up her cunt and began to slide it in and out. She'd just worked herself into a moaning, shivering mess of desire when Brad stepped through the door she'd left unlocked, two small packages in his hand. "I see you're being naughty again, using those toys that belong to me. The tight, wet holes that are also mine. Come sit over here. Maybe when you feel the weight of my collar around your neck you'll realize you belong to me. Only me."

Moving awkwardly, she got out of bed and sat in front of an antique washstand, her gaze downcast the way a good sub's should always be. The plug still vibrated, even after she removed the dildo and set it aside. "You're my much-loved Master. I'm your obedient sub. I can't imagine being hotter than I am now, waiting eagerly to wear your symbol of ownership."

She wasn't so sure when she felt Brad wrap a wide metal choker around her neck and join the two ends with a click that sounded ominously final. The sensation of a metal ring brushing the hollow of her throat made her visualize Brad hooking a slender chain on it someday, threading it through the small gold nipple rings he'd personally inserted in holes made by a master piercer on their first stop after landing in Denver. Her whole breasts hurt, the pain a throbbing numbness that had started when Brad clamped her nipples then worsened after he ordered the piercer to push through sterilized needles that looked and felt as thick as the long wooden cocktail picks she'd seen Brad—her Master now—use to skewer olives off the appetizer tray the hotel chef had sent up to their suite. His gentle handling as he'd fitted the rings through the bloody holes had soothed her, reassured her that the pain would soon yield to incredible pleasure.

"Look, my darling." Her Master turned her head until she had a clear view in the mirror. She gasped. The collar he'd chosen left little doubt she was a rich man's sex slave, but it suited her perfectly. Her open robe obscured her vision, so she slid it off to get the full effect of the glittering choker fastened around her neck, the slender rings dangling from her reddened nipples.

Brad cupped her breasts, being careful not to irritate her piercings. "They look as red as cherries and nearly as swollen. I can hardly wait until they heal and I can play to my heart's content." Shifting his hot, possessive gaze to the collar that felt the tiniest bit snug against her throat, he slipped a finger into the oval ring that hung, a delicate ring beneath a large square-cut emerald. "I couldn't pick just one stone so I had the jeweler use a lot of them. They're real, and they're set in platinum. Nothing but the best for this Master's most prized possession."

The collar was a work of art, its smooth surface embedded with rubies, then diamonds, and finally brilliant blue sapphires in different shapes. She realized now why it felt so thick and heavy. It had to have been, so the craftsman who'd made it could secure all the beautiful stones. "It's beautiful, Master. I love it almost as much as I love you." She held her head high, and the collar seemed less oppressive than when he'd put it on her and locked it in place.

It felt right to go down on her knees, free Brad from his dark jeans and take him in her mouth. It didn't take him long to stiffen and fill her greedy mouth with his creamy essence.

"Next time we do it right," he growled. "I want us to make a baby."

\* \* \* \* \*

The wedding the following day was everything Keely could have asked for, candlelight and roses, soft music, and a minister with a mellow voice admonishing them to love, honor and cherish each other for always. Afterwards there were sensual finger foods and rich desserts. All happy memories to cherish, nothing sad to mar their wedding day. Jared was up once more, albeit on wobbly legs, standing beside Brad while they spoke their vows. Ninia stood beside him, dressed in pale blue and wearing a matching scarf over a long-haired light brown wig. She held herself proudly, a slave clearly content with her doting Master. Diana and Matt, her supposedly submissive rancher, abandoned their public BDSM play and held hands conventionally during the ceremony and the sumptuous feast that followed.

Brad came up behind her when they were finally left alone. "You're my beloved woman. The one I'll spend the rest of my life giving the pleasure you deserve," he whispered, taking her left hand and laying it over the collar that by now felt light, easy to bear as proof that she belonged to Him, her awesome Master who had no desire to enslave her. Only to love her and see to every one of her needs, sexual and otherwise.

"I love you, wife." Tenderly Brad brought her hand to his lips, sucked the massive diamond solitaire and its glittering platinum band between his full, sensuous lips.

"I love you too, Master. Husband," she added, liking the sound of the words—both of them. Keely was finding it easy to think of herself as slave, submissive, and lover. Her value as a person was neatly tied up in what Brad had made it, yet more precious now that he'd pledged not only his protection but his unconditional love.

As if he realized she'd turned a corner, Brad smiled down at her and squeezed her hand. He'd given her the gift of free will as well as all his love and support, and the moment she thought it might please him, she'd accept the role of slave to his Master. He'd done more, and she couldn't have been happier than she was today, when he'd taken her as she was, as an equal emotionally, a sub he'd cherish for life. Brad McTavish was the beginning and end of all she needed. All she wanted.

# LASSOED
༶

# Trademarks Acknowledgement

∽

The author acknowledges the trademarked status and trademark owners of the following wordmarks mentioned in this work of fiction:

Beechcraft: Beechcraft Aircraft Corporation

Chippendales: Chippendales USA, LLC

Jacuzzi: Jacuzzi, Inc.

Stetson: John B. Stetson Company

# Chapter One

୭

As she'd expected, Roped and Lassoed's decor reminded her of rugged Western males, from the grayed cedar siding on the walls to rugged cowhide-covered sofas and chairs that were so big they practically swallowed her up. Raucous country-western music wafted up from the bar downstairs, its beat primitive, at odds with lyrics that spoke of broken hearts, lost loves. The scent of leather and sweat surrounded her, another reminder this was a man's mecca.

Even though she'd been coming to the dungeon often since coming home, she sometimes felt like an intruder, a female player in a male world, especially lately since the two subs she'd been playing with had moved to Salt Lake City six weeks ago. Now she waited for the new sub her brother Brad had promised, all alone in the conversation grouping at the edge of the public playroom. Diana McTavish sat, her feet not quite reaching the floor, staring at the beaten silver handle on the flogger she'd bought before heading home from rehab. Why the hell did she suddenly feel so out of place?

"Patience, big sister. He's coming." Reaching over, Brad flicked the soft tails of the flogger. "Don't you want to use something more lethal than that cute little thing? Hell, when Jared and I were small you used switches on us that felt liked you'd used a chainsaw to get 'em off the tree." His grin reminded her of that time years ago, before Gareth, when her life had revolved around her family and the responsibility she'd taken for keeping the McTavish ranch running smoothly after their grandfather's death. Those had been good times, especially when she compared them with the nearly ten years she'd spent with Gareth.

She shivered. "I don't want to inflict more pain than is necessary. I've been on the receiving end…"

"You know, BDSM doesn't have to involve pain at all. It can be completely psychological. And with most Doms and Dommes, it's not the desire to inflict pain, but the need to exert mind control that drives them."

"I needed the pain to get off." She couldn't, wouldn't think about the beatings, the humiliation she'd endured in the name of orgasm. Those days were firmly in the past. After all, she'd spent almost two years working the painful memories from her brain and setting them free. "Never mind. I'm sure you know."

"Okay, sis." Brad bent, gave her a brotherly kiss. Concern still in his eyes, he rose, took her hands and gave her a steady look. "But I'll be nearby if you need anything."

Brad doubted she was taking the right path here. She read the concern in his dark eyes. But she'd made up her mind. While he was right to question her sanity about wanting to be within a hundred miles of the BDSM scene again, there was part of her, even after all the therapy, that made her feel she had to confront the yearnings within herself. Something she'd firmly decided would find its outlet this time through her attempt to play the Domme.

Play the Domme. The words made her shudder, because that's what she felt like this was. Play, not real. She'd played with the two submissives who'd moved on, felt a certain amount of satisfaction in bringing them pleasure. Not nearly as much satisfaction as she'd felt when she'd been on the receiving end of domination, though, before it had turned cruel and abusive.

There was no way she was going back down the self-destructive path of being a submissive. She worried that she'd find herself back in rehab, devoid of self. And she sure as hell didn't believe she could trust any man to lead her on that journey. Not after one man she'd thought loved her had turned both of them into monsters. Mockeries of what a loving Master and slave should be.

Of course there was Matt... She pushed that thought out of her head immediately. No way she'd try to resurrect the relationship with her high-school lover. He'd left her with a lot of beautiful memories she'd clung to for more than twenty years. But they were only recollections, albeit ones that had often kept her clinging to sanity when she was on the brink of falling into a hole so deep she couldn't claw her way out. It might hurt both of them terribly if she tried to rekindle the flame. No way could she drag him through the muck of her psyche.

But of course she knew why Matt had invaded her mind. She hadn't stopped thinking about him—about the past—since Jared mentioned him when he and Ninia had come to visit at the rehab center last Valentine's Day. He'd moved back home, to the ranch adjoining hers. And he came here regularly to play as a Dom.

Oh, God, if he were here tonight...

She couldn't stop fantasizing about his strong hands holding her body, bearing her down, taking control.

No! Damn it, she was the one in control tonight. Tonight and always. Almost everybody in the lifestyle knew hardcore subs and Doms did not become switches. But she was going to do this. She had no choice.

Brad cleared his throat. "Here comes your new sub, all ready for some pleasure through pain." Brad gestured toward the door to the dressing rooms.

The sub stood, head angled down. He was a tall, slender cowboy type, and he was completely naked except for a sound secured inside his cock by the PA ring that ran through its purplish head. She couldn't fault his looks, all blond and pale skin and white, straight teeth. But he didn't make her hot. "Oh," Diana said, even less sure now that this had been a good idea.

"Come on, sis, male subs are scarce around here. I had to borrow him from Ninia's old dungeon in Cheyenne. Most folks who come here are Doms, or female subs."

For a moment Diana forgot she'd embraced the concept of staying in control. Looking at "her" sub, now kneeling at her feet awaiting instruction, she couldn't help remembering the years when she'd serviced Gareth as a slave. Or the feeling of self-loathing that had grown from a tiny kernel to the point that she hadn't been able to function.

Tightening her grip on the flogger so as not to toss it aside and run, she firmed her chin, held her head up high. She had to do this. Had to prove to herself that she could exert control over a man. That not all men were like Gareth, out to hurt and humiliate her for their own twisted pleasure. Rising and placing her hands on the sub's shoulders, she tried to summon up a voice that suggested control—authority. "Go in the playroom, slave, and bend over." Uncertain what should come first—Diana had never taken part in public BDSM scenes because Gareth had refused to allow it—she looked first at the fucking table. The St. Andrew's Cross had possibilities. She shuddered at the sight of the new fucking machine that had been delivered earlier this week. Brad had mentioned that he wanted to buy one when he visited her at the rehab center near Denver and took her to a rodeo buddy's BDSM dungeon there where they saw one demonstrated by its inventor.

How Gareth would have loved using the thing on her! Diana's pussy ached at the thought of being restrained while the twin dildos pounded in and out of her pussy and ass. With Gareth at the controls, the machine would have produced unspeakable pain. With someone not wanting to inflict hurt on his or her slave, she imagined it could produce incredible pleasure.

"Mistress?" Her sub sounded uncomfortable yet cooperative.

She knew she had to punish him. "I didn't give you leave to speak, slave." A succession of thwacks with the flogger left his bare butt red, drew her gaze to his asshole, quivering already. With anticipation? "Is that your ass telling me it wants a fucking?" she asked, ringing the puckered opening with a finger before slipping one finger then two past his anal sphincter.

"Oh yes, Mistress."

Why was it she got the feeling he was playing a game, not getting personally involved in this scene? Diana laughed at herself. Obviously this was a club scene between two strangers, no emotional connection on his part or hers. This was strictly sex, him submitting, her dishing out whatever pain and humiliation it took to bring him satisfaction.

She stroked his slender, hairless body, trying to enjoy the power that came from being able to sample him, take pleasure from the simple act of sliding her fingers over his smooth, taut skin. It surprised her how his ribs were prominent when she explored him there, not padded with hard muscle the way she remembered Gareth's. This sub was vulnerable, the way she'd been for so long under her ex-husband's cruel control.

Her submissive moaned at her touch, the sound almost a purr. He shivered yet held the bent-over position she'd specified. Slowly, her fingers following a drop of sweat as it worked its way down his smooth, slick back, she traced a path along his spine, over his buttocks and down the insides of his thighs.

Her nostrils flared at the distinctive aroma of sex, the sweat and male musk mingling with the taste and smell of her own arousal. None too gently, she dragged her hands up his thighs, finding and cupping his taut balls with one hand while she wrapped the other around his steely erection. "Lie down on the table, slave, I want to taste you."

He rose. Apparently no stranger to being restrained, he placed his feet in the stirrups and his wrists in the manacles on either side of the table. His cock rose straight up, the sound drawing her attention as she clamped the manacles and strapped his knees and ankles. "Helpless. Do you enjoy knowing I can do anything I want with you, take you any way I choose?"

"Yes, Mistress."

"Good." Her motion smooth thanks to months of aerobic exercises they'd made her do as part of her rehab therapy, she straddled his face, bringing her pussy flush against his slightly opened lips. "Use that tongue on me. Make me scream with pleasure."

It had been so long. Too long since Gareth had tied her to the bed and eaten her until she hadn't been able to resist coming. She'd thought of those moments of ecstasy as payback for the ever-deepening pain that preceded and followed. The ecstasy that had come less often as he'd became more vicious, she more codependent. Toward the end Diana had escaped into her own world, imagined it was Matt doing it to her.

Just as she found herself doing now. The feel of her submissive's lips and tongue on her clit, her outer labia, brought back pleasure along with the pain that now was only in her head. And oh, now he was tongue-fucking her pussy and making her breathe hard at the sensations. She was feeling the sub's lips and tongue, but it was Matt fucking her in her mind, tricking her into coming, making the ordeal be over.

It was ironic that her therapist was pretty sure she'd fallen in love with Gareth out of desperation. Her need to be loved and cared for had driven her into a relationship that quickly morphed into a horror chamber, and when she'd taken all she could, she'd fantasized about Matt this way, to make her misery bearable.

The sub licked harder, drove his tongue into her pussy as though he wanted to control her. She wouldn't let him. Lying flat over him, she took his penis and sucked it, hard. She used her tongue to set the sound to vibrating. When a few drops of his salty cream escaped around the sound, she lapped it up like a starving bear who'd found the honey tree.

She was close. Had to take him now, feel the heat of his sex in hers. Rising, she found a condom in the drawer at the side of the table and started to roll it onto his erection. Then she remembered the sound, guessed that if she fucked him while he had it in, it would hurt him—badly. "Take out the sound."

"Can't." He gestured with his head toward his manacled wrists. "Mistress."

"Oh." Of course he couldn't. He must think she was an idiot. "How do I take it out, then?" Gareth hadn't been into piercings or tattoos—said he didn't need them to attract his slaves.

The sub's shy smile almost made her want to untie him, order him to take over, fuck her any way he liked it. But then, that wasn't the point of this first sexual encounter. "Take out the Prince Albert ring. It holds the sound in place. Then just tug on the end of the sound and it will pop right out. I'm sorry, I should have asked whether you wanted it in or out."

"It's okay. The thing looks neat, but I can't imagine you'd enjoy being fucked with it in place." Diana knew it shouldn't matter to her whether the way she fucked her sub was painful to him or not—but it did. Standing between his widely spread legs, she loosened the captive bead and worked the Prince Albert ring out of his distended flesh. Then she slid the sound out. All nine or ten inches of it, way more than the length of his cock. "What?"

"The sound goes all the way inside, not just into my cock." His erection didn't wilt at all, she noticed as she smoothed a condom over it.

"You aren't to come until I say so," she whispered as she straddled him, sank down on his cock and began to move.

Diana was in control. It gave her a sense of safety, not satisfaction. But her flogger was within reach, and she clasped her fist around its leather handle. Slowly, deliberately, she set the pace, trying to pay no attention when her sub strained his hips upward. Sweat glistened on his brow.

He wanted to come. She could tell by the desperate look in his eyes that she'd pushed him to the edge. Strangely enough, she didn't care.

The prospect of fucking another helpless sub had appealed. The reality left her, well, not cold but no better than lukewarm. "You may come," she told him, realizing now that she needed more than a helpless male to achieve the climax that came easily with her trusty dildo.

Once, twice, three times she raised her hips and slammed down hard on his eager cock. His heart pounded against her hand as she stroked his chest. Then his body tensed.

He was coming. And she needed to punish him because this wasn't doing it for her. She lifted the flogger, brought its silken strands down hard on his chest, his flanks as he strained upward and came.

When it was over she noticed the vein in his neck throbbing, the flushed skin pulled taut over his bland, handsome face. Fucking like this was nothing like what she'd imagined on lonely nights in the room at the psych hospital. Lifting herself off the sub, Diana allowed a moment to mourn. Then she loosened the manacles and freed him from leg restraints that had held him helpless for her pleasure.

Pleasure? Her body still needy, seeking a release that wouldn't come, she bent and brushed her lips over his. "Thank you," she whispered as she walked away.

* * * * *

"Have fun, Di?" Brad looked up from the stack of invoices on his desk and motioned for Diana to sit down. He frowned, though, when he saw her expression. "Hey, what's the matter?"

She didn't know, but it felt damn funny to be talking about sex with one of the younger brothers she'd practically raised after their mom had died. But she had to talk to someone, and it felt ludicrous to be shy in front of a BDSM dungeon keeper, never mind the fact he was her brother. "I don't know. It's…it's just that I'm not sure I'm cut out to be a Domme, but I can't risk handing over control of my life to somebody else."

"Don't you remember I know most of what he did to you?" Brad clenched his fists so tightly the knuckles turned white. "I'm sorry for biting your head off. I guess, in addition to feeling guilty that I didn't step in and do something before it got so bad… Never mind, talk to me if it helps. Jared, too. That's what brothers are for."

Diana felt the tears coming, searing her cheeks. Crying didn't help. She'd learned that in the time she'd been away. Crying was a fucking sign of weakness, weakness she never intended to show again, even to her closest friends and family. The therapists had taught her that, but they hadn't helped her with her deeper issues. They hadn't understood the lifestyle that pervaded her whole family, that her brother Jared seemed to handle with his wife in a healthy, loving way. That Brad seemed to manage with such joyful male abandon. The shrinks had tried, but they hadn't been able to sell her on the idea that BDSM was at the root of her problems. All she'd gleaned from them was how to do and say the right things so she could come home.

She guessed that was why she still felt so fucked up, as if she was still fighting through the darkness by herself. It probably had a lot to do with the fact that her brothers still watched over her so closely, unless they were giving her payback for having run herd on them when they were wild schoolboys. She grabbed a tissue from the box on Brad's desk and scrubbed fiercely at the evidence of her frailty. "I'm sorry. God, but I need to come, and having a sub who has no passion of his own doesn't cut it for me."

His expression serious, Brad looked out toward the dungeon playroom. "Take a look. It seems your sub prefers guys, or at least swings both ways."

Diana followed Brad's gaze to a St. Andrew's Cross where the man she'd brought to climax hung, writhing with what she guessed was pleasure while one Dom fucked his ass and another jerked a chain connected to his nipples with wicked-looking clamps. "Oh no! He has to be in agony. Aren't you going to stop them?"

Catching her chin in one hand and turning her away from the observation window, Brad made her look him in the eye. "He's a sub, honey. From what I see, he enjoys taking it rough. Most of the male subs I've observed seem to need more of the S&M element in their play than the women."

Images rolled around in Diana's brain, confusing her even more. The nameless sub, seeming to enjoy torture far greater than she'd ever be willing to inflict. Herself, cringing under Gareth's cruel onslaughts until one day she woke up in a hospital, broken and battered, finally ready to charge him with abuse and call a lawyer to get him permanently out of her life. Her youngest brother Jared and his slave, Ninia, whose mutual love overshadowed Ninia's need for full-time slavery and occasional humiliation. Even Brad, whom she'd watched earlier when he serviced a pretty redheaded sub Diana thought she recalled having been in the same school class as Jared, was stern in the dungeon scene, but never cruel.

"I know. I still don't think I'm cut out to cause another human pain, not after all I went through. But I know I dare not pick another Dom. I can't be sure of my judgment, and I don't think I can ever trust a man that far again. You and Jared don't count."

"We're not men? Sis, a long time ago we quit wearing short pants and jumping when you cracked the whip over our butts. And we both grew up to be Doms."

"I don't know. I need to be pushed sexually, but not cruelly and not in a way that makes me a laughingstock. Maybe I should just forget about sex."

Brad rubbed his thumb across Diana's hand. "You know, have you ever considered going more vanilla, with an Alpha guy who'd realize you need a little domination and would work hard to fulfill that need? Maybe you should give some thought to settling down and raising a family."

She'd given up that dream long ago. "It's pretty much too late for that, Brad. After all, I'm almost forty years old." Actually, she'd turned forty last summer. She was pretty sure Brad knew that—he'd always been good at math. But she wasn't quite ready to admit it out loud without the modifier.

"Why, you're just a baby. Did you know we have members in this club that are pushing seventy and still going strong? Not only men, either. You got your life back from that bastard, now make something of it. You deserve to live and to enjoy all the pleasures of life. Not just sex, but love and affection, companionship, and so on. Tell you a secret. I've been thinking a lot about persuading someone to be my lifetime sub, giving up rodeo and settling down to raise a family."

Diana and Ninia had talked about Brad's seeming change of direction just the other day. Ninia had mentioned she thought Brad had fallen hard for one of the subs who he played with regularly at the club. Glancing toward the playroom to see if she could see the woman he'd been playing with earlier, Diana didn't see the pretty redhead.

Instead, her breath caught in her throat when she saw a familiar face. *Oh no*. She didn't know if seeing Matt Rogers here was an answer to her earlier fantasies, or an embarrassing nightmare about to happen.

She couldn't tear her gaze away from his huge, rugged body. The years had treated him well. Other than a short beard that matched his dark brown hair, Matt looked pretty much the same as he had when they graduated from high school more than twenty years ago, except that now he'd packed on more muscle and had a few new scars. When they were kids, he'd favored worn-out jeans and skintight T-shirts. He looked damn good now in that pair of brown rough-out chaps and matching vest. His beautiful sex was even more impressive than she remembered. Of course she'd never seen the massive, satiny-looking cock and low-hanging testicles displayed so brazenly. Her mouth went dry, and her pulse started racing as she remembered sweet times with him, times that came back as clearly as if they'd happened yesterday.

"Is he married?" Where did that come from? Matt had left town right after graduation, after she'd told him she couldn't marry him or anybody else until her brothers were on their own. He'd gone to college first then played pro football until he'd retired almost a year ago. He'd been a temptation before that, since he'd spent off-seasons at the ranch his grandfather had left to him.

So many times she'd caught glimpses of him, wanted to go and welcome him home. But she hadn't dared to do it. Gareth would have killed her and him both, even though Matt had several inches of height and at least fifty pounds of solid muscle on her miserable ex. "Not that it matters whether he is or not," she said, but she wasn't quite able to mask the regret that she'd let Matt get away.

Brad followed her gaze, obviously aware as soon as he saw Matt that she'd singled him out from the others at play. "No, he's not married. Never has been, as far as I know. He plays here with the unattached subs, almost as if he's going through the motions." Brad paused and stared briefly at the scene where Matt and another man were making their sub writhe with pleasure. Then, his expression serious, Brad turned back to Diana. "You loved him, didn't you?"

She never thought she'd been so transparent that a twelve-year-old could tell, and she wasn't about to let Brad carry around misplaced guilt. "Puppy love. It was the wrong time for us. He had college and a dream of playing football in the pros."

"And you had us to take care of." Brad touched her cheek, a gesture he used to make back then, when he was trying so hard to be a man despite his tender age. "Maybe it's time for the two of you to get together now."

"I don't think so. He's obviously a Dom, and I'm pretty sure I never could rest easy, anticipating the day he'd turn mean." Still, she couldn't help watching Matt through the observation window, imagining his hands on her as she grew wet, needy. Almost as needy as she'd been when they made love underneath the stars. *Stop it, Diana. It would never work.*

But Brad's suggestion just wouldn't go away. Watching Matt commanding the sub's shattering release in the erotic scene made her hot, hotter than she'd been in years. Longer than she could remember. She couldn't even put her finger on the exact time Gareth had killed her desire for him. "How long has Matt been coming here?" Since she'd been visiting Roped and Lassoed almost weekly now for close to a year, she wondered why their paths hadn't crossed before.

Brad hesitated a minute, she thought. But when he spoke, his tone was thoughtful. "A little over year now, except for a few months when he was doing product endorsements out East after retiring from playing football. He told me he wanted to try the lifestyle. I thought then that he was doing it because of you, because word had gotten to him that our whole family is into the BDSM lifestyle. You'd just gone back to rehab, after testifying against your scumbag ex." Brad reached across the desk and took Diana's hand. "Life goes by too damn fast. If you want the guy, go grab him. Frankly I think he's ready to settle down, just waiting for the right woman."

When she thought about that, Diana knew she was no Domme. She'd never have the balls to go up to Matt or anyone else other than a club sub she'd never have to see again. And she'd never be able to tell him she wasn't about to be a slave to any Dom, ever again. Sadly, she looked away. Matt hadn't been right for her when they were kids, and he wasn't the man for her now. "I'd better be getting back out to the ranch. You and Jared did a great job keeping up with things while I was gone, and you've been cutting me a lot of slack since I've been home. Now it's time for me to be pulling my share of the load." Determined to get out of her brother's office before she started to cry, Diana grabbed her gym bag and made for the door.

When she opened it she merely ran into a brick wall, only it wasn't a wall. It was Matt Rogers. His huge body glistened with sweat, and she couldn't help noticing he still had on the chaps and vest. Now he'd added jeans and a Stetson that shadowed the gorgeous dark brown eyes she'd been seeing in her dreams for so many years. "Hello, Matt. I was just leaving." It took a mighty effort for her to tear her gaze away from his.

He made no move to let her by. Instead he set his calloused hands on her shoulders. "No hurry, Diana. I saw you come into Brad's office and decided to welcome you back home. I've been meaning to drop over to your place, but somehow the time has never been right. You know we're year-round neighbors now."

Yes, she knew. "Jared told me months ago, when he brought his wife down to Denver to introduce us. I'm sorry you quit playing ball, I remember how much that meant to you." *Quit acting like a ninny, spouting out all kinds of useless drivel when all he's doing is saying hello to an old friend.*

"It's okay. I had a lot of playing years, more than most tight ends in the NFL. Even more important, I'm still pretty much in one piece. Now that I've broken the ice, I'll ride down from my place and we can visit." Pulling her to him, he bent and brushed his lips over hers, a friendly kiss that still sent waves of desire coursing through her body. Then he stepped aside so she could pass.

God, how she wished they could turn back time.

Then, as if he had every right to do so, he reached out and pulled her to him, bent and kissed her, hard. The gesture was simple, deliberate, almost casual, but it sent waves coursing through a body she'd thought minutes earlier would never feel desire again. When he lifted his head, she met his gaze, saw the brief flash of intensity in his eyes. Before drawing away, he caressed her waist. When he stepped aside, she felt the magnetic pull that wanted to propel her back into his embrace.

## Chapter Two

He'd set out to become a Dom because that's what he'd thought Diana would want. It had shocked him to see her in the club last night, playing Mistress to a sniveling one-hundred-and-fifty-pound weakling. He'd deliberately avoided coming to Roped and Lassoed on Wednesdays, because he hadn't wanted to watch her playing with the two subs. But last night was Thursday—his night. He supposed she'd come in specifically for the new sub.

It hadn't surprised Matt at all that the chemistry that had nearly made them do foolish things when they were kids was alive and well. At least for him. For her, too, he thought, recalling the way her breathing grew ragged and her eyes glazed over with desire when she stared a second too long at his exposed genitals while he was playing the scene with a sub and a rancher he often paired up with for menages.

This was his time. Time to step into the void in her life. He'd be fucked if he'd lose Diana again. As he had done nearly every day since he'd come home to stay, Matt trotted up the worn horse trail to a spot where he could see her house in the distance.

He ground-tied Midnight, his thoroughbred mare, and looked over the split rail fence that separated his land from Diana's part of the huge McTavish ranch. It was almost a cruel coincidence that her ranch bordered the place he'd inherited five years ago from his grandfather. At first he'd tortured himself, coming here nearly every day he'd spent at the Rocking S during off-seasons, hoping to get a glance of her. He'd given up after a while, sick at heart because he'd heard whispers at the saloon outside Laramie that she'd completely submitted to her cruel Master, that she rarely left the hundred-year-old log house he glimpsed in the distance.

Until he'd come home to stay and heard Diana was in rehab, her now-ex-husband in prison. His heart broke when he heard what she'd been through. And every time he thought about Gareth Bender, Matt wished he'd come back a month sooner. If he had, he'd have killed the sadistic motherfucker with his bare hands. Instead he vowed to step in and be all Diana needed in a lover, even to the point of joining her brother's BDSM dungeon and setting out to become a Master.

Matt had enjoyed learning about the lifestyle when observing scenes there. Truth be known, he eventually participated in some scenes and fit right in. If Diana wanted a Master, he'd be one, but no way would he ever hurt her. He wouldn't let anybody else do it, either. Her ex wouldn't be out of prison for a few years, but when they let him loose, Matt intended to be there. If Bender was fool enough to come back to Laramie, Matt would warn him to stay miles away from Diana. He'd back up that warning with his fists—or his gun, if need be.

What the fuck was he thinking? From what he'd seen last night, Diana wanted a slave, not another Master. Matt didn't think he could play that role, being tromped under a Domme's stiletto heels.

He looked up. The sun was taking its time to rise. The air had a cold edge to it that told him winter was almost upon them, and some ominous-looking clouds hung low in the western sky. So far they'd had a warm fall, but he had the feeling the balmy days were history now that it was mid-November. He bet that by nightfall they'd be getting their first big snow of the season. He'd better get back home and make sure the horses were rounded up and in the barn.

Then he saw a figure on horseback, moving erratically. Diana? He doubted it. She'd been one of the best barrel racers on their high-school rodeo team. Still, it looked like her, dragging a surly calf toward her barn.

Maybe he wouldn't go home. After all, he'd told her last night he'd come see her, and she hadn't offered any objection. He whistled for his mare and swung into the saddle.

"Let's go see our neighbor, Midnight." He flicked the reins against her glossy, black neck. The mare seemed to understand everything he said—something most women couldn't, he thought wryly—and took off at a leisurely pace through an opening in the fence and down the hill toward Diana's place.

What the fuck? As he got closer, he realized Diana wasn't dragging the calf along. The damn critter was attacking her. Her horse reared, lashing out with its front hooves at the crazed beast. "Come on, girl, we've gotta get there fast." Matt spurred Midnight to a gallop and grabbed the lasso off the saddle horn. He wasn't gonna lose his woman to this loco calf, any more than he was going to lose her to some sniveling sub.

* * * * *

"Damn you. I swear I'm gonna turn you into a steer. Stop it," Diana yelled, a lasso coiled in her hand as she struggled to stay on her pony and hold the satellite phone to her ear at the same time. "Finally you come to the phone. Brad, I need you out here now. East pasture."

"On my way." The phone went dead then sailed onto the ground.

"Hold on. Don't let go." The shouted order made sense. Too bad she couldn't comply. Her mount bucked wildly, spooked by the devil calf. She tried to hold on, but it was no good. She hit the almost-frozen ground hard, instinctively rolling into a ball to protect her vitals from the crazed bull calf. In all the years she'd spent on the ranch, as a child as well as when she'd moved back here with Gareth, she'd never run into a situation like this before. She rolled up tighter in a fetal position and closed her eyes.

She'd never been so scared.

"You okay, hon?"

"No. I mean, yes." She opened her eyes, just a little, and saw a set of dancing jet-black hooves. It wasn't Brad, unless he'd been halfway here when she called. And she didn't recall the high-strung black horse from her visits to his barn. "Matt?"

"Yeah. Hold on there. I'm gonna try to get a lasso around the critter's neck and pull him away from your horse."

"Thanks." They'd both done rodeo in high school. All the kids had. She didn't remember Matt being particularly good at roping, but then he'd only done spring rodeo because of football. *God, let him have practiced since then.* Diana turned her head enough to get a glimpse of him galloping toward the calf, his lasso poised to throw.

Oh no. He missed. Twice. Now the calf was coming at him. Matt leapt off his horse and grabbed it around the neck. Diana struggled to her feet. "Idiot! That crazy SOB has to weigh five hundred pounds. Hold on, I'm coming to help." She scrambled around in the dirt. Had to find her lasso. There it was. Re-coiling it, she moved as fast as possible, considering it felt as if her ankle might be broken. Had to get where she could throw it before Matt lost, calf won.

The muscles in Matt's neck bulged. He let out a bellow louder than the little bull. Then he slammed him to the ground and straddled his neck. Infuriated, the animal twisted and struck out with his hooves, but Matt held on.

"Hold on. Let me help you hog-tie him before he gets loose again." Diana moved closer, trying to avoid sharp hooves and hobble his rear legs at the same time. She got one, then the other tied. Not tight enough, though, that the bull couldn't lash out at her. "Matt, choke him."

"I'm trying, damn it. He must've gotten into some locoweed." He sounded out of breath.

Who wouldn't be, after spending ten minutes holding down something twice his size? "I'm gonna try to tie his front legs, too. Brad's on the way."

The calf's frenzied movement slowed. "Try now. I won't let him loose." A powerful engine roared in the distance. "That Brad?"

Diana nodded. No time to talk. She managed to loop first one front leg and then the other, but she didn't have the strength to force all four legs together. Even though it was barely forty degrees outside, sweat poured from her body. "I can't," she cried, tugging as hard as she could on the rope and seeing the hobbled legs edge closer together. "Can't."

The truck engine roared then stilled. She'd never been as glad to see anybody as she was when Brad came up beside her and grabbed the ropes. "Let go, I've got him."

Diana scrambled backward, avoiding the bull's flailing hooves. The two men worked together as if they'd been doing it all their lives, and soon the animal lay helpless on the ground with Matt and Brad standing over him. "Is he going to break loose and come after us again?" She found it hard to believe the bull was just going to stay there peacefully until somebody came to cut him loose.

"He's not gonna get a chance," Brad said, his gaze shifting from Diana to Matt, and back to the frenzied calf. "I've got a vet coming. If I don't miss my guess this guy had a feast on some locoweed up in the high pasture. Damn shame, I'd thought this one might be a good breeder."

Matt snorted. "He might be better as rough stock for the rodeo circuit. I thought he had the best of me, and I've wrestled down defensive linemen almost as big as him and laid them out on the ground."

"Yeah, but the weed makes cattle go bonkers. Hope the weather holds a few more days, because we need to send some wranglers up to find and poison the stuff. Don't want a whole herd turning into killers." Brad dusted off his Stetson and set it back on his head. "Have you got enough crew to send a few guys up there tomorrow, sis?"

"Yes." She glanced down at the struggling animal. Somehow she couldn't dredge up a lot of sympathy for him. He'd damn near killed her. If it hadn't been for Matt coming along at just the right time… No, she wouldn't think about that or she'd turn into a sniveling, helpless lump, unable to hold the faith in herself that she'd worked so hard to build up during the past year. "Matt, I can't thank you enough," she said, meeting his dark, serious gaze and barely succeeding in keeping her voice steady.

"Your smile's more than enough thanks, honey. I'd been up on the hill trying to decide whether you'd toss me out if I came visiting, but then I decided I could live with rejection. When I saw this ornery critter trying to take out his frustration on you, well, I knew I'd made the right decision."

Brad took off his gloves and held out a darkly tanned hand to Matt. "Yeah, you did. And I owe you. No one can run the books the way Diana can. Jared and I would hate to lose her great business sense when we just got it back again."

Matt grinned. "Give yourself and your sister some credit, too. If it hadn't been for her getting rope around his legs and you hog-tying him, I'd have probably given out before much longer. I can only imagine how my arms and shoulders are gonna ache by tomorrow."

Gorgeous arms, shoulders broad and powerful. What a pity for them to hurt. Diana pictured herself rubbing that hard male flesh with pungent liniment, reveling in his strength…his ability to control her.

*Idiot. That's just what you don't need.* Still, Diana couldn't help fantasizing, wishing she trusted herself—and Matt—to cherish and protect her, never cause her the pain that visited her every night, reminding her she never dared be another man's slave. Ever.

Then Doc Johnson pulled up in his battered SUV. While he worked with Matt and Brad to load the calf into the back of Brad's truck, Diana retrieved her pony and Matt's beautiful jet-black mare, taking up their reins and heading for the back of the big pickup. When she saw her satellite phone on the ground, she picked it up and flipped it open.

It didn't surprise her that the phone was dead. Or that her poor pony was limping. They'd both taken a beating. She was glad Matt's mare seemed to be okay. "You've got another patient," she told the vet. "Want to see if you think he's in shape for me to ride him to the barn?" No way could she walk, not with all the scrapes and bumps and bruises. But she wouldn't risk the little gelding who'd bravely tried to fend off the crazy calf.

All three men turned from the bed of the pickup. Doc Johnson bent and examined the pony's forelegs closely. Then he moved around and took a careful look at the rest of him. "I'm pretty sure nothing's broken. He's got some cuts and bruises. I wouldn't suggest riding him right now, though."

All eyes turned to the truck bed where the loco calf was securely tethered. The pony backed off. Diana didn't blame him for being afraid. "We can't put him in there," she said. "He's afraid."

Matt took his mare's reins. "Midnight's not hurt. I could ride up to the house and pick up my horse trailer."

"Or you could ride to my place and get mine. It's closer." Diana's pulse raced at the forbidden fantasy of having Matt there, seducing him in front of a crackling fire.

Brad looked at the pony. "I think he'd be better off walking without carrying a rider. I doubt if this guy's ever been loaded into a trailer. After getting attacked the way he did, he's going to be skittish. I'm afraid he might hurt himself more, fighting us while we load him."

"You're probably right. Why not tie him onto the big black's saddle and lead him to the barn?"

Matt took Diana's hand. "How about riding double? The pony would probably be more comfortable if you stay close by."

"All right." Even though she'd only been riding the pony a couple of months since she'd moved back home from Brad's place, Diana thought he might feel more secure with her company. She tried to squelch the excitement that coursed through her veins at the idea of taking a slow ride holding on to Matt's hard, powerful body. When Matt held out a hand and lifted her up behind him as if she weighed nothing, her heart raced and her pussy clenched with irrational anticipation.

"Hang on. We're gonna take it nice and easy. Brad and the doc will meet us at your barn." The muscles in his back flexed when he tightened his thighs around the mare's sleek midsection.

Easy... Did he mean it in a sexual way, or was it just her wishful thinking? Diana held on, let the smooth walk of the mare and the heat of Matt's body lull her into a state of sensual enjoyment. And the sort of almost desperate need she'd sworn never to allow herself again.

The need that made her want to race into the house and hide the moment she dismounted, slid into his waiting arms and felt his heat surrounding her.

\* \* \* \* \*

Matt couldn't believe his luck. For having been in the right place at the right time to act the hero, he was now here in Diana's house, alone with her except for the purring gray cat that had twined itself around her legs when they stepped through the door. It sat by the hearth looking almost like a statue, its green eyes focused on him as though he somehow posed a threat to its mistress.

Diana had issued the impromptu brunch invitation to them all, but Brad had begged off because he was meeting a special sub at the club. Doc Johnson had gotten an urgent call from another rancher just as he finished patching up her pony.

Midnight was in a clean stall in the barn, being fed and rubbed down by one of her ranch hands. And Matt was here, his legs stretched out on a cozy couch in front of the fire while Diana warmed them some food and her cat watched him. Yeah, he knew she was as skittish as her pony after their run-in with the calf. But she'd let him in here when she could have retracted the invitation and sent him home.

That gave him hope. It was obvious her ex had done a number on her. Had to have since she'd spent all that time in a rehab facility. The fear in her still resonated. What Matt hated was that something about him seemed to make her draw back, withhold herself. Looks-wise, she hadn't changed much since they'd been teenagers. Her dark hair was longer now, and he'd noticed a few fine lines on soft skin that hadn't seen much sunlight lately. She probably had lost a few pounds—understandable considering all she'd been through—but her curves were still lush, enough to tempt any red-blooded man to explore them. *Rogers, you have it bad.*

He wanted her so much his balls ached. If he had to play the sub to her Domme, he'd do it. At least he'd try. He only hoped she wouldn't drag him into the dungeon to show him off as her slave in front of everybody in the local BDSM community. The tempting smell of something beefy distracted him, reminded him he hadn't eaten for hours and that he had another hunger he needed to feed.

"Come on in the kitchen. Stew's ready."

Now commands like that Matt could live with and love. Getting up and stretching, he hurried toward the sound of Diana's voice. When he saw the steaming bowls of beef stew and a tray of biscuits she was setting on the table, his mouth watered. "Your wish is my command. That smells real good."

"Eat up. You want milk or beer?"

"Milk." If he was going to make this work, he had to keep his brain sharp.

She poured him a glass then grabbed a beer and sat across from him. "I've got half a pound cake for dessert."

Small talk. Diana was nervous. Matt could tell from the tone of her voice, the way she avoided eye contact. "Sounds good. Sweetheart, I'm not about to bite you."

"See that you don't." She smiled, but from her tight expression he could guess the seriousness of her discomfort.

He reached over and took her hand. "Look, I've wanted you ever since we were kids, but the time was never quite right. But now I'm home, and you're free. I still want you, and I'll do whatever it takes to wipe that scared look off your face."

"I-I'm not ready. Don't know if I ever will be, but if I ever am, I doubt I'll go looking for another Master." When she hesitated and nibbled at her lower lip, Matt wanted to pick her up and hold her like a baby until he could cure her of her fear. "I don't ever want to be under someone else's control again."

"Even if I'm willing to let you call the shots?"

When she set her spoon down, he noticed a tremor in her hand. "I don't know. Part of me wants to say yes, but I'm afraid." At least when she smiled at him this time, a lot of the tightness had disappeared from her expression.

"Don't be. There's no way I'd hurt you. All I want is to bring you pleasure. Whatever it takes."

"Right now I want us to eat. We'll talk more later."

He could do that. The stew smelled great, tasted even better. And the biscuits reminded him of the ones his grandma used to make, big as his palm and dripping with butter. "As I said, your wish is—"

"My command. You said that before." As if she needed something to distract her from him, she slid a jar his way. "Try the jelly. It's homemade."

"By you?" The spoonful he set on his plate jiggled, a translucent blob the color of purple berries he'd helped pick when he was a kid.

When she laughed, her whole face lit up. "By Jared's wife. Ninia. She brought that over when I got back. She's quite the little homemaker, and Jared's 24/7 slave."

"I'll have to thank her, too, next time I see her." Matt smeared jelly over the biscuit and finished it off in three giant bites. "Mmmm. Everything's delicious. My housekeeper sticks pretty much to beef and beans and tortillas."

"Then you need to learn to cook."

That sounded like a command, but he squelched a smartass comeback. "Want to teach me?"

"It'll cost you."

His freedom? He was ready to give that up. Money? He had plenty of that, but so did she. "I think I can pay the price."

They weren't talking about a few lessons in her kitchen. He knew it, and he had the feeling she did, too, especially when she stood and gave him the once-over. "We'll see. I think you need to rest and let those bruises heal. I know I do. Come on."

Was she inviting him to fuck her? Matt stood and slid the chair back to the table. Somehow, the idea of letting her have her way with him appealed, even if that meant she was going to tie him to the bed and torture him before… "I'm coming," he said, enjoying the way her tush filled her jeans as he followed her through the living room and up the stairs. Out of the corner of his eye, he noticed the cat had silently joined the procession.

## Chapter Three

"Take off your clothes."

Hell, it should have been him ordering her to undress. But it didn't matter. They'd both be naked in her big, comfy-looking bed soon enough. "Tell me how you want me to do it."

She grinned. "Slowly. Make me hot for you. Pretend you're one of the Chippendale dancers entertaining a crowd of panting women."

He could do this. Never mind that exhibition wasn't his bag and he'd never aspired to be a male stripper. Imagining the beat of a bass guitar, he unbuttoned his shirt and slid it off then flexed the muscles in his chest as he peeled off his T-shirt. "Like this?"

"Take it off. Take it all off." She obviously was enjoying his impromptu act. Her tongue darted out and moistened soft lips he longed to taste, to feel on his own lips, his body. His balls felt like they were about to burst, and she hadn't touched him yet.

She'd seen him naked and aroused before. Not just years ago but last night, before he'd walked out on the ménage scene and caught her coming out of Brad's office. Still, he hesitated once he got rid of his belt and began to shove down his loosened jeans.

"Mind if I do my socks sitting down instead of dancing?" he asked, glancing over at the bed.

He loved it when she smiled. "Not at all. I don't need you getting any more battered and bruised than you already are."

Given permission, he sat on the edge of her bed and took off his socks before standing and sliding his jeans and underwear down and off. "What do you want me to do now?"

Her lips curled in a lascivious smile, and she apparently couldn't drag her gaze off him. "How about undressing me now?"

Her looking at him like that had blood slamming to his groin so fast that he felt dizzy. "Sure thing," he said, reaching for her with every intention of ripping away every stitch she had on.

She stepped back. "Easy, there. I didn't say I wanted you to use brute strength. Go easy and maybe you'll end up getting what you want."

He'd get that, all right, even if she teased him into a blind frenzy. Slowly he undid the snaps on her shirt and went to pull it off when the cat leapt up on her shoulder. "What the hell?" Matt had wrestled a five-hundred-pound bull calf high on locoweed. No way was he going to let a ten-pound furball intimidate him. "Get down, cat," he ordered.

The cat hissed. Diana laughed. "He might like it better if you called him by name."

"I don't know his damn name." The animal's soft gray fur stood on end and his ears lay back against his head. Snarling, he lashed out at Matt with bared claws. "Ouch, you sonofabitch."

Diana reached up and petted the cat. "His name is Blue, short for Blue's Clues. Don't frighten him."

"Then he shouldn't be up there scaring me. If it weren't that I'm afraid he'd claw you, I'd show him who's boss."

She rubbed her cheek against Blue's. "I'm the boss here, and you'd better not forget it. Here, Blue, make nice to my friend Matt."

"You should've named him Green." Blue regarded him quizzically, with eyes that glowed with emerald fire. "His eyes certainly aren't blue."

"It's his coat. In the cat world, all gray cats are referred to as blue. He's a Russian Blue, and all Russian Blues have green eyes. Come on, pet him. Show him you're a friend."

Matt's hand still stung from where Blue had nailed him, but he held it out in surrender. To get to Diana, he obviously had to get through her watch cat. "Good kitty. Come here," he said as he tentatively scratched Blue under his chin. Blue purred. "I think he likes me."

"He likes everybody unless he thinks they're threatening me. I got him when I was in rehab." She reached up and took Blue in her arms, snuggling him the way Matt wanted to snuggle up with her. Then she set him on the floor. "Go on, Blue, it's time for your morning nap. Matt's not going to hurt me."

No, he wouldn't hurt her. Ever. No matter how much he wanted to rip her clothes off her and taste her from head to toe. No matter how crazy she made him. "May I finish undressing you now?" he asked in his most docile tone, trying to tamp down the urge to take her now—his way. Out of the corner of one eye he watched Blue curl up on a chair by the window and cover his eyes with one paw.

"Since you ask so nicely, yes." She raised her head. "No touching, though."

His cock throbbed. His balls ached. His fingers shook as he took off her shirt, her jeans—and the flesh-colored scraps of lace that hid almost nothing. He couldn't help it. Diana was as beautiful as he remembered her, even with the handful of scars on her breasts and belly that hinted at past abuse. As soon as Matt had her naked, he went on his knees and buried his face against her soft pubic curls, inhaled the musk of her arousal. He dug his fingers into his palms so as not to spook her with his desperate need to take charge.

"Oh, that feels good," she said when he found her clit and teased it with his tongue. "Come on, let's get in bed so I can taste you, too."

When he imagined how her mouth would feel on his cock, he practically lost it. Instead, he licked her one more time then stood, ready to do her bidding.

"It looks to me like you want some pussy," she cooed as she stretched out across the bed, her head resting on his belly. "That will have to wait. I want to suck your big, hard cock first."

"Feel free." He'd take it as long as he could. Her warm breath tickled his cock head before she opened her mouth and took him in. "Oh, yeah. Like that." It took a lot of effort not to come then and there, especially when she wrapped her hands around the base of his cock and squeezed him. The pressure built in him but he tamped down his lust, concentrating instead on other emotions that had lain dormant for years and deepened by events beyond his control.

Love. He'd never stopped loving her. Fury for what she'd put herself through to feed her need to submit sexually. Frustration that in getting cured, she now couldn't see submitting to him. He tried not to heed the urgent message from his body, to take this slow and show her he was hers for the taking.

God, but it was hard. "Sweetheart, I can't take much more. Please." *Please fuck me now. Please quit driving me past sanity. Please trust me and let me make love to you the way I need to.* "Please," he croaked again, "please stop."

If she didn't, he was going to come in her mouth when where he wanted to be was inside her hot, wet cunt. The way he'd been twenty-two years ago when he claimed her virginity with his own. He was about to lose it when she raised her head and lapped the drop of lubrication that had settled on the tip of his cock.

"Mmmm." Gracefully, she rose and straddled him, rubbing his cock head along her slit before inserting it in her cunt and lowering herself onto him. "I think you've gotten even bigger here."

He didn't know or care. All that mattered now was her heat enveloping him, the delicious friction when she moved up and down, slowly then faster. She'd better not want him to wait much longer before giving him permission to come.

Instinctively he reached out for her waist, wanting to direct her movement. "No. Not yet."

He understood from the panic in her voice that she wasn't ready to hand over control of their lovemaking. That was okay. He laid his arms out, the way they'd be if she'd tied them to the headboard. "I'm not moving. Take what you need."

When his words sank in, she smiled. "Thank you." Then she moved on him again, her tight pussy milking his cock. He didn't know why, but not being able to touch her anywhere else heightened the sensation of them fucking. Determined to hold out until she took her fill of him, Matt caressed her with his gaze, imprinting her on his memory now, replacing the nostalgic images he'd carried with him through the years.

God, but she was still every bit as beautiful as she'd been when they were kids. Still as soft and sweet-smelling, as giving. Her pale skin glistened as she moved on him, varying the tempo, making memories that were brand-new yet colored by the long-ago past they'd shared. She bit her lip, as though holding back from saying whatever it was she had on her fertile mind. He hoped it was him, the feel of his cock throbbing in her hot, wet cunt as she hurried up the pace, slammed into him harder.

She tossed her head. Her expression tightened, and sweat beaded on her forehead. She licked her lips. Her cunt tightened on him like a vise. "Now. Come for me."

It was as though a thousand rockets burst in his head when she screamed out her pleasure. God himself couldn't have stopped him from coming now. "God, sweetheart, I love you," he muttered, shooting wave after wave of hot, slick seed into her spasming cunt. He barely remembered her fear, his promise not to touch her.

But he kept still. His restraint paid off when she snuggled up beside him and said, "You may hold me now." When he stroked her back, the raised scars there made him clench his teeth so as not to spoil the afterglow.

\* \* \* \* \*

When she woke several hours later, Diana slipped out of bed. Funny how she'd slept so well with Matt in her bed, when she usually tossed and turned so much that Blue had taken to sleeping on the lounge chair by the window. He was still there, one eye half open as if he were looking over her and Matt while they slept. Careful not to wake Matt, whose chest and arms were sporting some nice bruises where her calf had nailed him, she got up and grabbed a robe.

It was getting colder. Fast, she realized when she looked at the clock and saw it was hardly past noon. When she went to turn up the thermostat, she glanced out the window. Snow was coming so hard and fast, she couldn't even see the barn. Apparently Nature was taking care of that locoweed she'd been planning to send a crew up to eradicate.

"Hey, where'd you go?" Matt sounded surprised, not angry. "You were doing a great job keeping me warm. Is that snow coming down, or are my eyes playing tricks on me?"

"It's snow. Looks like the start of a blizzard. If you need to get home to take care of your stock, you probably should do it now."

"I have a ranch manager who takes care of that. Got him when I inherited the place while I was still playing football out east. If you can use an extra hand here, I'll stay." He shot her a playful grin. "I really hate to leave, in case you should need me to warm your bed."

He had a nerve! Still, she didn't want him to go. She'd miss him terribly if he left. "If you want to warm my bed, you're gonna have to dress and help me make sure the wranglers get all the cattle to safety in the barns. Come on, get the lead out."

"Yes, Mistress. One thing for sure, you've learned to give orders."

She only wished the hired help obeyed as well as Matt did. "What I need right now is for you to go with me and make sure my help does what I say. They're not nearly as obedient as you."

"Okay." He got up and pulled on his clothes. "You want me to be your enforcer, then?"

"You could say that." His smile warmed her more than the long johns and clean jeans she put on. "Stupid cowboys don't seem to think a woman can give them orders, especially since I was away so long."

Grinning, he handed her the socks he'd taken off her and suggested she might put them on when she started shoving her bare feet into a pair of roper boots. "I have a way of commanding respect, except from you. Comes from being six foot six and two hundred fifty pounds."

She doubted that. There was a lot more about Matt Rogers than size that made men hesitate to cross him. An inner strength, a strong sense of chivalry. And a sense of protectiveness toward weaker people that made her pretty confident he not only would take care of her against potential bullies, but also would protect her from himself. "Come on now. You know you're nothing but a great big pussycat." Smiling, she patted Blue and headed out the door.

# Chapter Four

By the time they'd satisfied themselves that the stock was being taken care of, snow lay three feet deep in the barnyard with some drifts already over Diana's head. It was still coming down strong, no sign of letting up anytime soon. Diana had gotten no arguments from the ranch hands about how she wanted the stock sheltered. She hadn't expected to with Matt scowling at them over her shoulder. Yeah, size did matter to a bunch of itinerant cowboys.

Despite the cold wind that swirled around them and blew snow into treacherous drifts, she laughed out loud. Her pussy twitched when she thought how tight a fit Matt's cock had been. Apparently size mattered to her, too. "Ready to go inside?" she asked.

"I'm always ready," he whispered in her ear, tickling her with his warm breath as it evaporated against her icy skin. "Want me to carry you?"

A long time ago she'd have giggled and thrown her arms around his neck, but life had made her wary. "I can walk, thank you." She noticed how he shortened his steps so she could follow in his tracks. Oh, how she wished…

Wishing didn't cut it. Diana accepted that she needed his strength, and also his willingness to let her maintain control. Control over the ranch hands as well as his big body when they made love. As she watched Matt shed his gloves, jacket and boots inside her mudroom, she saw Blue twining around his legs. She might not have given Matt her entire trust, but apparently her cat had. He followed them into the kitchen and nibbled at the cat food in his bowl by the sink.

Matt stood by the window, watching the snow swirl wildly in the wind. "I called up at my place and asked my housekeeper to send me a change of clothes. One of my ranch foremen should be coming on a snowmobile any minute."

"Why?"

"Because it's freezing cold outside, and I like having clean, dry clothes. You don't mind, do you?"

She did and she didn't. While his presence gave her confidence, it also made her feel dangerously dependent, especially when she pictured him wandering around naked, tempting her beyond resistance while a blizzard raged all around them. "I guess not. Your man may have to stay here. The storm's getting worse, not better."

"That's understood. He'll stay in the barn with Midnight. That way he can keep an eye on your stock, too. It looks like we may be stuck here for a while." He held his hands over the stove, close to her yet giving her the space she needed. "Can you use some help? I could call back and have him bring a few wranglers. I have more than I need."

"Not really. As long as they know they've got you to answer to, the cowboys will do their jobs. Cook will fix grub for the men. I just need to keep us fed." She leaned back, rested the back of her head against his rock-solid chest. "Coffee and some more of that stew sound all right for lunch?"

"Yeah. And maybe a piece of that cake you mentioned." When he nuzzled her hair, he sent shivers down her spine. She loved it, the desire that overwhelmed her fear and made her want to drag him back to bed.

\* \* \* \* \*

Matt stretched when he got up from the table. His bumps and bruises were hurting now, and he had no doubt Diana was suffering, too. "I'll get the door," he said when he heard a loud knock over the storm's roar.

When he came back, he joined Diana on the couch and gazed at the fire in the grate. "Do you have enough wood to keep this going?"

"On the porch. Brad and Jared brought it over last week, after they cut down a dead tree close to Jared's barn."

"Good." When Blue jumped up between them and started to purr, he reached down to pet him and collided with Diana's hand. "I think he likes to see us together."

She glanced up at him. "Seems like he does. You know, Blue's been my best friend since Brad brought him to me."

Her tone was wistful. Matt covered her hand with his. "I think he knows I want to be here for you, too."

"Maybe. What's in that big duffel bag?" She had to be desperate, starting a conversation about his clothes.

"Some jeans and shirts. Underwear. Some cold-weather gear. No way did I want to wear anything your ex might have left lying around." It wasn't the time or place to show her the bag of toys he'd had his housekeeper pack.

"You wouldn't have found anything of Gareth's. I had it all burned. Brad and Jared took care of that chore for me since I was in the hospital, but they brought me pictures of the bonfire." She curled her fingers around his, almost as though she trusted him. "Besides, none of his stuff would have fit you. He only seemed omnipotent to me because he had me under his boot heel. You—any big, powerful man for that matter— could have torn him apart without breaking a sweat."

Matt wished he could soothe the hurt that was still evident in Diana's voice, in the defensive way she slumped her shoulders. "I should have, the first time I came home and heard how he abused you. I will, if he ever comes near you again."

She laid a cheek against his forearm as they stroked Blue together. "You'll have to get in line behind my little brothers. I doubt my ex will show his face again around these parts. He made me his slave, but he cringed at the thought of anybody dishing out any kind of pain to him." She sat up and stared into the fire. "He did it because I let him. Because hurting me helped me come—to a point. He fed my need for punishment while he developed a finer and finer edge to his sadistic nature."

She must have heard that drivel in rehab. Her ex was a sadistic bastard. He'd been born that way, and that's the way he'd eventually die. Matt couldn't help hoping Gareth would meet his end at the hand of a fellow prisoner he was bound to cross, sooner or later. As for Diana, it was obvious to Matt she'd wanted love and protection after having given up her own youth to raise her younger brothers. Somehow Gareth had appealed to her needs, sucked her into a relationship that had nearly destroyed her.

While Matt had seen subs who got off on the need for punishment, he was willing to bet that, with the exception of a playful spanking now and then—that made his cock harden to think about doing that to her—Diana mainly enjoyed the psychological feeling of being taken over, controlled for her pleasure. Not harmed, and definitely not humiliated. It was just that somewhere along the way she'd confused the things her parents had enjoyed with her own needs. Gareth had completely fucked her up about it.

As she recovered from the horrors he'd put her through, she'd had no one but her brothers, both hardcore lifestyle Doms, to relate to. For the first time, Matt felt a tendril of hope penetrate his unease with the idea of being her submissive. Maybe that wasn't what she wanted at all. Maybe all he and she needed was each other.

"You're no masochist, sweetheart. You're a beautiful woman I'd kill for the chance to take care of."

Her smile reinforced the hope inside him, but it was obvious when she spoke that she didn't want to pursue his line of thought any further. "When we were kids you wanted to settle down, play football and have babies. Did you?"

That question hit him in the gut. "I played in the NFL for eighteen years. The nearest I've come to settling down has been since I retired last February. No wives or exes. No kids. How about you?" He knew from the tremor that ran through her that he shouldn't have asked.

"I wish…no, it doesn't do any good to look back. I haven't been pregnant now for over five years. I lost it in the third month, just like I lost the other baby the first year Gareth and I were married." Her shaking grew worse, made Blue jump off the couch and stare at Matt with what looked very much like a feline threat.

"I'll never hurt your mistress, big cat." When he spoke, Blue dropped his guard and padded over to the hearth, where he curled up on a round cat pillow.

When Diana's trembling worsened, Matt couldn't help clenching his fists. But now wasn't the time to come on like the high-school bully, snarling and pounding his chest and committing all kinds of mayhem. Even though seeing her like this made him want to put his fists through someone. Something. Anything solid he could destroy. He eyed the solid-looking door to one side of the fireplace that probably led to a downstairs bedroom.

When she looked up and met his gaze, her tears started flowing. Then came heart-wrenching sobs that tore at Matt's heart. Diana needed comfort, not raw male fury or idle promises of retaliation against her tormentor who fortunately was out of easy reach. Matt took a deep breath, let love for her shove his anger from the forefront of his mind.

Then he slid over to the spot Blue had vacated and took her in his arms. "It's all right, honey," he murmured, bringing her into the shelter of his body. Slowly, as he stroked her back, she began to melt into him, as if confirming her need for love and protection. As her tears subsided, she snuggled closer, confirming his earlier thoughts of what it was she really needed.

"I hate being so weak. I'm forty years old. It's too late…" Blue jumped up in Matt's original spot, nuzzling Diana's hand and earning a gentle scratch behind the ears.

Matt recalled their lovemaking this morning. He hadn't used a condom and she hadn't suggested it. "Maybe not, sweetheart." Or maybe her last miscarriage had damaged her, ended her hopes forever. The last thing he wanted was to rub in something Gareth might have done. He spoke slowly, wanting her to quit crying and consider other possibilities. "Even if it's too late for us to make a baby, we're plenty young, healthy and rich enough to adopt one. Hell, we can adopt as many as you want."

There. He'd told her as plainly as he could that he wanted her forever. That he'd take her as she was, squelch his need to control her, even go on his knees and be her sex slave if that was what she wanted. He wished she'd stop trembling, say something, even if it was just to tell him he'd lost his fucking mind.

Diana could hardly believe it. Matt had just offered her the moon. To stand by her side, raise a family now when she'd long since abandoned hope.

Maybe what was hard to believe was how easily she *did* believe it could happen. Her thoughts about him had been nearly constant while she was in the hospital and more so since her return. She'd cried buckets when she considered all they might have shared when they were younger. Matt had always been a loving, decent man, and she'd always been wildly attracted to him.

Nothing much had changed in twenty-two years. They still had the passion—and the love—that had begun before it had the freedom to bloom. "Do you mean it?" she asked, almost afraid to hear his answer now that he'd had time to reconsider.

"Yeah. I meant every word. Here, let me wipe away those tears before you flood Blue with them." Very gently, he stroked her cheeks with his bandana then pretended to wipe down the cat's coat as if she'd gotten it wet. "If you want me to, I'll be your slave. Do whatever it takes to keep a smile on your beautiful face."

She wasn't beautiful. Too many harsh Wyoming winters had done numbers on her skin, and there was nothing more she could do to get rid of the scars Gareth had left on her. The physical ones as well as the ones that had turned her into an anomaly, a woman afraid to trust even the kindest of lovers.

But she trusted Matt. He saw her and saw beauty. He wanted her enough to let her take the lead. He even cared enough to promise her the child she'd always wanted, whether or not it shared their genes. "I'll try," she said quietly, doubts still swirling around her mind as memories of times gone by collided with hopes for a future with him. "Right now I just want you to help me ride out the storm."

"As I told you, your wish is my command." Drawing her close, he took her mouth, pulling away only when Blue let out a screech and jumped off the couch. When Matt broke the sensual yet unthreatening kiss, she glanced at the hearth and saw Blue sitting there, an indignant scowl on his face that went well with his laid-back ears. "We don't have to have a kid, come to think of it. Blue's good enough for me. How about you?"

"He's my baby, all right. But I'd love to give him a brother or sister of the human persuasion." Diana felt freer than she had in years. For once she didn't beat down the hope that rose in her. "Maybe we can give it a try someday."

Matt squeezed her hand. "I'm game if you are. Did you realize we might have already done that this morning?"

For the first time she thought about having fucked him, giving no thought to protection at the time. "Oh no."

"Would you mind? I wouldn't."

Things were moving too fast. Diana's attempt at making a switch from slave to Domme wasn't working. She wanted Matt to take her, exert the control he'd been demonstrating at the club last night. She needed his hands and mouth on her, his huge body dominating her, claiming her for his own.

He needed that, too. She sensed deep down that he was no sub, any more than she was a Domme. And she couldn't imagine him morphing into a cruel Master like her ex. But then, in the beginning, hadn't she felt that way about Gareth? Then again, she hadn't known Gareth nearly all her life, as she had Matt.

And she and Matt had been together before, and he'd been every bit as loving and considerate then as he was now, a big, gentle brute of a man who'd never given her reason to feel a moment of fear. Diana realized any fear she'd felt in the time Matt had been with her today had simply been the greasy stain of Gareth lingering in her head.

"If only…" If only they could go back in time, make love as equals the way they'd done so long ago…

"We can do it, you know. Even if we don't succeed, it will be fun trying." He stood and held up his hand. "Take me upstairs and have your wicked way with me."

# Chapter Five

The snow kept falling, tiny diamonds in a fast darkening sky. Blue followed them upstairs, apparently not willing to let Diana out of his sight. The cat apparently sensed they were in for a storm. Animals could smell danger in the air, Matt remembered his grandfather saying one summer night long ago, when the horses had been practically tearing down their stalls during a vicious hailstorm.

From all the signs outside, Matt figured they were in for a blizzard the likes of what he hadn't seen for years. Lights flickered and went out, only to come back dimly a moment later. The fire he'd just started struggled to life, its feeble flame flickering in the small fireplace grate, illuminating the fear on Diana's face.

"We'll be fine. This house has stood a hundred years or more. It's not about to crumble now. Come here and let me hold you." After he spoke the words, she snuggled closer, as if something he said made her loosen up inside. "You okay, hon?"

"I'm mad. No, not at you. At myself. I'm no sniveling girl who's never braved a storm. I spent a lot of years running this place, and before I crashed and burned I was a damn fine ranch manager. Brad even said so."

"It's natural to be wary of storms like this one. Don't beat yourself down over it." Matt said, his tone reasonable. "I know you grew up here, and that you're perfectly capable of handling the place on your own. But now you don't have to."

"I know. And I thank you."

"Don't thank me, Di. Just trust me." Matt appreciated that the fear Gareth had planted in her had crept beyond the bonds of their relationship into doubting everything about herself. Those doubts gave her irrational insecurity about things she'd never feared before. "Your place has weathered far worse storms." So, he realized, had she.

They stretched out together on the big bed, Blue curling at their feet. The feel of her silky skin against him, the tickle of her breath on his chest, the closeness of the cocoon that kept them safe from the storm, even the cat's loud purr in the silent room made him feel incredibly content. When she began to run her fingers over his pecs, his libido began to stir.

He made himself be still so as not to spook her. No matter how he tried, though, he couldn't believe his lover was a Domme. He had to admit, if only to himself, that the way she touched him had blood coursing through his veins, headed straight for his already half-hard cock even though she hadn't touched him there. When she took his hand and set it on her belly, he took it as permission to make some explorations of his own.

Her breasts were firm yet soft, the nipples small, almost virginal. He ringed them with a finger, amazed at the instant response. "You like that, don't you?"

"Oh, yes. I like you touching me almost as much as I like touching you." She slid one hand lower, dragging it along his belly and outer thigh. "You're so big. So strong. You should scare me, but for some reason you make me feel safe."

That had his sex at full attention, knowing he turned her on this way. Yeah, he'd had women want him because he symbolized mean and tough. He'd had them chasing him because they were football groupies. No one but Diane and his football coaches had made him particularly happy he'd grown bigger than most men, strong enough to intimidate the most fearless opposing players. Strong enough to allay her fears. "I'm glad, sweetheart."

She lifted her head, planted a long, sweet kiss on his lips. "Come on over here. I want to feel you on me, in me."

He wasn't about to deny her or himself. Being careful not to disturb Blue, Matt laid back the comforter and rolled over Diana. She was so tiny. So trusting now when before, she'd been afraid he'd cause her harm. Taking most of his weight on his sore shoulders and forearms, he bent and kissed her, a deep, wet kiss that left them both trembling with emotion. "You taste so damn good. Come on, tell me what you want." No way would he risk spooking her now, when he was kneeling between her legs, his cock poised at the edge of paradise.

She raised her hips in silent invitation, and he slid inside. Plain vanilla sex, no toys and no kink, yet she strained to meet his every thrust, dug her nails into his ass as he captured her lips again and tongue-fucked her mouth with the same slow rhythm he was using to fuck her cunt. She moaned and wrapped her legs around his hips, holding on tight, silently begging for more.

He needed her to come, like this, the way she'd exploded around him years ago when neither of them had known about the joys of oral sex, let alone the dozens of tricks that could drive them to limits they'd never known of back then.

And he wanted to make her pregnant, give her the baby she'd always wanted. Not just to make up for not having stepped in and saved her from the horror that had been her life with her ex. He wanted to give her all she'd ever wanted, to love and protect her for the rest of their lives and feel secure in her love for him.

What was it about her that had him ready to come at the slightest twitch of her hot, wet cunt around his cock? He held on, determined she'd climax first, needing to hear her little moans of satisfaction while he filled her with his life.

She stiffened, threw her head back against the pillow and tightened her grip on his butt. "Don't stop," she cried when he paused. "Oh my God, I'm coming." Her cunt spasmed around him, drawing out his seed in spurts that left him so drained he could barely manage to roll off her before collapsing on the bed.

\* \* \* \* \*

She must have been sleeping for hours when her satellite phone rang. She blinked then focused on the clock. Midnight. Awfully late for anybody to be calling. Good thing she'd had a replacement battery. Otherwise she wouldn't have been able to talk with anybody unless they'd known Matt was here with a unit unscathed by her calf. "Hello, Jared," she said, speaking softly to keep from waking Matt.

Jared sounded worried about her, but Diana reassured him. She was all right. More than all right. For the first time in years she felt safe, protected. Matt snored softly at her side, and Blue purred between them. "I'm fine. Matt's here. He got one of his stock men to come over and make sure the wranglers are taking care of the stock the way they're supposed to. You just take care of Ninia and that baby of yours." She listened as he explained Brad had holed up at his place with the redhead he'd rescued from the storm as it blew in from the west and made the roads too treacherous to drive. "That's good. At least he's not all alone."

For a good while after they lost the connection, she lay there and watched the fire. So much had happened, good and bad. It had nearly killed her to see her baby brother come home from Iraq missing the lower part of one leg, but Ninia had handed him back the confidence he'd lost. For a long time Diana had wondered if Brad would decide to grow up and settle down before some crazed bull killed him, but it seemed her worries might be over on that score.

They came by their BDSM lifestyles honestly. Diana remembered her mom and dad playing Master-slave games she'd thought back then were things all moms and dads did. Brad and Jared had probably been too young to notice the subtle actions before Dad died, but like him, they indulged their need for danger and excitement. She guessed that since they chose activities where they couldn't control the outcome, they must have gravitated toward BDSM in their sexual lives. Seeking control from women more eager to submit than Brad's broncs and bulls, or the relentless enemy Jared had faced in Iraq.

Now it seemed they were finally growing up and building lasting relationships instead of passing encounters that answered their need for sexual control but not much else. Sexual submission came naturally to her, too, she reminded herself. She'd needed it so much, she'd gone on her own disastrous search for release that had only lasted until the pain subsided.

Was that it? For the first time Diana asked herself the question. Brad, Jared, even Matt had implied it to her. Or had she traded her need to be loved and protected, after having to be everything to everybody for so long, for the sacrifice of pain and degradation? Her actions had been desperate, pathetic. The counselors had spent months tiptoeing around what she now saw as truth.

But all Matt had to do was look at her for her thighs to liquefy. She didn't feel any compulsion for him to hurt her. She just wanted him to take her, make love to her. Being here like this with him felt right. Stuck in a blizzard with only each other and one small blue cat for company, she hadn't wasted a moment worrying. Matt would take care of her. Her whole body tingled with the sensual memory of their lovemaking. For the first time in years, she'd climaxed without being hurt, either physically or emotionally.

She glanced down at him, brushed a lock of dark hair off his brow. He smiled in his sleep then rolled over on his side, aligning their bodies. Blue got up, shifted positions and burrowed under the covers, apparently content to share their body heat now that the fire had burned down to glowing embers.

Yes, maybe now was the time for her. Time to find the sort of happiness it seemed Jared had lucked into. Laying a hand over her flat belly, she wondered how it would feel to have a baby growing there.

"Who was that?" Matt asked, reaching for her and making sure she was under the comforter. "Brad?"

"Jared. He and Ninia are snowed in. So's Brad, but he has company at his place. Jared said he brought home the redhead he was playing with last night at the dungeon."

"Keely?"

From Matt's tone, Diana guessed that surprised Matt. For a minute she wondered if he'd played scenes with this woman, too. "Have you…"

"No, sweetheart. Keely only plays with Brad or one of the club Doms, as far as I know. And only at Roped and Lassoed. Brad's been pushing her to go out with him ever since he came back from the summer rodeo circuit, but she's kept on saying no. If they're together at his place, my guess is she got marooned at the dungeon when the storm started rolling in. I doubt the rattletrap truck she drives would have made it back into Laramie." The way Matt stroked along her spine diverted her attention from what her brothers might be doing. "They're probably doing what we're doing now."

"Probably." She snuggled closer. Although Brad and Jared—Ninia, too—enjoyed the kinkier aspects of their lifestyle, Diana wasn't much into sharing—or watching, which brought Jared and Ninia to the dungeon often. "Do you enjoy the dungeon scenes?"

Matt pulled her on top of him and laid a playful kiss on her nose. "Jealous?"

"Maybe just a little."

"Don't be. If you ask me, I'll never go to Roped and Lassoed again. You're plenty of woman for me." He smiled up at her. "I only joined because I wanted to find out what turns you on, so that when you were ready, I'd be prepared. I needed to understand what made you want to be hurt."

It had taken a year for the shrinks to figure that out, Diana thought wryly. And they'd done a piss-poor job. "It's not that I want to be hurt, exactly. A little force goes a long way toward making me lose my inhibitions and..."

"And what? Get hot? Come? Tell me what you want me to do, and I'll do it. Diana, tell me how you want me to Master you." It startled her, but he wouldn't let her spook. "I learned how to play at Roped and Lassoed — just for you. We've shown I can play slave to you, that I'll be anything you want. Why don't I try being something you need? You'll still have the control, honey. A true sub always does." His deep voice poured over her like honey, his words providing relief for wounds she hadn't realized still festered. "Want to play switch? You have to tutor me at being your slave. I only learned to be a Master."

She gave him a playful jab in the ribs. "I don't have any toys. Just what's left of a torture chamber in the downstairs bedroom. I think there might be a St. Andrew's Cross and a fucking table, nothing as fancy as what Brad has at the dungeon." Diana hadn't been in that room, hadn't wanted to see it even though she knew Brad and Jared had stripped it of everything that wasn't bolted to the floor or wall. "We'll have to improvise."

"From the look of the weather, we're gonna be stuck here for days, so I had my housekeeper put in the backpack I take to the dungeon. I've got plenty of toys you can use on me. Meanwhile I need to feed you. Stay put. I'll toss another log or two on the fire and then see what I can rustle up in your kitchen. Gotta keep our energy up."

He slid out from under her and rose, magnificently naked. His fine muscles rippled when he picked up a log and laid it on the embers. Diana feasted her eyes on the gentle giant as he pulled on his jeans. "Come back up here soon, it's cold."

She didn't want to be cold again, ever.

*Lassoed*

\* \* \* \* \*

The door creaked as though no one had opened it for a long time. Matt stepped inside and clamped down the violent reaction that made him want to slam his fist through the stark dark gray walls. *The bastard kept her here.* Bars had obviously been torn out from the window frames, and the hardwood floor was scratched from where someone—probably Diana's brothers—had dragged out other torture devices.

The equipment she'd mentioned—a heavy iron St. Andrew's Cross and a solid-looking wooden table bolted to the inside wall—was here. Nothing short of tearing the room apart would do it to get either of the bulky pieces out.

He wanted to scream. More than that, he wanted to torture the bastard she'd married, worse than he ever thought of abusing her. And he didn't want to bring Diana in here to relive the nightmare that had been her life with Gareth Bender.

Matt forced himself to look more closely, ignoring the musty smell that came with long periods of disuse. He couldn't believe she'd offered this as a playroom after all she must have endured here.

Then he reconsidered. Maybe… Maybe Diana needed to revisit this chamber of horrors, experience the lifestyle she obviously wasn't ready to give up, with a man she trusted would never cause her harm. To exorcise the demons that had made her spend a year in rehab, and make new memories with him. Hurrying so she wouldn't wonder what he was doing, he took an incense burner and some sticks of incense off the living room mantel, lit it and set it on the table to freshen the smell. It didn't help. In fact he thought the floral scent made the room stink worse. He thought about opening a window just a little but changed his mind when he looked out and saw snow covering the lower half of the storm windows. There'd be no playing here. Not now. Not ever if he had anything to say about it.

In fact, if she gave him half a chance, he'd come back in here with Brad and Jared and get rid of all of it, even if it meant tearing out a wall to get it done. He'd turn it into a billiard room, or an office or entertainment center. Hell, if it would please Diana, he'd turn it into a fucking greenhouse. Something, anything that would banish what it had been from her mind. Forever.

Picking up the incense burner and extinguishing the flame, Matt closed the door as quietly as he could, set the burner back on the hearth and went to the kitchen. He raided the refrigerator and pantry to find some finger foods, and laid out apples, pears and two wedges of cheese. They went onto a tray with a roll of snack crackers and two bottles of spring water. Looking at the meager provisions that didn't require heating, he hoped to hell they weren't marooned here too long without electricity.

Blue hadn't ventured down here since they'd gone upstairs last night. He had to be hungry and thirsty, too, so Matt grabbed his food and water bowls and balanced them on the edge of the tray.

They ate in front of the fire. "Did you check out the downstairs bedroom?" Diana looked half excited, half terrified, but she managed to keep her voice steady.

Matt wasn't sure he could do the same. "It's in no shape to use. If you want some hardcore dungeon play, we'll go down to Roped and Lassoed once the highway department clears the roads. Meanwhile, you can try out some of my toys on me." He hoped he could persuade Brad to let them use the dungeon after hours, so no one would see him strapped up taking his punishment. "First, though, I think you need a good rubdown. Tell me where to find some lotion and then lie across the bed on your belly and let me do my magic." He'd forgotten to make it a question. As a matter of fact it had sounded a lot more like a command.

But then he noticed, with a surge of quiet triumph, the flare of arousal in her eyes when she turned and obediently stretched out on the bed.

The feel of his calloused hands kneading her back and shoulders practically made Diana come. By the time he finished taking care of her buttocks and thighs, she was purring louder than Blue.

"How does it feel?"

"Relaxing. Where'd you learn how to give massages?" She hated to think of some faceless lover teaching him.

He laughed. "Probably because I've had trainers give so many to me over the years. Hard games tend to leave guys, particularly ones as old as I was before I retired, with cramping muscles as well as the usual bumps and bruises. Roll over on your back and I'll do the other side."

When he gently kneaded her breasts, his breathing became ragged. She was sure he noticed how the nipples hardened, how she couldn't quite keep from squirming beneath his hands. For a minute it brought back memories of cruel clamps, a chain between them being tugged on. That had hurt so much, she hadn't wanted anyone to touch her there for a long time. But she wanted him to keep moving in that circular pattern, wiping out the painful history and making new, delicious memories to replace them. When he moved lower, his warm hands on her belly got her hot, so hot she could barely stop herself from begging for his cock.

She opened her legs. *Touch me, please. Make me come.* It felt so good when he tangled his fingers in her pubic curls, better when he slid a finger between her labia and found her clit. But she wanted more. She wanted to get him as frantic as she was, break the iron control that kept him from mounting her and claiming her pussy, her ass, whatever orifice would give him pleasure. But she didn't want to order him to do it. Tonight she wanted to be his sub, not a Domme bent on torturing her lover.

He slid up her body, taking her mouth. He tasted like the pear he just ate, and the sweet scent stayed on his breath. "I want…"

"Say it, sweetheart." His tone was so gentle, she couldn't be afraid. He took her hands and brought them to his lips. "Don't be shy."

"I want you to take me. All of me."

"Not quite all. I'd love to eat your sweet cunt while you suck my cock, and I'd die to come in you the way I did this morning. I'd never ask you to take my cock in your—" He hesitated, and she thought she saw the hint of a blush on his tanned cheeks. "Your butt. I'd hurt you."

Causing her pain had never bothered Gareth. He'd hurt her often in many ways, much worse than when he'd used her ass. After a while she'd begun to like it, or at least the vibrator he'd often put there while he was using her pussy. "I wouldn't mind."

Matt dragged her hands down and made her curl them around his huge, thick cock. "Yes, you would. This is the downside of being too damn big. If I tried to stuff myself up your ass, I'd split you apart. I even have to be careful when I fuck your hot little cunt." He raised her hands, setting them on her shoulders so he could look her in the eye. "If you want anal sex, you'll have to settle for a dildo. One that's less than half as big as I am. I think I've got one in with my toys."

At that moment Diana knew she loved him. "All right. I guess we'll have to pass on that," she said with a nervous laugh. "Funny. Your oversize equipment fits just fine where it's supposed to go. You know, I came this morning for the first time without someone hurting me. Really hurting me. Not a little twinge like I felt when you slid it into me."

"Then how about we see if we can do it again, with me being a little freer about loving you all over?" He smiled, as though he remembered how fast her nipples responded when he massaged her.

"No clamps!" she said before she could hold back the words.

"Relax, hon. I don't even own a pair. Relax. We're stuck here for several days without TV or movies or video games. How about letting me see how many times I can bring you to climax without damaging your beautiful body?"

His grin was contagious, so contagious she threw her arms around his massive neck and kissed him full on the mouth. With that, he knelt between her legs and joined their bodies. Again, no force. No kink. Vanilla sex, this time in missionary position.

But it didn't feel vanilla. Not at all. Her whole body tingled when he stroked her belly, her breasts, when he lifted her ass and altered the position of his penetration. Sweet words of love, dark ones of desire filled her ears and her heart.

He stretched her, made her pussy contract around his cock with every careful stroke. "Can you feel me touching your womb?" he whispered, still now that he'd fully penetrated her. His heavy testicles lay tight and taut against her ass.

"Oh, yesss." She was closer now to coming than she'd been after taking an hour's torture on the fucking table with her ex. Her nipples beaded up against Matt's hard chest, as sensitive as if they'd been restrained in clamps.

When Matt framed her face between his big hands and took her mouth, she came, squirming against him, wanting less gentle, more... "Fuck me, hard. Shove your huge cock all the way to my throat," she rasped out when he came up for air.

He did. "God, yes. Don't stop." She'd hardly gotten the words out before she contracted around him, digging her fingernails into his shoulders as waves of ecstasy coursed through her once again.

Laughing, he lifted her, keeping their bodies joined as he maneuvered them into a sitting position. "I want you to do that again," he commanded, balancing her on his left hand and fitting a long finger up her ass while he bent and sucked first one nipple then the other.

She felt conquered. Mastered. With none of the pain she'd been so sure had to happen for her to climax. "Now. Come again for me, honey. I'm about to—"

"Oh, yesss. Please come inside me." The staccato bursts of his hot seed against her womb triggered another series of incredible sensations that radiated from him to her.

Damned if she didn't come three more times before he began to soften inside her and collapsed, rolling her on top of him but keeping their sweaty bodies joined. It might have been her imagination, but she thought their hearts were beating in unison.

## Chapter Six

For the next three days their routine was much the same. Every morning they got up, took an icy shower, grazed on fruits and staples from Diana's kitchen, fed Blue and went back to bed. Afternoon was the same, except that on the third and fourth days they ventured outside to check on the wranglers and the stock in the big, thankfully gas-heated barn and got their first hot grub since the day the storm had blown in.

Diana noted that all was well, even the newly made steer who'd gone loco before the blizzard had rolled in. He seemed docile enough now. As Doc Johnson had said, a bull calf always calmed down once his balls were cut. She eyed the paint pony who'd gotten the worst of their encounter, then ladled some chili into a big bowl to take in the house for herself and Matt.

When they went inside on the fourth day, she heard her phone ringing. "They must have fixed the satellite," Matt said as he handed the phone over.

"Oh my God!" Matt shot her a questioning look when she practically screamed at whoever was talking to her. "Of course I want to go. Wait, let me ask Matt."

"What's wrong?" He caught her by the chin and made her look at him. "Come on, it won't help to hold it inside. Tell me what's wrong."

She brought the phone back to her ear. "Hold on, Jared. Don't hang up." She set the phone down and looked back at Matt. "It's good news. Nothing awful. Brad and Keely are getting married. The road's clear enough now that we can get over to the airstrip, and Jared's flying us all down to Denver for the wedding. I'm not about to miss my brother's wedding. Will you go with us?"

"If I can sleep with you in a warm, dry bed, sure. How long are we going to be there?"

Diana asked Jared then turned back to Matt. "Over the weekend. We'll be coming back after the wedding." When she named one of Denver's most luxurious hotels where Brad had apparently rented a penthouse suite, Matt whistled.

After telling Jared they could be over at the airstrip in about an hour, Diana set the phone down and looked at Matt. "I imagine there'll be some BDSM games."

He imagined she was right about that. Brad and Keely seemed to eat up kinky sex, watching and playing Master/slave games while being observed. Matt recalled one night when they'd worked every piece of apparatus, trying new positions, playing with a large variety of sex toys. The handful of members watching the show had been silent, as if they were eating up the act. At the time he'd wondered if there was any act too brazen for Brad and Keely to try.

Jared occasionally indulged his totally submissive wife with rough yet loving club scenes that usually featured Japanese rope bondage in one form or another, along with the skillful application of the cat-o'-nine. "Whatever it takes to keep my slave happy," Jared had said a while back when Matt had questioned him about how it felt to let a roomful of observers watch while he played with his wife.

Compared with Diana's brothers, Matt's repertoire of BDSM play was damn near vanilla, and he'd never gotten comfortable with group scenes. What he'd done, when he thought about it, was limited pretty much to restraining his partners and arousing them until they begged for release. Sure, he could use the cat, and he'd played some with toys. He wasn't big, however, on the club scene. Oh well, he could always hope this weekend in Denver would be monogamous in celebration of Brad's wedding.

"What do I need to bring with me?" he asked, pulling back on cold weather gear to take the snowmobile up to his place.

"Just yourself and some shaving gear. Hopefully the hotel will have hot water," Diana replied as she dug a few things from her closet and put them in a small garment bag. "I doubt if Brad will do this up formal, but if he does you can always go buy a suit. I'm sure that's what he'll do."

"Brad might be able to find a suit off the rack, although I doubt it. But I have to have my dress clothes custom made." Matt nuzzled her neck, sent shivers of anticipation down her spine. "I'm way beyond a 'long', according to the suit manufacturers."

She turned and dragged his head down for a kiss. "Another disadvantage of being six-six, I guess. But I'm glad you're big. You know where."

Yeah, he knew. They'd fucked vanilla for three days straight, and she must have come fifty or more times. He loved hearing her whimper with pleasure, scream at him not to stop as she was reaching her peak. It surprised the hell out of him that he enjoyed the quiet talks, the cuddling, as much if not more than the actual fucking. "Stop it or we'll be going back to bed," he warned her. "We don't have time now, but hold on to that thought until we get to Denver. Don't forget to put out enough food and water for Blue."

As he gave her a hard, possessive kiss, to make sure he left her hot while he was gone, Matt realized he'd once again slipped into the natural mode of a Dom, commanding her instead of making gentle suggestions. She liked it, though, if he read that flare of arousal in her eyes correctly. It made him itch to forget everything else and take her back to bed right now, but he wasn't about to ruin it now that he was ahead.

Diana was trusting him—at least a little. They'd come a long way in three short days.

At home he packed some casual stuff as well as a dark gray suit and black overcoat. Normally he didn't worry about his looks, but today he wanted to see Diana's face light up with pride when they went out on the town. He thought back, trying to remember the last time he'd dressed up as he tossed a pair of black wing tips into the duffel bag that held his shaving kit. He'd be using that as soon as they checked into the hotel. While he liked his Van Dyke beard, it seriously needed trimming. The rest of his face and neck would benefit by losing the scratchy four days' worth of stubble he could feel even through his gloves.

On the way out he glanced at himself in the mirror, wincing at the mountain hermit look he had a good start toward acquiring. Diana's tender body must be hurting, he thought, a wave of guilt coursing through him until he reminded himself about those delighted squeals that came out of her mouth as she reached climax after climax.

*She must love me. Otherwise, she'd have screamed bloody murder the first time I got this ugly mug anywhere near her.* Matt fired up the snowmobile and gunned the motor, sending snow swirling around him as he headed back to Diana's place. Before going to pick her up, he stopped by the barn and gave some last-minute instructions to his ranch foreman and her wranglers. No need to bother his woman with unnecessary work when he could do it just as well.

Settling her luggage alongside his and bundling her up on the passenger seat, Matt sped toward the airfield he'd noticed near the road on Jared's portion of the McTavish family's large spread. It wasn't until he saw the sleek Beechcraft with its twin propellers rotating and stirring snow on the edges of the tarmac that he remembered. He was scared stiff of flying, especially in small planes.

"Only for you would I do this," Matt told Diana as he helped her off the snowmobile in the covered hangar. "I guess I never told you I'm a white-knuckle flyer."

She stood on tiptoe and managed to lay a quick kiss on his cheek in spite of the fact he was loaded down with her luggage as well as his. "Hold my hand. We'll be okay. Jared's an excellent pilot and so is Brad."

Once he got inside the plane, Matt noticed that both men were in the cockpit, which reassured him a little. He glanced around the twelve-passenger seating group, liked the soothing beige and navy colors that reminded him more of a living room than a plane. Ninia wore dark slacks and a loose jacket, and a long blonde wig he'd never have guessed wasn't her real hair if he hadn't seen her in the club a few weeks back, bald as a cue ball. She shot a smile their way when they found seats on an overstuffed love seat and buckled up. Keely, in the chair beside Ninia, looked ill at ease, and her worn jeans and jacket seemed out of place inside the multi-million dollar airplane.

He managed not to turn into a shivering shadow of a man when the engines roared and the plane began to ascend, a fact he attributed to Diana holding his hand, one of her soft palms below it, the other above. He felt surrounded by her love, safe for the moment.

*****

"You did fine, big guy." Somehow Diana loved Matt more now, knowing he wasn't all powerful, unafraid of anything and anyone. "Shall we make a detour to the toy store?" she asked as they deplaned at Denver International Airport. "Ninia said she and Jared were going there and invited us to join them."

"What are the bride and groom going to be doing?" he asked as he helped the other men unload the luggage.

"Brad needs to take Keely shopping for some clothes and buy her a ring and collar." Diana remembered when Gareth had padlocked a leather collar around her neck, knew Brad's choice would be something with class. Something Keely would be proud to wear in front of their vanilla friends as well as at the dungeon. "She's been at Brad's since the blizzard hit, and apparently all she had with her was on her back. Fortunately she was able to fit into a few of my things that Brad got me for when I came home from rehab for the occasional weekend, even though I'm taller than she is. Otherwise she obviously would have frozen."

Matt shook his head. "I'm surprised she didn't freeze on the way from Brad's to the airstrip. Jared's wife is pregnant, isn't she?"

"Yes. She's due in April. She hardly shows yet." Diana couldn't help the edge in her voice. Of course she was happy for her brother and his wife, but she couldn't help being the least bit envious.

When their cab pulled up in front of the toy store Brad had recommended, Matt handed the cabbie a folded bill and asked him to wait. "What we're getting won't take long."

Jared and Ninia's cab stopped behind them, and Jared helped Ninia out. He seemed a little wobbly on his feet, more so than she'd seen him for months. "I hope Jared didn't overdo it, flying us down here today. Apparently he insisted on going out himself to check on his horses the morning after the blizzard started. Somehow he gouged his good leg with a grappling hook. Ninia says she has to fight him to get him to realize his limitations. She wasn't happy."

"I hope he's okay, too. For selfish reasons. He just gave me the most comfortable trip I've ever taken in a small plane, and I'm expecting an equally pleasant ride home."

Diana laughed. "Brad's as good a pilot as Jared. We'll get home in one piece. Trust me."

Half an hour later they got to the hotel and went to look over their loot in one of the two smaller bedrooms in the suite.

"I'm ready for a nice, warm soak in the Jacuzzi, how about you?" Diana asked.

"That sounds great after four days of taking cold showers. Later, though. Right now I have to shave. How about us taking a little rain check on that hot tub?" He laid out a beautifully crafted cat-o'-nine across the bed. "I bought this for you to use on me."

\* \* \* \* \*

While Matt shaved, Diana lifted the coiled whip. Remembering the feel of a similar one lashing her back as being mildly painful but extraordinarily stimulating, she imagined herself using it on Matt. She'd use the pair of handcuffs she'd bought to secure him to the bed, give him the sense of helplessness that had always brought her to the brink of climax, anticipating the punishment that usually accompanied the closing of the cuffs on her wrists. Sometimes her ankles as well.

The metal balls on the ends of each of the nine slender tails at the end of the whip felt smooth against her fingertips, the braided leather supple, almost as if it were alive. She slid her hand up the cat until she reached its handle, savored the power that flowed through her when she gripped it.

"I see you're ready to dole out my punishment," Matt said, stretching out on his belly on top of the king-size bed with its black satin comforter. "Go on, do your worst."

"Put your arms over your head." When he did, she put the cuffs around each wrist and then fastened the other ends to the sturdy wood headboard. The metallic sounds they made when she clamped each of them shut was ominous, a prelude to the main event. "I want you to come when I say so," she said as sternly as she could manage.

Then she raised the cat. It felt heavy in her hand. Unwieldy She stared at his tanned skin, registered each small scar put there by opponents' cleats over the years, the one large one on his right shoulder where he'd apparently had surgery to repair a separation she vaguely recalled having read about in the Laramie paper.

"I don't want to hurt you." But she remembered the strength of orgasms she'd had when Gareth had whipped her this way. "I want to give you pleasure." Her words came out as mere whispers, but the emotion behind them surrounded her, floated around the luxurious room. Tentatively she swung the cat.

The metal beads clattered as they moved in slow motion, making contact with the flesh on Matt's tight ass. He winced but voiced no complaint, even when she raised the whip and administered several more hits, each harder than the last.

She stopped in midair when she saw the blood. Streams of it flowing in an eerie pattern along welts that seemed to grow before her eyes. Throwing the cat to the ground as if it were a rattler about to strike, she climbed on the bed, laid her hand over the worst of the welts.

"It's okay, honey."

"No, it's not." It was never okay to hurt anything or anyone. Especially someone you loved.

She couldn't help it. She began to cry. Long, pitiful-sounding wails. Cries of sorrow for his pain. For her ineptitude. For her damnable memories that had nudged her to hurt him in her misplaced quest to reject her own submissiveness and dominate her partner.

"Damn it, I'm okay." The bed shook as he bucked. His muscles contracted when he wrapped his hands around the headboard and jerked until it gave way, leaving the cuffs on each wrist—but no longer attached to the shattered wood. Splinters of what used to be a carved mahogany headboard surrounded them as she kept on sobbing, her tears mingling with his blood until he turned around and gathered her in his arms.

"I'm sorry." Sorry for starting this in the first place, sorry for not thinking to release the cuffs. She hoped he'd turn on her, punish her so badly she'd never dare to hurt him again.

Instead he held her as if she were precious, as though he was worried more about her than his own bleeding back. "It's all right, sweetheart. I'm tough."

It wasn't all right. Diana pulled away and stood. She picked up the cat and laid it in Matt's hands. "You're no sub, any more than I'm a Domme. Obviously I don't know how to use this. I don't ever want to try it again." Her tears still fell, staining her cheeks, the salty smell mingling with the blood — his blood — on her hands. It almost made her puke, but she managed to get the key and take both sets of cuffs off his bruised wrists.

He met her gaze, smiled, made her feel even more guilty. "There's a trick to using the cat. I'll take you to Roped and Lassoed, show you how to do it so it doesn't draw blood."

"Here. Take the cuffs. Tie me up and whip me the way I whipped you."

His grip on her shoulders tightened, and his lips curled in a snarl. "That's not going to happen. Get it in your head that I'm never going to hurt you. You don't deserve it. Come here. Let's try out the Jacuzzi before I call maintenance to have them send up another bed."

He gathered her in his arms, carrying her back to the bathroom and climbing back into the Jacuzzi. "Remember this. I'll never hurt you. All I want to do is love you. Bring you pleasure." He took her mouth, so gently it almost broke her heart. With his hands he stroked along her back ever-so gently, returning her cruelty with kindness. And love.

As they made love surrounded by swirling, steaming water, it felt as though her hang-ups were being washed away along with Matt's blood and her tears. He left no part of her untouched, using his hands and mouth to invade every orifice but her pussy. That was for his beautiful cock. When he stiffened and began to spurt his seed into her body, she came in waves of sensation more intense than she'd ever experienced from pain.

In that moment Diana knew the difference between the anger of one who loved her and the one who abused her.

"You know, I don't need toys or punishment. All I need is you," she said later when they lay in bed, his big body curled around her like a spoon. "You make me feel new. Protected."

"I'm glad."

\* \* \* \* \*

Keely looked radiant with her new gold collar and the whopper of a diamond solitaire and matching band Brad had just slid on her finger. Matt liked the soft-looking pink dress she was wearing. Even more, he liked the triumphant grin on Brad's face. He'd staked his claim and he was proud of it.

Still limping from the accident he'd had the morning after the blizzard started, Jared hovered over his pregnant wife. Matt figured he'd do the same if he and Diana were lucky enough to make a baby. Ninia's collar glowed, its amber center stone reflecting the sun's rays. She, too, wore a rock big enough to choke a horse, and a pair of diamond earrings she'd mentioned that Jared bought her the day she told him about her pregnancy.

Both women were beautiful, both years younger than Diana. Still, he saw his woman as the most gorgeous creature on earth, especially now that the shadows of her past seemed to have faded in the last few hours since the traumatic, emotional purging in their hotel room. Matt smiled down at her, loving the clean, fresh scent of the perfume he'd bought her last night in one of the hotel's boutiques. The swirly skirt of the blue dress she had on drew his eye to her shapely legs. No stilettos, just normal black heels. Before the year was over, Matt vowed he'd drag her to an altar—any altar—and make her his wife.

Oops. He needed to buy her a ring, one at least as flashy as the ones her brothers' wives had on. Good thing he'd saved an obscene amount of his seven-figure-a-year earnings. He'd need a lot of it to make sure his woman had everything her sisters-in-law did, without using any of her own fortune to buy it. He'd also need to refurbish his grandpa's place, make it fit to bring a bride. That wouldn't happen until spring came along.

"Wasn't that beautiful?" Diana squeezed Matt's hand. Tears sparkled in her eyes, but they were happy tears today. "I guess both my little brothers have grown up now."

"Yeah. I think you're right." Soon, he thought, there'd be another wedding, one that had been twenty-two years in the making.

# Epilogue

It wasn't fall yet, and the work on Matt's house was nowhere near done. That didn't matter, though. At least Diana had a ring on her finger—a headlight of a diamond Matt had bought the week after Brad and Keely's wedding. And they had a roof over their heads. Her place, where this whole crazy thing between them had begun again on a snowy night nearly nine months ago, with the beginnings of a new entertainment center and glass-walled greenhouse that already filled the space where the former torture chamber had been.

Her words that had made them move the wedding up two months resonated in his brain. "We're going to have a baby." The news had sent them both over the moon, and they hadn't wanted to wait until their new home was finished before making it official.

The summer sun beat down on Matt's head despite the canopy of tall evergreen trees overhead. His suit was damn hot. No wonder, since it was August. None of that mattered when Brad and Jared escorted Diana to him. She had that radiant look he'd first noticed three months ago, just before she'd told him about the baby, and he felt ten feet tall when he looked at her and their child who was growing beneath her heart.

"Who gives this woman?" They'd decided on traditional vows to go with their mutual decision to go vanilla, leave the BDSM lifestyle to her brothers and their wives.

Brad and Jared answered as they laid their sister's hand in Matt's, and the ceremony commenced.

White roses centered the bouquet Diana handed over to Keely when it was time to exchange rings. Hers was platinum like her engagement ring, studded with diamonds that sparkled in the sun. Matt slid it on her finger then brought it to his lips. "With this ring I thee wed." He said it first. Then she slipped his ring onto his finger and repeated the words.

His was plain, a circle of platinum. He liked the weight of it on his finger, the sentiment she'd had engraved inside it. *Love forever. Your honey, Diana.*

The food tasted great. The vintage champagne he'd ordered from Denver flowed cold and bubbly. The small country-western band Diana had hired alternated between sentimental ballads and hoedown dancing music. Matt ate it up, the family and friends and the good wishes that so obviously thrilled his new wife. He even endured eating that first bite of gooey wedding cake out of Diana's hands, then getting her back by smearing her face the way she'd smeared his. The kiss that followed brought more hoots and hollers—and that feeling in his groin that made him figure he ought to get rid of the company and hurry his bride off to bed.

A baby cried in Ninia's arms. Their nephew, born on Easter Sunday, apparently didn't appreciate the solemnity of the occasion. Jared hurried to his wife and took the baby, who seemed to calm down. "Let me take him inside for a nap."

Ninia smiled at Matt. "If you don't mind, I think little Jared's ready to go home."

*Yes.* This public celebration had gone on long enough. Nearly four hours by Matt's estimate. "Maybe we ought to wind this down," he said. "I think the honeymoon's about to begin."

* * * * *

Alone at last, Matt scooped Diana into his arms and carried her to the upstairs bedroom where a warm breeze floated in from open windows. Blue lifted his head as if to say, "What took you two so long?" Then the cat moved to the foot of the bed, as if he knew his mistress and her new husband wanted space for themselves.

Matt undressed his wife for the first time, then shed his own wedding finery and joined her on the bed. Blue purred at their feet. Yeah, Matt thought as he cupped his hands over her growing belly, this was going to be good. Really good. Sort of like what he'd dreamed of years ago, only better.

*The End*

## Also by Ann Jacobs

A Gift of Gold
A Mutual Favor
Another Love
Awakenings
Black Gold: Dallas Heat
Black Gold: Firestorm
Black Gold: Forever Enslaved
Black Gold: Love Slave
Captured (*anthology*)
Colors of Love
Colors of Magic
D'Argent Honor 1: Vampire Justice
D'Argent Honor 2: Eternally His
D'Argent Honor 3: Eternal Surrender
D'Argent Honor 4: Eternal Victory
Dark Side of the Moon
Enchained (*anthology*)
Gates of Hell
Haunted
He Calls Her Jasmine
Lawyers in Love: Bittersweet Homecoming
Lawyers in Love: Gettin' It On
Lawyers in Love: In His Own Defense
Love Magic
Mystic Visions (*anthology*)
Out of Bounds
Storm Warnings (*anthology*)
Tip of the Iceberg
Wrong Place, Wrong Time?

## About the Author

Ann Jacobs is a sucker for lusty Alpha heroes and happy endings, which makes Ellora's Cave an ideal publisher for her work. Romantica®, to her, is the perfect combination of sex, sensuality, deep emotional involvement and lifelong commitment—the elusive fantasy women often dream about but seldom achieve.

First published in 1996, Jacobs has sold over forty books and novellas, some of which have earned awards including the Passionate Plume (best novella, 2006), the Desert Rose (best hot and spicy romance, 2004) and More Than Magic (best erotic romance, 2004). She has been a double finalist in separate categories of the EPPIES and From the Heart RWA Chapter's contest. Three of her books have been translated and sold in several European countries.

A CPA and former hospital financial manager, Jacobs now writes full-time, with the help of Mr. Blue, the family cat who sometimes likes to perch on the back of her desk chair and lend his sage advice. He sometimes even contributes a few random letters when he decides he wants to try out the keyboard. She loves to hear from readers, and to put faces with names at signings and conventions.

Ann welcomes comments from readers. You can find her website and email address on her author bio page at www.ellorascave.com.

### Tell Us What You Think

We appreciate hearing reader opinions about our books. You can email us at Comments@EllorasCave.com.

# Why an electronic book?

We live in the Information Age — an exciting time in the history of human civilization, in which technology rules supreme and continues to progress in leaps and bounds every minute of every day. For a multitude of reasons, more and more avid literary fans are opting to purchase e-books instead of paper books. The question from those not yet initiated into the world of electronic reading is simply: *Why?*

1. *Price.* An electronic title at Ellora's Cave Publishing and Cerridwen Press runs anywhere from 40% to 75% less than the cover price of the exact same title in paperback format. Why? Basic mathematics and cost. It is less expensive to publish an e-book (no paper and printing, no warehousing and shipping) than it is to publish a paperback, so the savings are passed along to the consumer.
2. *Space.* Running out of room in your house for your books? That is one worry you will never have with electronic books. For a low one-time cost, you can purchase a handheld device specifically designed for e-reading. Many e-readers have large, convenient screens for viewing. Better yet, hundreds of titles can be stored within your new library — on a single microchip. There are a variety of e-readers from different manufacturers. You can also read e-books on your PC or laptop computer. (Please note that Ellora's Cave does not endorse any specific brands.

You can check our websites at www.ellorascave.com or www.cerridwenpress.com for information we make available to new consumers.)

3. *Mobility.* Because your new e-library consists of only a microchip within a small, easily transportable e-reader, your entire cache of books can be taken with you wherever you go.

4. *Personal Viewing Preferences.* Are the words you are currently reading too small? Too **large**? Too… ANNOYING? Paperback books cannot be modified according to personal preferences, but e-books can.

5. *Instant Gratification.* Is it the middle of the night and all the bookstores near you are closed? Are you tired of waiting days, sometimes weeks, for bookstores to ship the novels you bought? Ellora's Cave Publishing sells instantaneous downloads twenty-four hours a day, seven days a week, every day of the year. Our webstore is never closed. Our e-book delivery system is 100% automated, meaning your order is filled as soon as you pay for it.

Those are a few of the top reasons why electronic books are replacing paperbacks for many avid readers.

As always, Ellora's Cave and Cerridwen Press welcome your questions and comments. We invite you to email us at Comments@ellorascave.com or write to us directly at Ellora's Cave Publishing Inc., 1056 Home Avenue, Akron, OH 44310-3502.

Make each day more *EXCITING* With our

# Ellora's Cavemen Calendar

www.ElloraSCave.com

Cerridwen, the Celtic Goddess of wisdom, was the muse who brought inspiration to storytellers and those in the creative arts. Cerridwen Press encompasses the best and most innovative stories in all genres of today's fiction. Visit our site and discover the newest titles by talented authors who still get inspired - much like the ancient storytellers did, once upon a time.

Cerridwen Press
www.cerridwenpress.com

*Discover for yourself why readers can't get enough of the multiple award-winning publisher*
*Ellora's Cave.*
*Whether you prefer e-books or paperbacks,*
*be sure to visit EC on the web at*
*www.ellorascave.com*
*for an erotic reading experience that will leave you breathless.*